This Side o

A Child's F

Rachael Trask

Dedicated to

Mai MacIntyre, 1648 – 1655, the inspiration for this book

My husband, for his unwavering love and support

And to all who went before

Short Pronunciation Guide

A lot more Welsh was spoken in Mai's time than today, and what they used to call 'the Wengi' – that peculiar combination of Welsh and English. For non-Welsh speakers, I have attempted to compile a (very) rough guide to pronunciation of some of the Welsh words you will come across in the book in the hope that it will aid fluency of reading.

Welsh	English	Pronunciation
Mai	May	My
Mamgu	Grandmother	Mamgee (g as in girl)
Cyflym	Swift/fast	Kuvlim (the name of Alexander's horse)
Cefn-yr-Afon	Behind/back of the river	Kevn (Kevin without the i; uh and roll the r a bit; Avon – but a as in cat) Kevn-uhr-Avon.
Tŷ Mawr	Big House (lit. House Big)	Tea Mowr (ow as in cow; roll the r a bit)
Cwtch	Hug/cuddle	Kootch (oo as in book)
Bach	Little/Small	As in the composer, J S Bach, (ch as in the Scottish loch)
Alys	Alice	Alice
Wengi	Mixture of Welsh and English	Wengee
Llygaid	Eyes	Ll tip of tongue to back of lower front teeth and blow gently through sides of tongue; ugh; eyed: Ll-ugh-eyed!
Coch	Red	Korch (ch as in the Scottish Loch)

Table of Contents

Part One: His Brother's Child

I Am Not Your Father

Sunday, 25th April, 1655

Never before had her face been so close to his. Nose to nose, helpless, she dangled for the eternity of a few moments, choked by the grip around her throat.

'I – am – not – your – father! You are nothing to me! NOTHING!'

He flung the wretched child across the hut. Her mouth clipped one of the wooden roof supports but the glancing blow did little to reduce the momentum. Her head and back slammed against the wall, expelling whatever remnants of air remained in her lungs. Dazed, she slid down to the earthen floor.

Sarah flew at him, screaming, 'You have no reason to treat my child like that!'

He turned instantly, catching her off-balance with a sharp back-hander to the side of her face. She sprawled to the ground, banging her temple on one of the stones surrounding the central fire pit.

Hands on hips, he stood between them, sneering, as his eyes darted from one to the other, then he dropped onto his stool.

They deserved it! Was it not he, Herbert Henry MacIntyre, who had taken over the family's welfare when his brother had gone off to fight for the King? Was it not he, Herbert Henry MacIntyre, who'd endured almost seven years of 'Oh Herbert, you must be so proud of Eric?' every time he stepped out into the settlement?

Oh, yes! Brave, wonderful Eric! Left his wife and three children – and her pregnant with that useless thing over there to go off and get himself killed. Was it not he, Herbert Henry McIntyre, who'd had to pick up the pieces?

Little Mai's senses began to return. Her breathing was shallow. As the shock wore off, the pain in her ankle, awkwardly trapped beneath her bony bottom, encroached. She wanted to cry – but not in front of him. Never! It was the first time she had dared to speak to him directly. She thought he was in a good mood. She was wrong. Like her mother, she was used to his clouts, his kicks, his punches; some form of violence every day. This was different. Never, ever would she speak to him again.

What had she done? She'd called him 'Father'. That's what other children called the man of the household. She had heard them around the settlement, although she had never heard Fitz or Pat call *him* anything.

She was trying to be nice. It was of no consequence now. Whatever it was she wanted to ask him had flown clear from her mind.

Her breathing began to ease. With the deepest breath she could muster, she took hold of her leg, just above the ankle, with both hands. Grimacing, she wiggled her bottom, and little by little, managed to ease the twisted ankle from beneath her. Only then did she notice her mother lying on the floor.

Sarah struggled to prop herself up on one elbow and, somehow, managed to haul herself to her feet. Her entire body quivered, legs barely supporting her as she staggered to the other end of the rough wooden table, as far as possible from him. She reached out and steadied herself with both hands, palms flat on the table surface. The waters gushed from between her legs into a puddle on the floor and she collapsed onto her own stool. Something damp trickled down her cheek. She tapped the side of her face, flinching as her fingers made contact with the gash and the graze. Her inspection of the red liquid on her fingertips was interrupted; she doubled over in pain, groaning, cradling her swollen belly with both arms.

Herbert, more inconvenienced than concerned, snarled at her:

'Reckon that baby's on the way! Better tell that thing on the floor to fetch Mamgu.'

Sarah opened her mouth to speak but her throat was dry. No voice came. She nodded in Mai's direction.

It was difficult and excruciating, but the little girl managed to find her way to her feet. Her left foot pointed inward but, as long as she didn't place her heel to the ground, she could just about walk. Limping heavily, she left the hut.

'At least this one will be mine! Taken long enough!'

Scowling at Sarah as she doubled up with another contraction, he sat, brooding his lot.

What had he done? His duty! And look what he'd saddled himself with.

The grass was a little more forgiving under her feet than the hard floor inside. The tiny dwellings were arranged in a circle around the larger communal hut. Mai skirted her way around it until Mamgu's home came into view. The old woman was outside, tending to the herbs growing on her little patch of land.

Mai approached her, hobbling, barefoot. Mai was always barefoot.

'Oh, my goodness me, Mai bach! What in Heaven's name have happened to you, then? Have you had a fall or something?'

Mai said nothing. Mai rarely said anything. She reached out, grabbed Mamgu's hand and tugged. Mamgu noted the urgency on the child's face.

'What is it, my little lovely? Baby?'

Mai nodded and tugged again.

12

'Wait here one moment, Mai.'

This was worrying. The baby was not due yet, surely? With the sense of urgency demanded by the occasion, she dashed into her hut and donned her sackcloth apron, reserved for midwifing. Two deep pockets, raised and stitched from the hem, contained the items she would need.

Mamgu swiftly returned outside to little Mai. A little stooped with age, Mamgu was nevertheless stocky and still very strong. Sweeping the child up with ease, saddling her on her hip, she hurried over to the McIntyre hut. The graze and bruise on Mai's mouth did not go unnoticed but she said nothing for now.

'Well, I don't know, indeed I don't. You were a big baby. I was afraid you would kill your Mam when you was born, but there's nothing of you these days, is there, Mai?'

Mamgu brought all the MacIntyre children into the world. Fitzgerald and Fitzpatrick, fifteen and fourteen years ago, with barely a twelve month between them. Then Miriam, twelve years ago. Shame about Mai. Born only a few days before the news of Eric's death at the Battle of St Fagans. Never knew her father. Lovely boy he was, too. Better man than his brother by far! Poor Eric never even knew Sarah was expecting when he took the King's shilling. Oh dear. Well, what's done is done. There's another baby to deliver.

Outside the MacIntyre hut, Mamgu popped Mai to the ground, mindful of her injured ankle, however that had happened, and peeped through the door space. She rushed over to Sarah and assessed her injuries: her face bled from a gash on her right temple, and there was grazing and bruising to the cheek. Something untoward had gone on here. The injuries to both Mai and Sarah were no coincidence but, just as she was about to tackle Herbert,

Sarah doubled up with another contraction and Mamgu noticed the damp patch on the ground.

'Right, Herbert, get out – now! And let down that door on your way out!'

A formidable woman was Mamgu – and a match for any man. She not only delivered all the babies, brewed medicinal potions from her herbs and held story-telling classes for the children, but she was uncommonly deft at the gelding of horses, too. These days, in some English communities, she might well have been thought of as a witch, but in Cefn-yr-Afon and round abouts, she was simply revered as a woman with the wisdom of the ages. Fortunately, most of Wales had escaped the superstitions of the witch hunts.

Herbert was not about to argue with her, even if he was being ejected from his own home. He scuttled from the hut like a frightened rabbit, briefly pausing outside to undo the twine and let down the roll of the woven reeds.

A few cracks in the weave and at the sides of the door allowed some dappled afternoon sunlight to fall inside the hut, complementing the gentle glow of the fire. It was darker now, but not so dark that Mamgu and Mai could not see what they were doing.

Now that the brute had left, Mamgu's face softened as she turned to Mai, placing a gentle hand on the child's shoulder.

'No place or time for a man, this, Mai bach. Could you help me, do you think? Would you like to stay and see your new baby brother or sister born?'

For the first time since Mamgu could remember, she saw little Mai's face light up and, at the corner of her mouth, a painful twitch: the merest hint of a smile. There was little, if anything, to smile or laugh about in this family; certainly not since Herbert had taken over.

Under normal circumstances, given the time, a woman about to give birth would present herself at Mamgu's hut. Mamgu possessed an old birthing chair – the only one in the settlement. Mamgu examined Sarah. It was clear to the old woman that there was no time. Sarah would have to give birth here and now.

Despite the pain of her injured ankle, Mai did everything she was asked. She fetched all the cloths that Sarah had been saving up for this time from the shelf, as Mamgu busied herself preparing a bowl of hot water from the pan boiling over the fire; she allowed the water to cool a little, damped and rung the cloths and, with the utmost care, wiped Sarah's face clean and mopped her brow. She took the opportunity to wipe the graze on little Mai's mouth. At Mamgu's instruction, Mai stood by her mother's side, stroking and mopping her brow as the labour progressed.

Mamgu examined Sarah again. As she expected, the baby's head was already crowning.

The three legged wooden stool did not provide sufficient support for Sarah to give birth.

'Sarah, you are going to have to stand up and lean on the table.'

Sarah was not receptive. Mamgu put her arm under Sarah's and tried to pull her to her feet.

'Sarah, come on, my lovely. You have to get up! I can't help you deliver of your child like this.'

Mai tried to encourage her mother:

'Come on, Mam. You have to do as Mamgu says. She's trying to help you.'

With a flicker of registration in her eyes, aided by Mamgu's strength, the woman struggled to her feet and turned to the table. She leaned over, supporting her weight with her elbows and forearms on the table surface.

'Quick, Mai, – come and see!'

15

This was happening fast – very fast indeed!

Mai hopped to Mamgu's side.

Another strong contraction, accompanied by a long grunt and a howl of pain, and Mamgu guided the baby's head into the world. She satisfied herself that the cord was not tied around the neck. So far so good. A few breaths and another two contractions in quick succession brought the baby into the safety of Mamgu's experienced hands.

It gave a huge cry without intervention.

A safe delivery – one of the speediest she'd ever experienced. Mamgu was triumphant!

'Sarah, you have a beautiful baby boy! Mai, you have a lovely little brother!'

Mai, grinned from ear to ear. At Mamgu's instruction, she fetched an old shawl from the shelf. Mamgu remembered it being used, not only for all the MacIntyre children, but for Sarah herself. She took her small shears from one of her apron pockets and cut and clamped the cord.

Baby was swiftly wiped clean, wrapped in the shawl, and placed safely in the centre of the table in front of his mother for the time being.

Another quick couple of contractions delivered the afterbirth into a shallow earthenware bowl placed between Sarah's feet and, when all was dealt with, Mamgu aided Sarah to her cot as Mai watched her new little brother with wonder. Mamgu propped up Sarah with a straw-filled sack and helped her to put the baby to the nipple. Crying immediately subsided as he began to suckle.

Mamgu finally had time to take a good look at the new mother. No reaction. No expression. No joy. The years of Herbert's disgusting brutality had taken their toll, but there was something more. Sarah just gazed vacantly into space. Mamgu looked down at Mai.

'This is your step-father's doing, isn't it?'

Mai plunged straight back into the reality of her existence. Too terrified to say anything, she did not respond. That said everything to Mamgu. She would deal with Herbert, but she needed to keep the child out of his way as much as possible. Mamgu had an idea.

'You know, Mai, you were a great help to me just now. How would you like to come and help me when other babies are born?'

Mai remained silent but looked up at Mamgu. She nodded, enthusiasm alight in her eyes.

'That would be very good for you and a great help to me. And I think you should come to my classes to hear my tales. What about attending Meg's school, too? You could learn reading and scribing and stitching – like Miriam is doing up at the Old Priory. How does that sound? You should be mixing with the other children.'

Initially, Mai beamed and nodded vigorously. Then her expression changed. Mamgu understood.

'Don't you worry about Herbert MacIntyre, my lovely. I'll sort him! Here. Something for you.'

She dug into her other apron pocket and pulled out a little doll made of coloured corn.

'I always have one on me. I make them for all the little girls.'

Mai took the corn dolly. She gazed at it with the wonder of a child who had never before received a present from anyone and clutched it to her chest. She had something she had never had before: a gift to treasure. She took it to her cot.

The baby had gone to sleep at the breast, Sarah barely aware of him. Mamgu took him and covered Sarah's modesty. She gazed at the sleeping bundle in her arms.

Hopefully, this little boy will have a better life than the other children, being his own. Hopefully.

Two strapping, fair-haired lads, laden with three freshly caught rabbits and a few fish between them, crashed in through the door space. They stopped dead in their tracks at the sight of Mamgu holding the new baby.

'Fitz, Pat, you have a new brother.'

Both wide-eyed and mouths agape, the brothers stared at the baby, then at their mother, staring into space as if she didn't know where she was. They couldn't miss the state of her face but, for now, kept their counsel. Fitz nudged Pat with his elbow and gestured a nod to Mai's crooked foot.

It was Pat, as usual, who spoke first: 'But it's not due yet, is it? Wondered why the door was down so early in such fair weather.'

'Well, he is here now. Babies will come when babies will come, my boy. He's small, because he's early, but he's quite healthy. Now one of you go and find Herbert. I suppose he has to know. He won't be far.'

They dropped their haul on the table, turned and ran out together. Safety in numbers where their step-father was concerned. They still bore the scars of his beatings from when they were younger. He was more than handy with his belt. The boys stuck together. They could probably take him on individually, but neither was prepared to risk it. Not yet. Together, though, they could handle him, and he knew it very well.

Herbert was not difficult to find on an early Sunday evening – in the communal hut, drinking with a couple of his cronies. He was still sober. Just.

He eyed them with the same disgust that he held for Sarah and Mai. He was a lot more wary of these two, though.

'What d'you want?'

'Mamgu sent us over. You're needed at the hut.' Fitz told him.

'Baby's here. Boy.' Pat added.

'Is it now? That was quick!'

The other two men cheered as he picked up his mug from the table and gulped down the remaining ale in one go.

'See you, boys!'

He followed Fitzgerald and Fitzpatrick out.

Mamgu was waiting for them, the baby now settled in his crib.

'Herbert, you have a son.'

'So they say. Let's have a look then. Oh yes! Looks like I did a good job there!'

Mamgu couldn't help herself:

'It appears that you have done a very good job in this household indeed!

Fortunately, he had supped sufficient ale for the irony and sarcasm to go straight over his head. He was ecstatic.

'Seamus! I'll call him Seamus! My son, Seamus!'

He continued to inspect his new son as he lay sleeping in the crib, ignoring Sarah altogether.

Mamgu put on her most authoritative voice:

'Now, Herbert, I have a proposition for you. Young Mai, here, has proved very useful and helpful in delivering your little Seamus. A real asset, she's been. Bright as a button, so I think it would be a good idea if she becomes my assistant when I am doing the baby delivering. I can give her a penny or two and it will be a little bit of extra income for the family. She can be trained for a proper trade when she is old enough. What do you say?'

19

Herbert, at that moment, wasn't sure what to say. That thing? Useful? He'd never heard such nonsense.

'How can she learn all about your trade? She's an idiot. She can hardly speak! All she's good for is keeping the fire going and turning the spit!'

'Now you listen to me, Herbert MacIntyre. I've seen with my own eyes how bright and intelligent this child is. And if you think that she's an idiot ...'

Oh God - the Mamgu glare.

'... I am here to tell you that there is only one idiot in this household – and it is not Mai!'

Fitz and Pat could barely contain themselves. Fitz made some pretext about going back out to hunt for more rabbits, and yanked his brother outside. As soon as they were out of the hut, they scarpered to the edge of the woodland, howling with laughter as they went. Had Mamgu thought before she spoke, she might have reined in her words, and as much as Herbert would have loved to clout the woman for her insolence, he held his ire.

'And you'll pay her, you say?'

'Well, I can't spare much, but something's better than nothing, is it not?'

'I s'pose.'

'And, what's more, if you agree, I won't charge you for delivering Seamus. And another thing!'

Jesus! Don't the woman ever shut up?

'She needs an education if she's ever to be a midwife in her own right. I think she should go to Meg's school to learn reading and scribing and numbers and things. She can learn to stitch as well. And she should come to my own classes to listen to my stories.'

What? This was too much!

'Hang on now, Mamgu. You can't read nor scribe, and you does alright for yourself.'

As far as Mamgu was concerned, every minute that Mai was away from Herbert was a minute more she was safe from one of his backhanders. Meg Summerlee had discussed with the settlers a few months before that the best hope to raise their children out of poverty as they grew up, would be some kind of education, even for the girls.

Initially, the settlers regarded the prospect as nonsensical. Educating boys, yes – there was some sense in that. But girls? Ridiculous! Pointless! Unknown for their sort. Meg persisted with her argument. The settlers argued that classes should be held in the afternoons; mornings were for chores. Otherwise, the way it was put to them, most eventually saw the sense of the proposition and agreed. Herbert had not, so Mamgu took the opportunity to have another go at him, but with her fury somewhat cooler – on the surface, at least.

'I'm from a different time, Herbert. Things is different these days. And who knows how much she could earn or what else she could do on top of the midwifing if she had an education. Just look at your Miriam. Up at the Old Priory with Meg and her family, learning all those things in return for her service. I'm told she's doing really well. Showing great promise, she is. Meg will be here on her rounds in the morning. I'll fetch her to see Sarah and tell her she can expect Mai at class on Tuesday afternoon.'

Oh God. Meg! You daren't argue with Meg lest she set God on you.

From Herbert's experience, it's best to stay out of the way of the Summerlee family but, if you can't, just be polite as you can and agree with them. The four of them up at the Old Priory, so God-fearing it was scary. They reckon that Meg – and that sister of hers – would be nuns if it was allowed. It's not allowed. But they could still set God on you.

In truth, it wasn't so much Meg's piety that frightened Herbert, but his own lack of it.

'That's settled then. Mai, I will see you in the morning, when I come back with Meg. And, Herbert, I've given Mai a little present – a corn-dolly, for all her help today. Anything happens to it, my man, and I'll know where to come!'

She flounced out before tempers were ignited again and he, or she, had a chance to say anything further that either of them might come to regret.

The boys had disappeared. Sarah and the baby were both sleeping soundly, so he could turn his vindictive spite on Mai. It was a bit early, but dusk would soon be descending on the settlement.

'Right, you. Go and get those hogs in!'

He held the door aside to allow the hogs through. Mai limped outside and, small as she was, she ushered the two great black and white sows inside. The girls knew exactly what to do and trotted into the hut of their own accord the moment they were called. Mai followed them. Herbert waited, holding the door aside with one hand and the end of the sectioning rope in the other. As soon as Mai came through the door space, he kicked her backside into the hogs' section, roping it off behind her.

'And whatever that fool of a woman says, you're useless. From now on, you sleeps with them and you eats with them. It's all you're worth.'

She would have liked her precious corn-dolly with her, but hogs love corn. It was safer in her cot.

Hognights

Mai slept surprisingly well. Being with the hogs was nowhere near as bad for her as Herbert had intended, or hoped, but she was not going to let on. The straw was deep and fresh and the earth floor was not really any harder to sleep on than her cot. The hogs were somewhat confused to have her with them at first. Mai knew how clever they were.

One of them, Mai called 'My Girl' because she always seemed to show some affection for her. Mai loved her. The other, she called 'Arabella', after the old widow-woman who lived in the next hut. They both had a grumpy nature. It was said that Arabella (next door) lost all her family in an outbreak of blight before Mai was born and it had made her bitter. Mai thought Arabella (the hog) was a bit grumpy because they kept taking her babies away, but one of her tusks was bent at a strange angle, so perhaps it irritated her. Perhaps it was both. She seemed to get better over time until she was near to the birth of her next litter, though she was never particularly nasty.

My Girl seemed much more resigned to the situation. She was lovely and warm. She let Mai cuddle up to her, being careful not to roll on her, and she put herself between Mai and Arabella (just in case of accidents, Mai thought).

By the time Sarah and Herbert rose in the morning, the hogs were back outside and Mai had already set the fire. Sarah should have remained abed after the delivery, with one of the local women coming in to help but, with Herbert's reputation, nobody was willing to enter the property. Sarah had to carry on and manage the bleeding as best she could. She was just about able to care for the baby, but not with any great interest. She half-heartedly got on with her chores. Nobody had eaten supper the evening before so they were all hungry. Fitz and Pat had not returned overnight. Sarah settled the baby and got on with gutting and preparing the fish for breakfast. She was doing what she had to do, but in a world of her own. When the fish was ready, she began to serve for the three of them but Herbert stopped her.

'Oh no you don't! I told you yesterday! That thing eats what the hogs eat!'

He grabbed a raw, half-rotten turnip from the pigswill and threw it to the ground. As Herbert and Sarah ate their breakfast at the table, Mai sat on the floor and picked up the turnip. She tried to bite into it but yelped in pain. Her tooth had loosened when her mouth hit the roof support and it almost came out altogether.

'Shut your noise! What's the matter with you?'

Not that Herbert could care less.

Mai pulled at the wobbly tooth, then gave it a sharp tug. It came clean away. She held it up to show him.

'Oh,' was Herbert's only response. He carried on eating his breakfast. She gave up trying to eat. As if it wasn't bad enough, the taste of blood in her mouth made it worse.

From then on, all Mai ate, at home, was raw turnip, roots and scraps from the swill.

Later that morning, Mamgu visited with Meg. Sarah barely acknowledged them. Mamgu was worried. The baby seemed content enough, but Sarah was still in her far-away world. The side of her face was a mess and looked as though it would take some time to heal. Blood was congealed around the main site of the wound and on her cheek. Meg dampened a cloth in a bowl of warm water and bathed it for her. Sarah flinched. Then Meg turned her attention to Mai's ankle. It was still swollen, but Mamgu noted that it was not quite as bad as yesterday, although it was still turned inward and Mai

24

could not put her heel to the ground. Meg turned to Herbert.

'This child needs shoes – support for her feet.'

'And some clothes!' Mamgu interjected.

'And where do I get the money for that? We don't have it to spare!'

Mamgu turned on him, jabbing the dreaded forefinger in his direction.

'Don't you go telling me that nonsense, Herbert MacIntyre, because I knows you has a bit put away!'

Meg was still examining Mai's ankle. She was concerned that tensions were running a bit too high.

'Don't worry, I will sort out something. But this is not good. How did it happen?'

She looked into the child's eyes. Mai's expression told her nothing.

'Dunno. She just tripped and fell over, I think,' Herbert lied.

They all knew it was a lie, as was the 'coincidence' of Sarah's 'fall'.

'So be it. Mai, I will see you at my class tomorrow afternoon. And I will try and get you some footwear and a new dress as soon as I can. And, Herbert, before you ask', she went on, pursing her lips, 'it will cost you nothing. Nothing at all.'

Mamgu and Meg said their goodbyes and left the hut but, once outside, Mamgu put a hand on Meg's arm to stop her.

'You know, Meg, I am so fearful for that little girl. Herbert treats her terrible. She's such a bright little thing but her life is constant drudgery. It is for all of them but I know Herbert treats her worse. I don't know why he seems to hate her so. Her life is hardly worth living. She isn't loved. I mean, I'm sure Sarah do love her, an' all, but she daren't show it. What was the point of the poor child ever being born, I wonder?'

Meg smiled.

'There is always a point to human life, Mamgu.'

Neither Mamgu nor Meg noticed the child follow them out, overhearing their conversation. Mai had never given a thought to her life. She just accepted her existence as it was. But, as much as she loved the hogs, what was the difference between her and them if she was going to be treated no differently?

She was deep in thought as Meg left, with Mamgu accompanying her on the rest of her rounds.

The following afternoon, Tuesday, ensuring that all her chores for the morning had been completed, Mai went over to the communal hut, where lessons took place. Benches and tables were arranged around the circular wall. Mai sat on a bench behind one of the tables near the door space. There were eight other children, five girls and three boys varying in age between about five and ten. Mai had never been allowed to attend before. She was never allowed to play and only knew the other children by sight. They knew her, but only to laugh at. It was generally assumed that she was 'slow' and an 'idiot' because she never spoke to anyone. Why should she? Nobody ever spoke to her. But Mai listened. The children generally followed their parents' example. They laughed when she limped in but she ignored them and they were hastily reprimanded by Meg.

'You will welcome Mai MacIntyre kindly if you wish to continue your learning.'

They all did, otherwise they would be set to work at home. Meg handed out wax tablets and feather quills that she had fashioned herself. She told the other children to write out their names and whatever letters or words they could remember from their last lesson. She came over to Mai and sat next to her. She etched out 'Mai' on the tablet.

'This is your name written down, Mai,'
She showed her which letters made which sounds and how to hold the quill.

'Now, see if you can copy it, Mai.'
Mai wrote her name almost perfectly. Meg was delighted at how quickly the child picked it up. She told her the sounds of the letters and asked her to copy them a few more times. Then she showed her the first few letters of the alphabet; a (as in her name), b, c, d, e, and asked her to copy them. Leaving Mai to get on with her scribing, she went over to the other children and checked their work, correcting as necessary and setting them more work to copy.

'Children, what is the day today?'
Mai did not know but the other's, in unison, said, 'Tuesday'. The days of the week had never been of any consequence for Mai.

'And tomorrow is…?'
'Wednesday.'
'Will you all be going to Mamgu's class tomorrow?'
Nods all round.

'Good! So, now, we can count on our fingers, can't we? One, two. That's when our stitching session is, girls. Two days after tomorrow, isn't it? Friday. Now, shall we count our fingers up to five? One, two, three, four, five.'
Lots more nodding and finger counting, including Mai.

By the end of the lesson, Mai could count all her fingers up to ten and had learned the days of the week. She could remember all the names. She was good with the counting, too, and, best of all, she could write her name!

'And, again, what day do the girls come to my stitching class?'

'Friday!'

'Mai, I hope you will come too?'

Mai nodded again. If the others were unkind to her, she didn't care. One day, she would be a proper midwife, helping to bring new babies into the world, whatever anyone said.

At the end of the lesson, as the other children left, Meg asked Mai to stay back as she handed in her tablet.

'Are you sure you know when Friday will be, Mai?'

Mai nodded and then whispered, head bowed, 'Two hognights after Mamgu's class.'

'Hognight? What's a hognight?'

Mai shrugged her shoulders.

'You know, Mai, this is really very good for a first attempt. You are quite clever, aren't you?'

Then she noticed something and took up the quill that Mai had placed on her table..

If we write the letters in your name backwards, it reads, 'I am. If we write it backwards and then forwards it reads, 'I am Mai'.

Meg wrote it out again and explained that the spaces between the letters showed the separate words. Mai beamed and nodded. She understood. Overjoyed, inside her head, she repeated again and again: I am Mai! Not 'thing'! Not 'that'! I am Mai! Whatever *he* calls me, I am Mai. I will always be Mai!

She limped home to resume her chores.

A Boy and His Horse

At Mamgu's class, there were a few more children. Sioned Jones, a particularly nasty-natured girl of twelve, and her ten-year-old brother, Ioan, saw Mai limping on her way to the communal hut and, laughed at her, copying her strange gait as they entered the classroom. Mamgu was furious and when the children were seated and quiet, she gave them all a good telling off.

'You never, ever laugh at Mai, or any other child in my class! And that applies to all of you! Do you understand me?'

They all nodded, shame-faced. They all liked Mamgu, but it was never a good idea to get on the wrong side of her.

A tall slender boy of about fourteen years of age walked in. His light-chestnut wavy locks flowed down to his shoulders; Mai thought he was the most handsome boy she had ever seen. He wasn't dressed in finery, so didn't look rich, but neither was he from a poor family. He bowed slightly towards Mamgu. She flushed and became quite flustered.

'Oh, Master Alexander! It is so nice to see you! Will you be joining our class today? I understand you have been away.'

'Nice to see you too, Mamgu. Yes, indeed. I was staying with my Aunt and Uncle in Monmouth.'

He had the most beautiful smile and polite manners.

'I always look forward to your classes. It's a lovely way to spend my Wednesday afternoons.'

'Your father has business up at the Big House this afternoon, does he?'

'Well, yes. He is usually up there on a Wednesday afternoon. I take the opportunity to ride out with him on my way here, but I'm sure that I would come anyway. I do so enjoy your tales.'

He turned his attention to Mai, sitting alone near the door space.

'Hello. Mai, isn't it? I am Alexander. I know your brothers, Fitz and Pat. Do you mind if I sit with you?'

He sat on the stool next to Mai. His big brown eyes were smiling with his friendly grin. She returned the smile and nodded, but it was too late. He was going to sit there regardless. She was grimy, dressed in rags and had a front tooth missing. Where most girls had long flowing locks, Mai looked as though somebody had dumped a pudding bowl on top of her head and roughly chopped around it with shears. They had, but a bit had been missed and a stray lock fell down her face over her right eye. Her hair smelt of smoke but Alexander didn't mind. There was something special about this dirty, scruffy little girl. Until now, he had only ever seen her from afar, as he rode through the settlement, always busy with her chores. She never played like other children. It seemed to him that she had been set to work from the moment she could walk. Sitting next to her, she enchanted him.

Mamgu called the class to order.

'Now some of you will have heard this tale before, but others haven't. It's some time since I have given this lesson so it will not do any harm to repeat it.'

She began her tale of Llewellyn the Great and how he united the country and became King of all Wales. While other children interrupted, chatted and fidgeted, Mai listened intently.

At the end of the lesson Alexander turned to her.

'Would you like to meet my horse?'

He took her outside to where the horse, a stallion of golden cream, with long, flowing white mane and tail, and big white feathered feet, was loosely tethered to what looked like a shepherd's crook, but forged from iron, stuck into the ground. He was contentedly munching on the grass. Mai had seen him before, when Alexander had ridden into the settlement, but not this close up. She had never seen so beautiful a horse.

The horse looked up, his huge brown eyes with long white eyelashes were gentle and kind. His forelock, swept to one side, revealed a white star between his eyes. He reminded her of the metal-heads' horses. She had seen them when they rode along the track past the settlement. This horse wasn't quite as big as those but, to a little girl, he was very big this close up; yet she was no more afraid of this gentle giant than she was of My Girl. She didn't know who to love more – Alexander or his horse!

'This is Cyflym. It means …'

'Fast,' whispered Mai, her voice barely audible.

Mai might not say much, but Mai picked up a lot of both Welsh and English words in the settlement. The two languages often mingled into what they called 'the Wengi. In the MacIntyre household, English was predominant.

'Yes, indeed. You can stroke him. He's very friendly.'

She stroked the powerful neck.

'He is fifteen hands and one inch high at the withers.'

He showed her how a hand was measured and where the withers are on a horse.

'He was a gift from one of my father's cousins when I was about nine years old. He was little more than a young colt then. We've almost grown up together! Perhaps, next week you could ride him after class, if you'd like. Shall I ask Mamgu if we can arrange it?'

Mai had never sat on a horse in her life! She couldn't believe it. Mai MacIntyre on a horse! She didn't know how to ride, but she was sure Alexander would show her. She wasn't in the least afraid of the beautiful Cyflym.

31

'Well, goodbye, Mai MacIntyre. I'll go and see what I can arrange with Mamgu for next week. But ...'

He put his forefinger to his lips. She didn't have to be told. If such a thing was ever to get out and reach Herbert's ears she would be in for another beating. Being well acquainted with Fitz and Pat, Alexander knew much about the goings on in the MacIntyre household.

Mai limped home while he nipped back into the communal hut for a word or two with Mamgu after the other children had left.

'You! Get some kindling on that fire before it goes out and then you can get your backside in that turnspit!'

Not a flicker of interest in what she'd been learning. Herbert just scowled his usual scowl and her mother carried on in her own world – wherever that was. Mai did as she was told. The rabbit was skewered ready on the spit over the flames. When the fire was roaring sufficiently, she got inside the wheel. This was the job of a small dog in the big houses – or a servant in the type of wheel that could be turned from outside. Here, it was one of Mai's jobs. She was the one small enough to get inside. Her hair was always getting singed by the flames so Sarah had chopped it off.

When dinner was ready, Herbert remained as good as his word and did not allow her to share the meal. He threw her some scraps from the pigswill and another raw turnip, part rotten. It was horrible. She had to run outside when it made her vomit and gave her the squits but it didn't matter. Learning her letters and reading and counting and stitching and midwifing will give her a future. Something better than this lay ahead. She knew it. There would be a life. There would be love. Not here.

Somewhere. One day. There would be love. There would be a reason to be.

Until then, she could endure what life she had been given.

Alexander trotted Cyflym along the track through the woodland. If his father had completed his business, he might bump into him on his way home from the Big House, or Tŷ Mawr, as it was called in Welsh and the Wengi. He spotted Fitz and Pat in the distance. They were coming his way, carrying a couple of hares and a duck. While the trapping of rabbits was permissible for the poor, hares were a different matter, even if trapped unintentionally. As he came alongside them, he reined in Cyflym, stifling a laugh.

'Not been poaching, have you, boys?'

Fitz had his tongue firmly planted in his cheek.

'Not today, for sure, Alexander! You can't see anything on us, can you?'

Alexander doubled up, almost slipping from his saddle!

'Ha! Do not concern yourselves about me, boys. You have enough to contend with. I will not be adding to your woes. Oh, and I have just heard Mamgu scolding the Jones children. They were teasing your sister. How did she acquire that injury to her foot? Looks nasty.'

They shrugged, but they, and he, were pretty sure how.

'Thanks, Alex. We will deal with the Joneses.' Pat said.

'Yes, I am sure – but take care, lads. They are but children themselves.'

They threw a wave as Alexander heeled Cyflym on. The boys ran the rest of the way home. Diving in through the door space, they dropped their spoils on the table and dashed out again before Herbert had a chance to say a word. Sarah barely noticed. The baby started to cry. She took him from the crib and sat down to feed him.

The Jones children were playing a game of tag around their hut. Fitz and Pat, as ever a single entity, waited unseen at the back. As the children chased each other around the hut, he first, with her very close behind, the boys pounced. Pat grabbed the boy by the scruff and Fitz, the girl, by the hair. They dragged them to the edge of the woodland and wrestled them to the floor.

'You two, both or either,' growled Pat, by far the most intimidating of the two, purely on account of his size, 'tease our sister, or hurt her, or do anything to her, ever again, and you will have us to answer to. Do you understand?'

'Well, do you?' Fitz hissed at the girl.

Struck dumb with terror, they just nodded. Fitz and Pat jumped up and hauled the two bullies to their feet, sending them both packing with a kick each to their behinds, lurching them forwards.

The girl was indignant.

'You'll be in trouble for this! We'll tell our father and he'll tell your Uncle Herbert and then you'll get it!'

'Really? I think not!'

Pat knew he was right. John Jones was a true weasel of a man; cowardly as you could find anywhere. He wouldn't be telling anyone. Their mother, Alys Jones, was no better. The couple had never instilled discipline into their children; they had always permitted them to run amuck. The result was a thoroughly nasty pair of children who would grow into thoroughly nasty adults.

Heaven knows, Fitz and Pat had copied some of Herbert's ways with their attitude to Mai for the first few years. They were so young when they lost their father that they knew no better. Now, as they were maturing, there had been an epiphany of sorts, and there was enough residue of Eric's influence, of his decency, to know when things had gone too far. Nobody took on these two, certainly not the Joneses. Herbert would never tackle the two of them now, for sure. They didn't feel quite ready to do anything about him for now, but it wouldn't be long. His time would come.

Now the weather was warmer, the brothers had taken to sleeping out in the woods every night. They fashioned shelters from reeds on the banks of the stream if needed. Anything to be away from *him*. Fortunately for Herbert, they were unaware of Mai's hognights. Had they known, Herbert's time would probably have come long before either of them expected.

A Tree for Mai

On Friday morning, Meg called around to the MacIntyre hut with Mamgu. Meg brought a dress that she'd stitched from a piece of sackcloth she'd scrounged. The dress was plain but the cloth was fairly fine woven and at least it was decent. Mai put it on over her ragged short-sleeved shirt. Meg had also fashioned some shoes for her. The soles were cut from old leather begged from the cobbler in town. The uppers, she had made from plaited reeds cut from the beds at the river bank and softened with goose grease. They gave support and protection to Mai's feet and ankles. She was not yet able to put her heel to the floor, and the toes were still turned slightly inwards, but the swelling had all but disappeared and the pain was now very slight. Mai was thrilled with her new dress and shoes. Herbert shrugged his shoulders and carried on supping his ale, while Sarah, other than taking instinctual, minimum care for the baby, still appeared to be oblivious as to what was going on around her. Meg and Mamgu worried but, other than monitoring the baby's welfare, what could they do?

The Jones girl was present at Meg's stitching class on Friday afternoon, but kept her distance. The other girls ignored Mai, not wanting to be associated with 'the idiot'. They had squares of coarse woven sackcloth and began stitching samplers with needles and thread provided by Meg. They already knew most of their letters and numbers and carried on stitching them below their names. Mai knew her numbers up to ten in her head but not yet how to scribe them.

Meg had already stitched 'i am mai' on the cloth and showed her how to stitch the 'i am' so that Mai could then copy her name: the same letters. She did it admirably. A bit wobbly here and there; it took her the entire session but, for a first attempt, it was an excellent effort. Meg was delighted.

At the end of the lesson, Mai handed in her work with great pride.

'You have done very well, Mai. We will see you next Tuesday afternoon, then. You know when Tuesday will be, don't you?'

Mai counted on her fingers. In her now familiar whisper she replied, 'Four hognights.'

Well, at least the child was speaking a little. But what, in the name of Heaven, could she mean by 'hognights'? It must be just how Mai interpreted the fact that, in the MacIntyre household, the hogs spent the nights inside.

The four hognights until the next letters and numbers class passed with the usual drudgery. Mai copied all her numbers, and the first five letters of the alphabet. Then they recited the names of the days of the week. That was a bit harder. Mai found it easy to remember Tuesday, which was letters and numbers with Meg; Wednesday, Mamgu's tales – and Alexander, which was best of all – and Friday, stitching with Meg. The names of the other days, when nothing happened, were a bit more difficult but she was getting there. The one she was absolutely sure of was the Sabbath, because everyone rested from their work in the fields. This time, though clearly unsure of herself, she got it right. Four hognights.

'Don't worry, Mai', Meg reassured her, 'you are doing really well. You have learned a great many things in a short space of time. You will soon catch up with the others.'

Inside, Mai was buzzing with the joy of everything life had in store for her – even if not yet. In the meantime, learning was something to enjoy, and she practised her counting and days of the week in her head at home, while she was carrying out her chores.

Wednesday was Mamgu's story day again. In the morning, she appeared at the MacIntyre's hut, demanding that following the afternoon's story session, Mai should come to her hut and help her with the stitching of cloths that were needed for the midwifing, as Mamgu called it. 'Mai needs to develop all her skills, you know.' She bustled out with, 'I'll see you later, Mai.'

Herbert gave Mai a clip around the ear and growled at her to get on with her chores.

In the afternoon, Mai dutifully turned up at Mamgu's class. This time, she told them how King Edward of England had conquered Wales, which Mai thought was not a very nice thing at all. Mamgu had a way of embellishing things and, while her hand-me-down history may have been less than entirely accurate, the children, perhaps with the exception of Alexander, weren't to know any better – and she certainly told a riveting tale. She followed it with a tale of fairies, pixies and goblins in the forest.

At the end of the session, Alexander whispered in Mai's ear, 'See you shortly' and left with the other children. Mamgu took Mai's hand and rushed her to her own hut. Rushing wasn't easy for Mai, given her infirmity, but she managed to keep up. Mamgu was very excited about getting stitching done! Would Alexander be there? There was no sign of Cyflym. When they arrived at the hut, they didn't go inside. Mamgu gave a quick look around and, satisfied that they weren't noticed by anyone else, hurried Mai over to the edge of the wood.

A little way in, not far from the track, just out of sight of the settlement, was a huge old tree, which must have been the biggest in the forest. Hundreds of years old, they said it was. For some reason, it was called Peter's Oak and had been so named for generations. Nobody now, not even Mamgu – for all her tales of history, had the faintest idea who Peter had been. It was just Peter's Oak, and that was that. Beneath its great branches, Alexander, atop Cyflym, waited for them, wearing a huge grin.

'Come on, then, Missy! Up you come!'

Mamgu gripped Mai around the waist and lifted her up, but her joyful expression changed. Passing the child up to Alexander, she felt Mai's bony ribs and hips through her new dress. This wasn't right. This wasn't right at all. Alexander noted the concern on Mamgu's face, and gave her a nod in acknowledgement, sharing Mamgu's unspoken concern, as he easily pulled Mai into the saddle in front of him. He might be just fourteen years old but he was educated, shrewd and wise beyond his years.

'Thank you, Mamgu.'

He heeled Cyflym forward and the horse plodded on. The woodland floor was shrouded in bluebells. Such a beautiful sight! Mai had never been this far along the track. A short while later, they arrived at a clearing; a meadow almost filled with wild flowers. Over the other side, not far from the hedgerow, stood another large oak tree, though not quite of the enormity of Peter's Oak. They rode as far as the tree. Alexander dismounted. He reached up and pulled Mai down from the saddle.

They sat down on the grass, sheltering from the sun under the oak tree's great boughs. Cyflym dropped his head to the grass and started to munch away.

'Mai? Do you know the names of the flowers?'

She shook her head. She recognised most of them but the only flower she knew the name of was the bluebell. She had heard people around talk about them because of the spectacle they made when they were in flower along the hedgerows and in the woodlands.

Picking them one by one, he said, 'Well, this one is a primrose … and this is a daisy … this is a buttercup… this is a celandine – and this is a dandelion,' pointing to one of the flowers with its dense head of long, thin yellow petals. 'They're called dandelions because it sounds like the French name for "lion's tooth". It's not a good idea to pick them, though, because they're said to make you want to piss if you do.'

She wasn't about to try it but she stroked the petals of the one he'd pointed out. She didn't know what a lion was but she imagined it must be some kind of animal; a quite small, gentle, furry one, she thought.

'Wait here!'

He jumped up. Her eyes followed him as he ran to the middle of the meadow. Cyflym lifted his head to check where his young master was going. When Alexander stooped to pick more flowers, the horse was satisfied that he wasn't going far and resumed his grazing. Soon Alexander was back with two posies.

'This', he held out one posy with a deep, exaggerated bow, 'is for you, Mademoiselle. And this is for Mamgu. They're called pansies.'

Each petal of the pansies was of three colours: purple, yellow – brighter than the sun – and white. They were so beautiful! They and the bluebells. She loved the bluebells. He went to the hedgerow behind the oak, where more bluebells were growing in the shade of the oak's canopy. He picked a few to add to Mai's collection then returned to sit at Mai's side and picked a few more daisies. He made a daisy chain and popped it on top of her head.

'There you are! Princess Mai! I wonder if this tree has a name like Peter's Oak. It's quite old but not as old as

Peter's Oak, though, so I shouldn't think it has. I've never heard anyone call it by a name, anyway.'

He turned to her with a broad grin.

'I know! We'll call it 'Mai's Oak'! How about that, then? Yes, Mai's Oak suits it perfectly.'

Mai was aghast. Nobody had ever been so kind to her. Except Mamgu and Meg, of course. But posies! Her own tree! And her very own prince! (Well, as far as Mai was concerned, Alexander was better than any prince that Mamgu could tell a tale of.) This was the best day of her life. Ever!

'Well, come along, little one. I shouldn't keep you out too long.'

They rose to their feet. He lifted Mai onto the saddle, she being careful not to damage the posies, then mounted up himself. He was only too aware of her misery and it broke his heart. From the feel of her ribs, Herbert must be all but starving her! Alexander would do anything, anything at all, to relieve the suffering of this sweet child, but what?

'One day, Mai, when you are of an age, I am going to come along and take you away from all this. We will be married and you will have the life of a real lady.'

She may only be a young child for now, but he really meant it. One day, she would be a beautiful young lady who deserves so much better than the miserable life she has now.

At Peter's Oak, he let her down from the saddle, her posies still intact and, having no hands free, she nuzzled Cyflym's neck, smiled her gappy smile and whispered her goodbye.

'Au revoir, ma cherie!' and he and Cyflym were off down the track at a canter. She didn't understand what he had said but it was something nice. She did know that she loved him. And Cyflym. Very much. At the edge of the woodland, she checked nobody could see her, and skipped and hopped her way back to Mamgu's hut, barely aware of the pain in her ankle.

She went through Mamgu's door space and held out a bunch of pansies.

'For you.' Her voice was a little stronger which pleased Mamgu no end. 'From Alexander.'

'For me? Oh! My goodness me! My goodness me! How kind! How kind!'

'And these is for me!'

The joy on her face warmed Mamgu's heart as she held out her own posy of pansies, bluebells and the other flowers.

'This is pansies, and this is a daisy, this is a primrose, this is a buttercup, and this is bluebells and this is a cela... cela...'

'Celandine, my lovely. It's a celandine.'

'Yes. But we didn't pick the lion's teeth because they makes you piss!'

Lion's teeth? Whatever they were. The only flower Mamgu knew that made you piss was a dandelion. Still, Master Alexander was well educated so he probably knew more than even she did.

'Right, my lovely. We'll pop these in water, shall we? Oh! Just look at your daisy crown! Pretty that is, isn't it?'

'And I've got a tree named for me. It's called 'Mai's Oak'. Like 'Peter's Oak' but not as big because I don't think I'm as big as Peter. Although we don't know how big he was because we don't know who he was. But we know who I am. I am Mai.'

'Yes, you are indeed! You are Mai! Is it the one in the meadow over by the far hedge?'

Mai nodded.

'Well, Mai's Oak will be there forever.'

Mai thought about that for a few moments, then she said,

'But I think there will be a time when nobody knows who it's named for, Mamgu. Just like nobody knows who Peter was.'

Mamgu could not believe the torrent of speech suddenly being emitted from the mouth of a child who had, hitherto, been regarded by all and sundry as 'slow' and 'an idiot' because she couldn't speak.

'Well, I s'pose eventually that will be so. One day. It's the way of the world. But for now, we know that it's Mai's Oak, don't we? Right then! We must put the pansies and bluebells in water.'

She busied herself by collecting a couple of wide-topped jugs and filling them with water from the trough outside her hut. 'We will press these others with a pansy and a bluebell to preserve them. You can keep them forever then!' She removed one pansy and one bluebell, putting them aside with the other single flowers.

She arranged the pansies and bluebells in the jugs and pulled down two old chopping boards and a selection of cloths from her shelves, placing them on her table. Mai studied Mamgu's every move as she folded a cloth and spread it on one of the boards, then carefully arranged the single flowers on the cloth, leaving a little space between each. She folded another cloth and put it on top of the flowers, then put the other board over that and placed the whole thing on the floor in a corner of the hut. Mamgu didn't keep hogs, so her hut was square. She trotted outside, returning a few moments later with a couple of large, heavy looking stones and place them on the upper board.

'There we are! In a few weeks they'll be nicely dried out to keep for ever. We must think of a way to display them. We'll keep them here for safety, though. You'd best be off home now, my lovely, or I'll have Herbert after me!'

That was unlikely – he wouldn't dare cross Mamgu – but he might take it out on her, so she returned home.

Herbert grunted as she walked in. Sarah was absent-mindedly feeding the baby. His eyes caught sight of the daisy chain sitting on her hair.

'What's all this rubbish then?'

He grabbed it and threw it on the fire.

She was home.

Two more hognights until stitching class.

The other children still avoided her, both at stitching class on Friday, and at reading and scribing class on Tuesday, and at Mamgu's tales class on Wednesday. Mai couldn't have cared less.

On Wednesday afternoon, Mamgu and Alexander pulled the same ruse. It was so joyful for Mamgu to see the child with a friend, and Alexander was so sweet. Mai was safe in his hands. She watched them ride away together, but Mai was even thinner now than last week. Mamgu went home to prepare a bowl of broth and bread for her. The poor child was not being fed while that fat, lazy man gorged himself and filled his gullet with ale.

Under Mai's Oak, Alexander's joyful mood changed to something more serious:

'Mai, there is something I must tell you. I have to go away at the end of August. I have had my lessons with a tutor at home until now, but I will be going away to school in September. It's in a place called Monmouth. That's why I have been away. I had to go there to see if it was suitable. My Aunt and Uncle live near there so I took the opportunity to spend some time with them. I quite liked the school. I will be gone a long time, I'm afraid, but I will be back next Summer. After that, I will only have one more year and I will have my qualifications to be apprenticed to my father.'

Mai was devastated.

'But when is August? I haven't learned my months yet.'

'The end of Summer, my sweet. I have to go, but when I have my qualifications, and have finished my apprenticeship, I can earn a fair amount of money and save up for a home for us. When you are of an age, we really can be married. What do you think?'

Her eyes glistened. Cruelty could not make her cry. It would not make her cry. Love was different. Even the love of a child. She looked at him and he stroked away the stray tear rolling down her cheek with his thumb.

'I think that I shall be very sad when you are away. I don't understand the ways of grown-ups yet but I know you have shown me a way of love I can understand. While you are gone, I will have my lessons and my dream of being happy one day. And Mamgu is making my flowers dry so I will always have them to remember you by while you are away. I will keep them safe with Mamgu because Uncle Herbert put my daisy chain on the fire as soon as he saw it.'

'Oh. I suppose he would.'

Like Mamgu, Alexander realised that a flood of words had cascaded from this little girl who, until now, had barely strung more than two whispered together and, otherwise; communicated with nothing more than a shrug of her shoulders, or a nod or a shake of the head.

'Come on, little one. Better go back, eh? We still have the rest of the Summer, don't we?'

That cheered her up a bit. He gave her a hug and lifted her up into the saddle. Like Mamgu, he noticed that she had lost more weight, even in the last week – barely anything but skin and bone. He set her down at Peter's

Oak and she patted and kissed Cyflym on the neck. Alexander looked down at her with his gentle smile and was off.

Mai returned to Mamgu's hut where a hearty meal awaited her. She said nothing, despite Mamgu's enquiries, but bolted down the food with gratitude. The poor little thing was starving. Then she opened up:

'Alexander has to go away at the end of the Summer, Mamgu. It's very sad. I will miss him and Cyflym very much, but they will be back.'

Mamgu was almost overcome with the warmth and joy she felt for the child. She wasn't sure who Mai loved most – Alexander or his horse. She suspected both equally.

'I know, my dear. I know. He did tell me. He will indeed be back. And you will have your flowers preserved for the memory until he returns, won't you?'

The Summer went on, with classes and Alexander, Cyflym, and their weekly meetings under Mai's Oak. Even though Mamgu was trying to supplement her food, Mai was not gaining any weight as far as either Mamgu or Alexander could tell, but she was doing very well with her classes. She could add up numbers on her fingers, but it was a bit annoying when she hadn't enough fingers and had to use her toes because she had to take off her shoes. She could remember most of the alphabet, even if she couldn't always get the letters in the right order. She was catching up with the other girls, too, in the stitching class.

Mai tried her very best at everything she did. She even helped Mamgu deliver a couple of babies although, from Mamgu's face, one of the births was not going to have a happy outcome and Mamgu had said, 'It's alright, my lovely. You pop along home – I can take care of this.' Mai intuitively understood what was happening. She heard gossip around the settlement that the baby had been born dead and its mother died later, although neither she nor Mamgu mentioned it. Mai was very sad about it, but it was not that unusual. Life could be so harsh. She loved the babies and small children and there was another baby due soon.

The dreaded end of August was approaching and Alexander would soon be gone. Mamgu had an idea:

'Mai, how would you like to make a gift for Alexander to go off to his school?'

Mai spent as much time as she possibly could at Mamgu's hut, making a feather waistcoat for him, with Mamgu fibbing to Herbert that she needed Mai to help her with stitching for the midwifing. Meg cut the shapes from the best sackcloth she could find and gave her the needle and thread. Mamgu had amassed a huge collection of duck feathers from the pluckings as she prepared her meals; ducks kindly provided by Fitz and Pat in gratitude for all she was doing for their little sister. She showed Mai how to stitch the waistcoat together, then secure the feathers with a special hook side by side, then each row of feathers was slightly layered over by the next. It was so fine and colourful. Mamgu invited Meg to see it before Mai gave it to Alexander. They were both suitably impressed with her handiwork.

On their last meeting before he travelled to Monmouth, Mai was to present it to Alexander. Mamgu wrapped it in a coarse linen cloth so that it would be a surprise for him when they got to the meadow.

Mai arrived at Peter's Oak with Mamgu as usual. He was intrigued by the parcel.

'What have you here?'

'Never you mind until you get to Mai's Oak!' Mamgu scolded.

He laughed as he pulled Mai up into the saddle. She was still no heavier. They dismounted at Mai's Oak and sat on the grass.

'For you, Alexander.'

She handed him the package and he unwrapped it.

'Oh, Mai! This is beautiful! So colourful and it will be really warm in the winter. Did you make it yourself?'

'Meg cut out the pieces, but I stitched it and Mamgu showed me how to do the feathers and I did them but Mamgu helped me when I got stuck sometimes. It was Mamgu's idea, though, and Meg found the cloth to make it.'

'You ladies have been conspiring, have you?'

He tried it on and it fitted beautifully, with a little growing room. Meg had judged his size well.

'Thank you, my precious little one – you are so clever. You must thank Meg and Mamgu for me, too. It's wonderful. I shall wear it with pride!'

At Peter's Oak, he dismounted and when she dropped down from the saddle, he put his arms around her, and gave her a huge hug.

'I am going to miss you, my dearest Mai.'

'I will miss you, too, Alexander. And Cyflym. But you will be back next Summer.'

'Yes. You can be sure of that. And I think we will both be taller!'

He remounted. She hugged and kissed Cyflym's neck, and as though he understood what was happening, the horse turned his head and nuzzled her. She sobbed out her heart at Mamgu's. Mamgu gave her the biggest cwtch and did her best to comfort her. Eventually, the tears subsided. Mamgu smiled at her.

'You just do your best with your learning for now, Mai bach. You'll be educated as he is by next Summer!'

Mai managed a giggle. Mamgu washed her face for her and, after a meal of broth and bread, she reluctantly made her way home.

As she approached the hut, a lump formed in her throat and her heart began to pound in her chest. Something was wrong. She didn't know what. She just knew something was wrong.

Baby … Gone

Mai entered the hut to find Sarah and Herbert alone. The crib was empty. She walked over to her mother and tugged her arm.

'Seamus? Where is Seamus?

It was the first time since Herbert had thrown her across the hut and struck Sarah that she had spoken to either of them. The slight progress that Sarah had made since that dreadful day had disappeared.

'Baby … gone … Baby … gone …' was all she could utter.

'Gone? Gone where?' pleaded her daughter.

Sarah's sad, grief-stricken eyes looked in Herbert's direction. Despite her vow to the contrary, Mai summoned up the temerity not only to look at him, but to speak to him.

'Gone? Gone where? Where is the baby?'

She expected a clout, but it was not forthcoming.

'Well, she was no use as a mother to him. She's no use to anyone, is she? Useless, just like you she is, now. Look at her! That baby has gone to a family that can look after him better. He'll have a good life with rich people. A lot richer than us! Relatives of them up at the Big House. A cousin of hers. Servant told Jonesy that they lost a baby boy and his mother was grieving so I told him they could have Seamus if they wanted 'cos she can't care for him proper. Related to that Cromwell what's running the country now, they are. He'll be well provided for.'

Had it not been for the devastating news she'd just received, she may well have been pleased that he had spoken to her at such length and, for the first time ever, with an almost civil tone. The feeling of nausea hit her hard; her legs wobbled beneath her. Unable to catch her breath, she fell to the ground as she tried to digest the information.

Seamus! He's given Baby Seamus away! Her beautiful little baby brother! She began to sob. Herbert hauled her to her feet.

'Get out of here if you're going to come that nonsense!'

He kicked her through the door space. She ran to Mamgu's and blurted out the tale through the sobs and tears. Mamgu's eyes almost popped from their sockets.

'He did what? Right! Let's get to the bottom of this, shall we?' and she marched, furious, not to the MacIntyre's hut as Mai had expected, but to the Jones' hut, Mai limping as fast as she could behind her.

'John Jones! John Jones!'

The short skinny man appeared at his door space.

'What's all this about Herbert MacIntyre giving away their baby, then?'

He smirked down at Mai, then looked Mamgu straight in the eye, with an air of defiance. Horrible man. It was no wonder his children behaved as they did.

'Give him away? Give him away? He never did give him away!'

'Then what? Where is the baby?'

'Ha! He sold him, he did. Got a fair whack too – and me and that servant of theirs – we all got our share.'

'What? I don't believe it! How could you? John Jones, you are evil beyond words, is all I can say! The lot of you are! Evil!'

She turned on her heel; fearful that her temper was about to explode. Mai limped as fast as she could behind.

'Maybe! But we got ours for it, Mamgu!' he laughed after her.

'He sold my brother, Mamgu! His own son! He sold my little brother!'

Mamgu stopped, crouched down, biting her lip – but Mai could see the tears in her eyes. She had never seen Mamgu so upset.

'I know, Mai bach. I know. And if the people he sold him to are related to that Cromwell what's in charge of the country now, since they killed the King, then I don't see as how we can do anything about it. I'm so, so sorry, my little lovely.'

Mamgu took a cloth from her apron pocket, wiped Mai's face, then her own, and pulled Mai to her, hugging her tight and stroking her hair. She took her back to her own hut to comfort her before confronting Herbert, which she would do in private – away from Mai, to avoid upsetting her any more. It couldn't have happened on a worse day, either. The day Alexander left. The Lord only knows what this would do to Sarah. What would Fitz and Pat say? By now, they had discovered that Mai slept with the hogs, but she had assured them that it was her own choice; she liked it, she was safe and warm – but don't tell *him*. Had Herbert over-stepped himself?

The next time Mamgu saw Herbert, he had acquired more than a few bruises. She gave him a few choice words of her own, but it made no difference. Baby Seamus was gone and Sarah grew even worse.

Mai was still counting the days of the week in hognights. She preferred it that way.

The Dying Days of Summer

The leaves on the trees were beginning to turn from greens to yellows and russets, but it was a warm Saturday morning. (Saturday was one hognight after stitching class, which was Friday.)

Mai crouched at the stream running behind the settlement, rinsing some pots. She finished her chore and put the pots beside her feet for a moment. The stream was almost still, barely flowing at this point, and deeper than elsewhere. Staring into the clear water, her reflection stared back at her. She'd never really noticed before.

That is me! I am Mai!

Mai MacIntyre was beginning to think of herself as a person.

Just as she was about to lift up the pots to take them back to the hut, a pedlar wandered from the track, making for the settlement. He hopped over the stepping stones in the stream and approached her. He was selling all kinds of silly charms such as lucky heather and rabbits' feet. Even Mai knew it was rubbish but everyone has to make a living somehow. He stopped.

'Hello! How are you today, my lovely? Is this Cefn-yr-Afon?'

She nodded and stood up to say 'hello', but before she knew what was happening, he lifted her up and gave her a huge kiss and cuddle.

'Aren't you a lovely little girl, then?'

This was not something she was used to at all. He meant no harm, but she didn't like it. He was old and scruffy and dirty and slobbery and he had horrible spots on his face and she was glad when he put her down.

'Many about, then?'

'A few. Most out in the fields, though.'

She bent down and picked up her pots, but waited a while so that she didn't have to walk with him. He jaunted merrily into the settlement. She followed from a distance. He went from hut to hut. Of those at home, some were interested in his wares; most were not, but he made a few pennies for his trouble.

Herbert was at home. Herbert was always at home if he wasn't supping ale in the communal hut with his cronies. Herbert was not able to do heavy manual work in the fields on account of a childhood injury to his shoulder: the one which prevented him taking the King's shilling.

The pedlar received no joy at the MacIntyre hut. After visiting all of the dwellings, he returned to the track, making his way to the next settlement.

It was ten days before Mai fell ill with the fever. Her mouth was sore. Two days later she began to break out in a rash of pustules. Others in the settlement were going down with it as well: smallpox, known to the settlers as 'the blight'. Meg was instrumental in setting up a hospital for the sufferers as far away from the huts as could be managed. Some of the men chopped down trees and built it from wood, which could be easily burned afterwards. Maria, Meg and Louisa, at great risk to themselves tended the sick. Marcus also did what he could to help.

'Meg, my dear, I fear 'that if it spreads to join up around her body, there will be no hope. We can only pray for her soul.'

Meg, heartbroken, knew her mother was right.

Three days later, Sarah gazed down at her desperately sick child. The blight would very soon take her daughter from this world. Meg was surprised that Mai had lasted this long. The rash of pustules covered the little body. Sarah felt no conscious compassion. The last seven years since she had heard of Eric's death, just after Mai's birth, had knocked every semblance of emotion from her, but somewhere, deep, deep inside her soul, tears mingled with the shattered fragments of her heart.

Mai, lying on a sack of straw on the makeshift wooden cot, in the hastily erected wooden shelter, drifted in and out of delirium and consciousness. She was vaguely aware of somebody sitting on a stool next to her, wiping over her brow with a cool, damp cloth. Meg? Yes. Must be. She wasn't sure, though. Through the blurred haze, she could just about make out somebody else standing at the end of the cot.

All feeling for her stricken daughter suppressed, Sarah's expression was blank as she braced herself.

'I have other family to care for.'

She spoke in little more than a whisper, but Mai heard her words and recognised the voice. Sarah turned and left.

Mai felt no emotion, either. Even if she'd had the energy, would she have felt anything? Unlikely. Her life on this Earth had been as purgatory. She had been treated no better than the swine. Only Mamgu, Meg and her beloved Alexander had shown her any real kindness – and dear Cyflym and My Girl, of course. Fitz and Pat had been nice to her when they were around, but they just came home with rabbit, pigeon, duck, fish or whatever else they could catch, and left straight away. She couldn't blame them. Now the nights were getting colder they began to sleep in the hut but were gone at first light. They just wanted to be away from *him*.

In this final moment of lucidity, with the end rapidly approaching, Mai understood that she would not see another day. The future she thought was hers had vanished. Oh, Alexander! Oh, Cyflym! Her eyelids closed and, for the final time, she drifted back into blissful unconsciousness.

Later that night, Mai's spirit departed her emaciated little body. She watched, bemused, as two women from the settlement washed and wrapped it tightly in linen cloths ready for burial.

'But I'm here! I'm here!'

The women did not hear her. They carried on. She walked through the door – as though it wasn't there. This was the moment the realisation struck her.

'I'm dead. But I'm not. I'm still here.'

On hearing the news that Mai had departed, Sarah showed no outward emotion. Herbert picked up the corn-dolly from Mai's cot and threw it on the fire. And who would keep the fire going and turn the spit now? Not Sarah, by the look of it. Down to him, no doubt! He could not allow the matter to vex him. He would have to fashion some kind of handle for the spit. Perhaps he should make a new spit. Yes. He would have to get onto that.

In the morning, Mai watched, unseen, dispassionate, as they lifted her body onto a cart with two others, a woman and her young daughter, who had also died overnight. She followed them as they led the pony and cart down along the track to the mass grave by the river, where her body would join other victims of the outbreak. The superstition of spirits being carried away by water still persisted.

Mai was never sure of her age. Even though she was very good at counting in Meg's classes, it never occurred to her to work out how old she was. She knew that she had been born in the Year of our Lord 1648, but how many years ago was that? She didn't know what year it was now. Apart from the passing of hognights from one class to the next, time meant very little to her.

A man from the church recited the names of the dead as they were rolled down into the grave. She saw her own body lifted from the cart. He read some words from his book that she didn't understand, and said that she had only seen seven summers, before her body joined the others in the pit, so perhaps she was seven years old. She didn't understand the rest. She just kept shouting at them, unheard: 'But I'm still here! I'm still here!' They shovelled lime on top of the new bodies, threw the water on the top and covered them over with soil. The hole was not completely filled in.

There would be more bodies. The family at the Big House lost one of their young sons to the outbreak. Even Meg's dear younger brother, Marcus, succumbed. His hopes of becoming a doctor like his late father, vanished. None was spared the indignity of the mass grave.

For Mai though, it was done. Her mortal remains were in the ground – yet she was still here. But what now?

Peace

'Child, come with us. We will give you Peace.'

Mai turned to the voice. A row of human-like figures, glowing white but strangely translucent, stood before the brightest white light she had ever seen. They looked human, but not quite. Only one spoke. They didn't look solid like real people. One of the figures beckoned to her. The speaker held out a hand. Man? Woman? She couldn't tell.

Again, 'Child, come with us. We will give you Peace.'

Mai, mesmerised, went to take the hand of the nearest being, the not-quite-a-person, but at the last moment, she jerked back.

'No! I am not going anywhere with you! I don't know you.'

'But, dear child, we can give you Peace. You are alone. You have suffered enough.'

Mai was adamant – and indignant.

'No, I am staying here. I don't want to go with you. Whoever you are, please go away!'

'Please child. This is what is best for you. You can have Peace. We can give you Peace.'

'No! My life is here. Go away!'

The not-quite-a-person tried again.

'But child, they can't see or hear you. Your physical life is over. There is nothing for you here.'

'There is a life for me here. I have a future.'

'Dear, dear child. You can come back and have a life again. Another life. A far better one than you had here. We know how you have suffered.'

Mai thought for just a few moments. Her response stunned them:

'But, if I go with you and I come back, I will be somebody else, won't I? I don't want to be somebody else. I want to be me.'

'Child, your spirit will still be you.'

'But I have told you. I would not be Mai! I want to be Mai. Mai MacIntyre. I don't want to be anyone else. I have a future. I know somebody will find me and I can be me. I just want to be Mai. Not – anyone – else!'

She turned her back on them and the light. Metaphorically, they were left scratching their ethereal heads. They could not force her to go with them.

'Child, who among humans – breathers – will find you? How can they? You have seen for yourself that they cannot see or hear you.'

'Somebody will. One day. I know they will. I just know it. I will wait until then.'

'Child, you will wait forever. Alone.'

'I have been alone for most of my life. In the end, when I did find some relief, some hope, it was taken from me. My learning with Meg and Mamgu, my baby brother, Alexander and Cyflym, My Girl and even Arabella. Everyone and everything I loved and who showed me any love. So, what was the point of me? Why was I born? Why was I? Why am I? No. I am staying here until I find my true life. Meg said there is always a point to human life and she is right. If I go with you, there would be no point to me. Mai. I am Mai. I will be no-one else until I have found my reason to be.'

'But, child, this is not life. You are not alive. This is death, unless you come with us.'

'I can think. I can feel my emotions. I can be. I am. I am Mai and, one day, I know that somebody in the world will find me or I will find them and I will have the life I was born for.'

'Well, you will wait a very long time, dear child. How long are you prepared to wait?'

'I will wait as long as it takes.'

'We will return to see if you change your mind. If you do, we will be here to guide you through the Light.'

'I will not change my mind. I preferred to sleep with the hogs. I prefer to wait. Thank you. Now please go away!'

Defeated, the spirits dissipated into the Light. The Light itself remained. Mai kept her back to it, watching and waiting.

The outbreak took one hundred and seventy-three souls in all; twelve from Cefn-yr-Afon, forty-eight from the two larger settlements on the other side of the town, and the rest from the town itself – as well as the boy from the Big House and Marcus.

Some weeks later, the body of an old pedlar was stumbled upon in the forest by dogs belonging to people from the Big House, out hunting. There wasn't much left of him.

Of all the victims, it was Mai that Mamgu mourned most deeply. She sat in her hut and cried for days. For all the cruelty and misery the dear child had suffered throughout her life, suddenly, there had been hope for her future. And Mai bach, bless her dear little heart, she tried so hard. For what? Mamgu sat weeping in her chair. She was inconsolable. Nicholas, the grandson whom she had raised alone since the rest of her family were wiped out by the previous outbreak, sympathised. He placed a gentle arm around her shoulders, but she would not be pacified. He brewed her some tea from her herbs and left her to her tears.

'Mamgu? Mamgu?'

Oh, my goodness! Meg!

'Come in, Meg, please.'

She was still sobbing but rose from her chair, sniffed, swallowed hard and wiped her face dry on her apron as Meg stepped through the door space. The reddened puffiness in Mamgu's eyes and blotchy skin didn't pass Meg unnoticed. She put an arm around her and guided her back to her chair. The still warm mug of tea sat on the table. Meg picked it up and handed it to Mamgu. She took it gratefully.

'It's not fair, Meg. It's just not fair. I cry for them all every day – but most of all I cry for little Mai. If she had been stronger ... if I'd have done more ...'

If, if, if.

'Mamgu, please do not distress yourself so. We all did what we could and we prayed. Stronger people than Mai were taken. And you know, she was happier than she'd ever been over the last Summer. She has gone to a better place. The Lord takes care of his little children in Heaven.'

As much as Mamgu loved the devout Meg, she couldn't help asking herself why the Lord did not take better care of them here on Earth. Nobody dared ask such questions though. Then something occurred to her; something that she had forgotten through all the misery and heartache.

'Oh Meg! Alexander! He should surely know! I do not know how to inform him. Nobody else will tell him. He will be heartbroken, poor boy. He said his school is in Monmouth.'

'I will make discreet enquiries, Mamgu. I know his Father knew he came into the settlement for your tales, but if he knew that Alexander was quite so friendly with the settlers, I fear the dear boy would be in much trouble. If I can find an address, I will write a letter to him.'

Alexander finished his studies for the day and returned to his dormitory. He had two letters. One from his father, and another one. Somebody other than his father had sent him a letter. That had never happened before. Who could be writing to him? He sat on his bed, broke open the seal and read it – over and over and over again, unable to comprehend its contents. Surely not! This cannot be. It cannot be! No! No! He struggled to catch his breath. He read it one more time.

'Dear Alexander,

It is with the greatest sadness that I have to inform you that an outbreak of blight occurred here recently. I am sure you will be aggrieved to hear that one of its victims was Mai MacIntyre, a child whose friendship I know you cherished dearly.

I cannot sufficiently express my regret and heartfelt sorrow, having to be the bearer of such dreadful news, but be assured that God is with you, as Mai is with Him.

Mamgu has been most distraught but she sends you her very kindest wishes and hopes that you will still come to her classes when you return home for the Summer. You are ever in my prayers.

Meg Summerlee

The colour drained from Alexander's face. 'Mai! Not Mai! My dear, sweet little Mai! She cannot be gone!' He bit his lip, breathing heavily.

His friend, Anthony, skipped into the room and jumped on his own bed.

'Hey, Alex! What's wrong? What's in the letter? You look like you've seen a ghost!'

He looked away from his friend. He could not let Anthony see his moist eyes and quivering lip.

Jumping to his feet, he grabbed his precious feather waistcoat and, passing Anthony as quickly as he could on his way to find somewhere quiet and private, he said:

'I've had some very bad news. My dearest friend at home has died.'

'Oh no! Sorry, Alex. If you need to talk …'

But Alexander was gone.

He dashed out to the gardens, sat down behind a secluded hedge, hugged his waistcoat tight to him, and sobbed his heart away into the feathers. He remained there for hours. He missed his evening meal, not that he could have eaten anything. It was dusk and the temperature outside had dropped. Alexander put the waistcoat around his shoulders. Anthony told his fellow scholars to leave him be as he'd had some bad news.

Somehow, Alexander went on with his studies. He wrote to Meg to thank her for informing him and telling her how sad he was and, yes, he would be sure to visit Mamgu when he was next home.

The following Summer, when the rawness of the grief had subsided, he did indeed visit Mamgu, and they reminisced about little Mai. He swore her to secrecy, to which she readily agreed, and told her of their now tattered plans for the future.

At least he left Mamgu smiling with happy memories.

Alexander rode Cyflym out on the track towards the meadow, pausing briefly at Peter's Oak. Riding on to the meadow, he paused again before cantering over to the tree: their tree. He leapt down from the saddle and took his knife from its sheath on his belt. Smoothing his free hand over the bark at about the height of Mai's head, he thought for a few moments, then began to carve. When he had finished, he stood back and reflected on his handiwork. M intertwined with a heart intertwined with an A. Underneath, he carved 1655, Although it was now 1656.

Mai floated behind him and whispered, 'I love you, Alexander.'

Alexander hadn't consciously heard her but for some reason said, 'I love you, Mai.'

He replaced the knife in its sheath on his belt, turned around and, stumbling right through her, threw his arms around Cyflym's neck. He cried and cried and cried. Mai stroked his hair with one hand and stroked Cyflym's blaze with the other. Cyflym looked straight at her.

He knew. He understood.

Mai adored Alexander's carving and, all through his Summer holiday, after Mamgu's classes on Wednesday afternoons, he returned there. His tears lessened with time, but the grief inside remained within him. The bitterness did not ease. That evil man treated the sweet, innocent child so badly that she didn't stand a chance. The thoughts stirred in Alexander emotions of which he never thought himself capable. There would be revenge. Herbert might not have been responsible for the blight but, if she had been stronger, if he hadn't starved her and worked her into the ground, she might have stood a fighting chance. One day, for all his cruel treatment of dear, sweet little Mai, Herbert MacIntyre would pay.

Mai stayed around the part of the settlement where Mamgu lived, only venturing through the forest as far as the meadow and Mai's Oak. She liked to go into the classes and listen, unseen, with the children who had survived the blight. She didn't go near the MacIntyre hut. Why should she? It had never been a happy place, apart from the day that Seamus was born. She wasn't loved. They didn't care. Even her mother didn't care for her. She followed Fitz and Pat whenever they came that side of the forest to go hunting and fishing. She did love them and their antics were so amusing. If only they knew she was there!

Alexander only had one more week before he would be returning to his studies in Monmouth. After telling her stories and dismissing the children, Mamgu asked him if he wouldn't mind staying behind for a word.

'Alexander, do you have a book that you could spare?'

'Indeed, I do, Mamgu? Are you taking up reading?'

The heat rising in her neck up behind her ears indicated that she was flushing. She let out a nervous giggle.

'Oh no, Master Alexander, you do tease! I'm far too old to be learning new things.'

'Mamgu, you are never too old!'

'Well, I think we will have to disagree on that, my dear', she argued, regaining the jovial upper hand. 'No, it is for you. I have something for you, but you will need a book. Would you bring one with you next week? Just a small one will do.'

He was bemused, but he had a small old schoolbook that he would be happy to fetch the following week. He left her, and he and Cyflym made their short pilgrimage to Mai's Oak. Mai was waiting at Peter's Oak and followed them.

The following week, after the lesson, Mamgu invited him to her hut. Outside, he took Cyflym's reins, removed the tethering stake from the ground and, proffering his free arm, accompanied her to her home. He just told Cyflym to wait and the faithful horse simply dropped his head and began to graze.

Inside, Mamgu removed the stones from the chopping boards on the floor in the corner of the hut, lifted them up, and said: 'Alexander, these have been ready some time, but I have kept them here for you. Dear little Mai would surely have wanted you to have them. 'She placed them on the table and carefully removed the top board and the cloths to reveal a small collection of perfectly preserved flowers.

'Now, then. These are from the posy that you gave to little Mai. I thought you might like to have them for a keepsake.'

He welled up, choked. 'Oh, Mamgu! How wonderful to have something other than my memories – and my feather waistcoat – by which to remember her. Something she gave to me, and something I gave to her.'

He gave Mamgu his little book, and she opened it, very carefully placing a single dried flower between the leaves and turning a few pages, repeated the process until all the flowers were safely stored.

'Mamgu, I can never thank you enough.'

'Alexander, in a few weeks, you gave Mai more love and joy than she had known in her entire life, and for that I, for one, will always be truly grateful.'

She took some twine and wrapped it side to side, top to bottom, around the book, to keep the flowers safely inside, tying it in a bow at the front. He took it from her with a loving smile, and she followed him outside, watching him as he carefully placed it in his saddle bag and mounted up.

'I will not be here next week, Mamgu. I return to Monmouth on Friday. I will be ever grateful to you for this.'

'Oh, just one thing before you leave, Alexander. What kind of flower is a 'lion's tooth'? I'd never heard of it.'

He gave her a cheeky grin.

'It's a dandelion, Mamgu. A dandelion.'

Mamgu was no clearer. Where did Mai get "lion's tooth" from, then?

Alexander turned Cyflym swiftly and left for the short pilgrimage to Mai's Oak, pausing briefly, as was now his custom, at Peter's Oak.

When they reached the meadow, he cantered Cyflym over to the other side. Dismounting, he walked up to the tree, stroked and gave a kiss to the carved 'M'. He retrieved the book from his saddle bag and sat on the ground.

Untying the bow and opening the book, he said out loud:

'I don't know if you can hear me, Mai MacIntyre, but I will treasure your memory with these flowers for the rest of my life.'

She laid her head on his shoulder as he opened the pages, studying each flower.

'I know,' she replied, unheard, as she stroked his hair, 'and thank you for the happiness you gave me; for the love I had never known before. Thank you for giving me the memories that I will always treasure.'

Alexander returned to continue his studies in Monmouth, taking his most treasured possessions with him: his feather waistcoat and the precious old schoolbook containing Mai's flowers.

He had an uneasy feeling. His father had been behaving oddly. On a number of occasions, strange men had come into their home. Alexander had noticed it the previous year, these meetings with strange visitors, but now the meetings were more frequent. His father had been visiting the Big House much more often than usual, too. The house took on a strange atmosphere with many whisperings and mutterings. He'd overheard something about more land being required, but why all the secrecy?

Something was seriously awry. His gut told him so.

Pogrom

On Monday, the twenty-fifth of September, less than four weeks after Alexander had returned to school, Maria Summerlee and her family received notice that they were required to leave the Old Priory. This came as a shock. They had resided at the Priory since the previous landowners kindly offered part of the building as accommodation after the much-respected Doctor Summerlee was killed in a fall from his horse, leaving Maria a widow with three young children. The new landowners had accepted the Summerlee's residence without question, but now required the entire building for the accommodation of their own visiting relatives on a regular basis. Maria and Louisa had been found accommodation at an empty house near Newark.

If Meg was not to continue her work in the little community of Cefn-yr-Afon, she took upon herself the decision to travel to Ireland, rather than Newark, where she felt her teaching and nursing skills might be of greater benefit to the poor. Secretly, she harboured other desires for her longer-term future

They were all suspicious about the turn of events. Something didn't feel right but none of them were in a position to question this decision, let alone ascertain what was going on. After much discussion, and with full understanding of the true reason for Miriam's refuge with them, the family decided to seek permission for her to accompany them to Newark. The thought of her returning to the MacIntyre home or, rather, the lustful attentions of Herbert, was unthinkable.

Maria Summerlee visited the MacIntyre home with Meg on Thursday. Herbert, as politely as he knew how, asked them to be seated. The stools in the hut were not particularly stable and Meg was a little concerned for her mother's dignity. However, Maria managed to remain reasonably graceful on her stool. It was she who spoke.

'Herbert, Sarah, I fear that we have to leave the Priory. We are told that our accommodation is required by the landowners for some of their relatives. We are to relocate to England. We are here to request that Miriam accompany us to our new home. She is doing so well with her studies. We really feel that she would benefit greatly from staying with us. I am sure you will agree.'

Meg, smiling, nodded in agreement. This was the truth to the best of their knowledge but Herbert was far from happy. Miriam would be useful in more ways than one at home if she wasn't to stay at the Priory. Developing nicely, she was. And with that idiot woman losing her wits, Mai gone and the boys out all the time, he had to light the fire and keep it going – and turn the spit – all his self these days! Still, he could hardly say no. This was clearly the one in charge and her manner of asking told him that, if Meg could set God upon him, this one could set God with all his archangels and bring up the fires of Hell to boot, should he dare to refuse. Sarah had no clue as to what was happening.

One week after receiving their notice to quit the property, Meg accompanied Miriam to the settlement to say goodbye to her mother, Herbert and her brothers. The following day, a carriage arrived to transport Meg to North Wales so that she could make the journey to Anglesey and then across the Irish sea to Dublin. Two days after that, Maria, Louisa and Miriam, their meagre possessions packed, boarded their own carriage to make the long journey across country to Newark.

The weather was unusually balmy for the time of year. The leaves on the trees were the colours of Autumn but, following a chilly spell, the nights became almost as warm as the Summer again. Fitz and Pat could comfortably resume camping in the forest for the time being.

Mai followed them as far as she felt able. She did not wish to wander too far from the settlement so stopped in the meadow clearing, waiting by Mai's Oak for their return. If only they could know that she was there. If only they could see her, or even hear her voice.

On the night of Saturday, the fourteenth of October, the dark sky was lit only by the stars and a sliver of the waning crescent moon. Suddenly, Mai heard voices, screaming and yelling. She rushed to the edge of the forest. Glints of metal flashed around the huts. Metalheads! Everywhere! Flaming arrows shot through the air, hitting their targets: the reed thatched roofs of the huts. All of the huts were aflame and people were screaming. A fiery orange glow hung over the settlement. Men, women and children rushed outside, defenceless against the swords, daggers and pikes that met them. They all fell as soon as they exited. Nowhere to run.

Herbert rushed outside but was felled by a sword, killed instantly. In the commotion, the two terrified great sows crashed out through the door, trampling over him, and made a successful dash for safety in the forest. Likewise, the sows in the other round hut got away. With sufficient time, the soldiers might have thought to kill them for a good meal, but the matter at hand was a different kind of slaughter so the hogs all escaped.

Mai heard the order shouted, 'No-one to be left alive!'

Sarah, in her own world, summoned sufficient wit to leave the hut, as pieces of its burning thatch fell in on her. Outside, she almost tripped over Herbert's lifeless body. It took a moment or two for her to register what was happening. At the very moment the fog cleared and clarity was restored, a male voice roared behind her.

She turned and stared straight at his pox-ridden, weather-beaten face. The metal helmet was dull but it still reflected the orange flames. Oh, those cold, hate-filled, black eyes! Sword aloft, ready to strike, his intent was maximum terror. Whether by design or by providence, Sarah denied him his victory.

She welcomed death.

The same fate fell to Mamgu, Nicholas and every other settler: man, woman and child. Each one mercilessly slaughtered, taken unaware. No chance of escape. Utter massacre.

As Mai watched the nightmare unfold, she became aware of hurried footsteps approaching through the undergrowth behind her. Fitz and Pat had camped in the forest on the other side of the meadow, close enough to hear the commotion and see the glow of the now raging fires. The screaming had ceased. It had all happened so quickly. They stopped close enough to see but not to be seen. Mai rushed to them. As soon as they processed the sight before them, and the horror hit home, Fitz called out, 'Mam! Mam!' and made to run into the settlement. Even knowing they couldn't hear her, Mai did her best to scream, 'Pat! Pat! Stop him. Be quiet! They'll hear you! She's gone! There is nothing you can do! You'll be killed yourselves!'

Pat chased after his brother, leapt forward and grabbed him by the arm, dragging him back: 'Fitz, no! Quiet! They'll hear us. She's gone! There is nothing we can do! We'll be killed ourselves!'

Fitz leaned back against a beech tree and slid to the ground, head in his hands, crying for his beloved Mam. Had she not suffered enough? Father? The beatings – and the rest? Miriam? Seamus? Mai? Was it any wonder that

71

she had lost her mind? Pat fell to his knees. The brothers both trembled uncontrollably, gasping for breath as they sobbed.

Herbert probably got what he deserved, or had he? Since they had given him that pasting, he was no longer in charge and he knew it. It had been a long time coming but he'd learnt his lesson. His behaviour had been less brutish. And their Mam, Mamgu, all the other innocent souls in the settlement? Good people, mostly, bar one or two. Their sobs subsided as they hid among the trees. They stayed quiet as mice, camouflaged in the undergrowth, sickened as they watched the bodies, men, women and children unceremoniously lobbed onto five carts and hauled away along the track that had carried Mai and the others, barely a year ago. Fitz and Pat followed behind from a discrete distance. The lime pit had been reopened and extended to accommodate the bodies. Nobody went near the gravesite, for fear of its association with the blight. A good place to bury so many.

The captain shouted: 'How many did we get?'

'Forty-nine, Sir!' came the reply.

'Thought it was supposed to be fifty-one.'

'Dunno, Sir, but we got 'em all. No-one got away. Apart from the hogs, that is!'

The captain told himself that there must have been a miscalculation on somebody's part but, just to be sure:

'I shouldn't worry about the hogs. They're not going to tell anybody, I shouldn't think!' Get some patrols to check the area for a few days, just in case. Perhaps they got it wrong – or maybe one of you fools miscounted. Anyway, they're not to know up there, are they? Not them getting their hands dirty! Oh yes – that reminds me – you need to make sure that these ponies and carts are all returned to them first thing, too.'

'Yes, sir. It will be done and a patrol organised.'

'Good. Now get this lot cleared up.'

Fitz and Pat watched, sickened and horrified, as the pit was filled back in. Then back to Cefn-yr-Afon, or what was left of it. The entire site was razed to the ground. All evidence of massacre, bar the scorched earth, gone. If this was what men who had fought for Oliver Cromwell were capable of, no wonder their father had gone off to fight for the King.

As daylight approached, rain fell and most of the spilt blood was washed away. The soldiers gathered on the track to march away; two officers, a captain and a lieutenant, on horseback. A strange thing to behold. They were dressed as Cromwellian soldiers, with their metal helmets and red jackets, but they looked dirty, unkempt, and their uniforms were ragged; not at all the smart soldiers, however much despised, they had once seen march along the track past the settlement, during the Wars.

When they were sure it was safe, the boys emerged from their hiding place, to inspect the desolate place that had been their home. At least they knew that Seamus was alive and assumed to be well, so perhaps Herbert had, albeit unwittingly, done him a favour. Miriam was safe in Newark and poor little Mai had at least been spared this horror.

Mai understood their feelings. As a spirit not yet gone through the Light, she retained all her Earthly emotions. She was still a child. A homeless child, waiting, alone, for the time when she would be part of a loving home and family. As Mai – not as somebody else.

Fitz and Pat looked at each other. There was nothing to be saved from the wreckage of their home or anyone else's. Anything not burned to ashes, and not worth the plunder, had been lobbed into the mass grave alongside the bodies. Still, they had their survival skills, their bows and arrows, their knives and a collection of coins, mostly pennies, but even the odd shilling, which they had saved from selling some of their 'ill-gotten' gains in the settlement and at the market in the town. It was in a pouch of pig-leather, buried and safely hidden in undergrowth. Only they knew where. They had been saving to leave for good and they certainly had sufficient for their needs for a considerable time.

'We can survive on what we can catch and gather from the hedgerows and forests,' Fitz said optimistically.

'Of course we can – and sell what we can't eat. We've been planning this for so long, anyway. It was just a question of time, and the time is here now.' Pat added. 'Trouble is, I doubt it's safe to stay around here. Those soldiers aren't sure they killed everyone. People know us and if they think anyone's left, they could come after us. As long as we stay around here, we're in danger.'

'But where do we go?' mused Fitz.

'How about we travel through the country to find this Newark place, where the Summerlees took Miriam. Who's to tell her that Mam has been killed? That the settlement is gone and she would have no home to return to, even if she wanted to?'

'How do we find Newark, though?' asked Fitz.

Pat's idea had been brilliant until it dawned on them that they didn't know where Newark actually was. They were quiet and pondered the matter for a while.

'Are we thinking clearly? Considering our Mam's just been killed and our hut is gone and all?' Pat asked.

''Course we are. I don't see as we've any choice, do we? It doesn't matter how, or even how long it takes us to get there. At least we have an idea of where we need to be and a reason to travel. We aren't vagrants. We need Miriam, though, even if she's with Meg's family for now. We need to be a family again.' Fitz had hit the nail on the head, as Fitz usually did.

Mai followed the conversation with great interest and completely agreed with them. Yes. A reason to be. Everybody needs a reason to be. A family what loves each other is a reason to be. Good for them. If they could find this Newark place, and find Miriam, they could make a home and somewhere for Miriam to go if she so desired. Mai dearly wished she could go with them but something told her that she must not leave the area of the settlement.

'So, how do we go about finding this place, d'you think?' Pat asked.

Fitz had the answer. Simple really. 'Well, we do know the place is in England, so I think we collect our stuff together and stick to the smaller forest tracks and just travel through the woodland, keeping hidden until we've gone far enough so nobody could know us. We can get to bigger tracks then and ask the way to England and keep going. We should just go North at first, I think. Don't know why. Just a feeling I have. There's no rush. When we're in England, we can ask the way to Newark. We can ask for odd jobs and stuff, and sell rabbits and fish and things to people along the way. Doesn't really matter how long it takes us. Finding England is the most important thing, We might even be able to pick up rides on carts. We should be able to earn our keep and sleep in barns or stables, maybe, if we're still outside when the cold weather sets in. We're just lucky it's warmer at night right now.'

It was true. They had no choice. They had to get away. At least they weren't wandering around with no purpose. Still, they had no concept of how far they would have to travel on foot, as Pat pointed out to his brother.

'Maybe we don't need to travel on foot,' Fitz suggested.

'What you talking about?'

'Horses.'

'Where the hell are we going to get horses?'

'The Big House.'

What? You gone mad?'

'Listen, Pat. They're going to be looking for us for a while. But we know this forest like the back of our hands, don't we? We can easily hide from their patrols. Give it a week or so and we can steal a couple of horses from the stables up at the Big House. I mean ...'

'But how do we manage it?'

'Wait for the Sabbath when they've all gone to church, isn't it? Easy! Sneak in, take the best couple of horses and whatever we need – feed and stuff – and we're on our way.'

'Think we can do it, Fitz?'

'I know we can do it, Pat!'

In the morning, the ponies and carts were returned to the Big House. well in time for the family to attend church. Bailiff Robert Lawson had a job to do. All records of the settlers and their tithes were to be destroyed. He piled the books into a couple of sacks, put them on one of the carts and drove over to the ruins of the abbey. There was a secret room in there, without windows. It had been stumbled upon, hidden behind a wooden panel, after the monks had left following the dissolution, but now, only a handful of people knew of its existence. Bailiff Lawson was one of them; but this was his job and his alone. Only he could be trusted with it.

He removed the panel and unlocked the door, then carried the sacks up into the room.

Suppressing any feelings of guilt – he had his orders, after all – he put the sacks in the centre of the tiled floor and set light to them. He added to the pile until all the records, all trace of the settlers – generations of them –

had been destroyed. He swept up the ashes with a shovel and placed them in the fireplace in the outer room. The tiles were scorched, but that could not be helped. Nobody would ever see them and there was no way of knowing what had been burned, or when, anyway.

When his job was done, he left the room, locked the door and replaced the wooden panel. Taking a deep breath, he drew himself to his full height and strode from the room, out of the ruined abbey walls and drove the cart which had, only the night before, taken the bodies of Sarah and Herbert MacIntyre and the others to their grave, back to the Big House. Bailiff Robert Lawson comforted himself with the knowledge that he had done his duty.

Dodging and hiding from the patrols was not difficult for Fitz and Pat; the searches were half-hearted at best and only lasted a few days. When they were sure it was safe, they executed their plan.

On the Sabbath, the boys crept into the grounds of the Big House and watched, hiding behind bushes, waiting for the residents and servants to go off to church; the family in a carriage and the servants following behind by cart. They could not believe that nobody had been left to guard the place. Much complacency had built up over the years in this rural area. As soon as the occupants of the house were out of sight, the two lads entered the stables.

Four horses were left in the stalls. Two were fine palfreys.

'Which ones should we take, Fitz?'

Fitz didn't need much time to think.

'I think we should leave the palfreys. They are too fine for the kind of journey we will be undertaking. We have no idea how long we will be travelling. These two are sturdier – and I think more placid. Fit for riding or pulling a cart.'

'Cart? You're not thinking of stealing a cart too, are you, brother?'

'No, that would be too much – and will make our escape from here slower. No. I was thinking of what we will do when we reach our destination. Horses fit for more than one purpose will surely be of more use – and, with us not dressed as rich folk, riding such fine palfreys would surely arouse suspicion. No, Pat. I think these two lads will serve our purpose well.'

The two horses, somewhere between a carthorse and a palfrey, looked tough enough to undertake the longest of journeys if they didn't work them too hard.

Fitz's horse, black with beautiful amber eyes, they called Llygaid.

'Eyes,' whispered Mai.

Pat's, a skewbald of white and red chestnut, they called Coch.

'Red,' whispered Mai.

They checked the horses' feet.

'Well now! There's a bit of luck, Pat!'

'Yes, indeed. Quite newly shod! Somebody up there's on our side, eh? Mind you, this is all a bit different to poaching, isn't it? I don't feel bad about poaching, so we can eat to live. But this isn't the same.'

'Pat, you don't have to feel guilty at all. They stole a lot more from us than ever we could steal from them, surely? They deserve nothing less. And we'll love these boys far more than ever they will.'

Pat had to agree with his brother. They knew the importance of the relationship between a horse and his master. Alexander taught them all they knew about horses and riding, and knowing how well his relationship with Cyflym served him, they took the matter very seriously. In contrast, the rich people, particularly men, were often hard on their horses, treating them with little or no compassion.

They tacked up the two geldings, took what they could without overloading the horses and with their hunting knives, bows and arrows, and the money they'd saved, were on their way, well before anyone would miss the horses. The tracks were damp and they would leave tracks, so they began by riding South for a few minutes, mingling their own tracks with those of the coaches and horses that had gone before them. They then slipped into the woodland, through the trees until they picked up a smaller track, doubling back on themselves.

'Farewell, my brothers. Take care.' she whispered.

Mai was uneasy about being too far away from her own territory for too long, but she did one last thing for them before returning to the meadow. All hell was let loose once the discovery of the theft was made. She hung around the stables, repeatedly whispering into everyone's ears, 'South. They went South. South. They went South.'

'Not sure why, Sir, but I have a feeling they've gone South,' the head groom told his master.

'Yes. I also have such a feeling. I'm not sure why, myself. Must be something in it, though. Don't want to be sending men out in all directions on a wild goose chase. They were hardly the finest palfreys, after all.'

Sure enough, when the groom checked for tracks outside the gates, there were no tracks heading North and the Squire ordered searches to be made South. Somebody must have seen them, but the searches were half-hearted. The thieves would be well away by now.

When she was sure her brothers would be safe, Mai returned to her own territory: the meadow, Mai's Oak, and the forest.

Journey

Fitz and Pat rode along the smaller tracks through the woodlands, following streams where they could to ensure they and the horses had fresh water along the way. They avoided the main settlements where they might have been recognised by people who frequented the market. Coming to a crossroads, they found the wider, main track heading due North. They were sure it was safe by now, so they followed it, being as gentle on Llygaid and Coch as they possibly could.

The boys concocted a story about having travelled from Carmarthen and, having no relatives in the area, their parents both now having passed away, they'd sold most of their possessions, bought the horses and were looking to stay with their mother's cousin and her husband, their only other relatives, who lived in Newark. It wasn't too far from the truth.

The track took them to Brecknock. It was a fine night, not too cold, so they found a suitable spot to set camp outside the town. The nights were getting longer and a bit colder now, but the hardy lads found a sheltered, wooded spot, built a fire and managed to catch a rabbit for supper. Here they camped for a couple of nights. It had been a long ride and they needed to rest the horses.

When they felt it time to move on, they rode into the town and asked for directions to England, being open and honest with regard to their story, but giving no more away than they had to. They were advised to travel East towards Hereford. A kind shopkeeper directed them on their way, having sold them a loaf.

After a day's riding, near Hay, they camped again and travelled on to Hereford in the morning. As they rode through the town, they were unsure whether they were now in England or still in Wales. It appeared to Fitz and

Pat that the locals were not really sure themselves: some saying Wales; others, England. Just as in Cefn-yr-Afon, there was some Welsh, albeit a different dialect, and Wengi spoken as well as English. However, when they asked for directions to Newark, nobody knew precisely the direction they should take. The general consensus was that they should travel East or North, or perhaps North-East.

They tried North-East and, just past Bromyard, they happened upon a farmstead. They could have done with a bit of work and, although the harvest was over, there was fence-mending to be done, and repairs to outbuildings in preparation for the Winter. The farmer, Josiah Groves, had been struggling alone, since his wife had passed away in childbirth,. The child, a girl, had also died. Despite grief and hardship, Josiah was hospitable and more than happy to have a bit of help in return for shelter, a good meal and some hay for the horses. Three nights, they stayed.

'Newark, you say. I don't rightly know, boys. It ain't on this side of the country though. I'd lay a penny or two it's eastward, meself. Get you to Worcester. A good day's ride from here, mind you, but somebody there will be able to tell you, for sure.'

He sent them off with a bit of food for a day or two, and a couple of bags of hay for the horses, for which they were most grateful. It took them another full day's travelling. The horses were bearing up to the journey admirably. Alexander had taught Fitz and Pat well.

Arriving at the Severn, they crossed the great river via the bridge and entered the City of Worcester. The weather was turning wet and Llygaid had managed to lose a hind shoe. They were able to arrange a bed for the night and stabling at a coaching inn.

Fitz and Pat stayed in the bar for a while, chatting to the other customers and to the innkeeper, Thomas Treadwell, before retiring for the night and sleeping in a comfortable bed. Josiah was right. Thomas assured them of the direction in which they should be travelling. Both Thomas and his wife, Anne, felt very sorry for them.

'Nice boys, they are. Rotten old thing to lose both your parents so young, isn't it?' said Thomas. All at the inn agreed.

After a good night's sleep, Fitz and Pat rose early, completed their ablutions, and paid the innkeeper, who wished them safe and well for their journey. Anne Treadwell, packed them chunks of bread, meat and cheese, enough for two days at least. They offered to pay for the food but she would have none of it. Poor boys. 'The least I can do, my dears.' Thomas, although sympathetic to the boys, was unsure of the wisdom of giving food away, from a business point of view but, as usual, his wife had her way.

They located a farrier who checked all the horses' feet, replaced Llygaid's missing shoe, and satisfied himself and the boys that all the other shoes were ride-worthy for a good while yet. They returned with Llygaid and Coch to the stables, saddled up the horses and were off.

The farther they travelled, the surer people were of the direction they should take. And so the journey went on, catching what food they could, sometimes camping out for an extra night or two to rest the horses: Bromsgrove, Coventry, Nuneaton, Leicester (they could just about afford one more night at a coaching inn), Melton Mowbray, Grantham.

If the boys had been occasionally misdirected, they were hardly to know but, at last, in early December, they arrived at their destination: Newark. After numerous enquiries they found their sister. She, Maria and Louisa were accommodated in a house on the outskirts of the town, where mother and daughter had set up a school to earn a living and pay their rent. Maria, on hearing their story was deeply upset and sent Louisa to fetch Miriam from her studies.

'I thought it was strange that we should be ejected from the Priory in so sudden a manner. This was no coincidence. I have no doubt that it was all planned. I shall pray for the souls of your dear mother and Uncle Herbert, and all the other souls. There is accommodation for you here and stabling for your horses, if you so wish, and, should you intend to remain in this area, you are welcome to stay until you can find your own accommodation. You look so tired, my dears.'

'Thank you, Mistress Summerlee,' said Fitz, 'that is most generous of you. We have nothing to return to, so we will be staying. Miriam is our only relative. We must ask, though, that you tell nobody of what we saw. We think that they were not Cromwell's soldiers, although once had been, from their attire.'

'But we are not completely sure,' added Pat.

'Even so,' Fitz went on, 'we know that those at the Big House are somehow related to Cromwell, and were involved in the massacre and destruction. And ...'

He hesitated.

'... and your horses were not yours to take?' she asked, with a tilt of the head and a wry smile.

'Indeed, Madam. I am sorry that we felt it necessary to take what was not ours.'

'In the circumstances, Fitzgerald, I think a sin such as this can be forgiven. I understand your predicament. Fear not. The tale you have given to others is the tale we shall tell. Nobody here knows whence Miriam came to us, but, you must make sure that your sister understands the story. We will protect you to the utmost of our ability.'

She smiled at them gently with a slight bow of the head. A knock at the door and their sister entered on Mistress Summerlee's command.

Miriam was so delighted to see them that she flung herself at them. With the surprise, the question of how, or why, they had travelled so far had not immediately occurred to her. Under normal circumstances. Maria Summerlee might have scolded her for lack of decorum, but these circumstances were far from normal.

'Miriam, my dear, please be seated. Your brothers have arrived, I am afraid to say, with some bad news. Some very bad news, indeed.'

Miriam's face dropped and she sat down, dreading what may follow. Fitz and Pat could not conceal their tears as they broke the news to their sister. Pat stood up to go to her but she leapt at him first, wrapping her arms around his neck, sobbing into his chest. Fitz joined them, and all three stood together, hugging each other, sobbing their hearts out.

Maria, herself unusually emotional, left the room to arrange accommodation for the boys, allowing the siblings to share their grief.

Farewell

Alexander was blissfully unaware of the events of the previous autumn. He only went home for the Summer recess, Christmas and Easter not being celebrated in Puritan Britain. There were a couple of other breaks during the year but they were too brief to be worth the travelling. Many of her fellow scholars were in the same situation. Besides, Alexander enjoyed the company of his friends far more than that of his parents. Furthermore, it was in his father's interest to have Alexander well away from home for now.

On the first Wednesday of Alexander's vacation, Bailiff Robert Lawson prepared for his ride out to the Big House. Alexander followed him to the stables to saddle Cyflym.

'Where d'you think you're going?' demanded his father.

'Thought I might ride with you and go on to the settlement. I usually do on a Wednesday when I'm home. You know I enjoy listening to Mamgu's tales. Corrupted history at its best!' he laughed, looking over Cyflym's withers towards him. Fortunately for Robert Lawson, he had his back to his son as he saddled his own horse.

'No point, son.'

'I'm sorry, Father? What do you mean? You've no objection to me going there, have you? You never have before.'

'It's not that, boy.' He reached underneath his horse and caught hold of the girth to fasten it, not turning to look at his son.

'Then what? Why should I not go?'

Robert Lawson tightened his lips as he tightened the girth, giving himself time to think of a plausible response.

'All moved on, they have. Gone. Nobody left. The settlement was razed after they moved out. Being set up for grazing now. Likely they'll put some of their own people on the land, eventually.'

Something was amiss. Unlike his father, and young as he was, Alexander, on a personal level, knew the settlers well. He had insight into their nature. They had been there for generations. They wouldn't have just 'moved on'. It was a desperately poor little community, but an established one, nonetheless.

'Father, were they forced to move on or did they go of their own volition?'

And then his father made his mistake.

'Oh, no-one forced them out, son. Just decided to move somewhere where they could prosper better, as far as I can see.'

He was lying through his teeth. Alexander knew it, and Robert Lawson knew that Alexander knew it. Robert had always underestimated his son, reckoning on neither his level of maturity nor his understanding of the settlers. They'd been forced alright. His father was the bailiff and he must have been up to his neck in the whole affair. That's what had been going on last Summer, and even further back than that. The planning.

'Well, I think I'll come along anyway, and perhaps visit Meg at the Priory.'

'Not there either. Their part of the Priory was needed for extra accommodation for relatives of them up at the House. Marcus Summerlee died in the blight, as you know, but his mother and sister went to Newark and the other girl went to Ireland.'

'The girl? You mean Miriam MacIntyre?'

'No, not her. She went to Newark, too. Took her with them, they did. No, Meg. She went to Ireland, I believe.'

What the hell has happened to these people? A whole community, established as long as theirs, doesn't take up and leave just like that. It made no sense whatsoever.

And Meg and her family gone too? It was all very suspicious.

'Well, as I'm here, I think I'll come along anyway, Father. I can just take Cyflym out for a while.'

'As you please, boy. As you please.'

Not a word was spoken between them until they parted company. Robert Lawson rode up to the Big House and Alexander rode on to the site of the settlement. At the edge, Cyflym stood stock still, refusing to move on. Alexander tried to encourage him forward but he was having none of it. The horse whinnied and stamped a front hoof. This was not Cyflym. The horse sensed something. The hairs on the back of Alexander's neck stood on end.

'Alright, boy,' Alexander reassured him with a gentle pat to his neck. 'You wait here then. You know something, don't you? If only you could talk, my lovely boy. If only …'

He dismounted, sharing Cyflym's trepidation, but wandered onto the site. He looked around; signs of scorched earth all over the place. He could even trace the shapes of the huts, including the MacIntyre's and Mamgu's.

'They're dead. They killed them all,' Mai whispered.

Alexander had a sinking feeling of dread. His stomach twisted into a knot. He wanted to vomit. They're dead. He just knew it. The devils killed them. It's the only explanation. Meg and the others were moved to get them out of the way. No witnesses. He was absolutely sure. He trembled all over, on the verge of collapse. Would his legs carry him over to Cyflym, let alone get him into the saddle?

He staggered over to his friend, and gripped onto the pommel before his legs gave way. He was light-headed; thoughts of massacre whirling around in his mind. For a few moments he rested, his arms taking his weight, but even they were trembling. Somehow, after some very deep breaths, he clambered up into the saddle, leaning forward onto Cyflym's mane, and rode on. He didn't need to use the reins to guide him; Cyflym knew exactly where he was going. He followed Mai.

At Mai's Oak, Alexander dropped from the saddle, patted Cyflym's shoulder and laid his head against the trusty horse's neck. Can it be true? Could they really have done what he believed? He took his book from the saddle bag and went up to the tree. His hand moved over the carving.

'You know, Mai, I think it's beginning to weather a little.' With great care, he placed the little book down on the grass and took the knife from its sheath on his belt. He deepened the grooves in the bark and stood back, admiring his handiwork. 'That's better, my sweet. It should last much longer now.' Cyflym eyed him, waiting for him to sit down on the grass before settling to graze.

'Hey, boy. Wonder why you didn't graze when we stopped at the settlement, or what's left of it. Not a bit like you.'

He was only musing. The notion that they had all been killed would not leave him.

He picked up the little book, untied the twine bow and opened its leaves to each flower in turn and, wistful, he smiled at the memories.

'Pansy.'

'Pansy,' she repeated.

'Daisy.'

'Daisy.'

'Buttercup.'

'Buttercup.'

'Primrose.'

'Primrose.'

'Bluebell.'

'Bluebell.'

'Celandine.'

'Cela... cela... the other yellow one!'

He stroked a dandelion on the ground.

'Lion's tooth,' he chuckled

'Makes you piss.'

'Oh, my lovely, sweet Mai. I know something dreadful beyond words has happened. Tomorrow is Market day. I'm going to ride into the town and see if I can find out any more. Somebody must have an idea. Must have! They didn't just move on.'

Pausing as usual at Peter's Oak, he returned home, arriving well before his father. he unsaddled Cyflym and turned him out into the field with some of the other horses.

'Nice ride out, dear?' his mother enquired.

'Yes, Mother. It was very pleasant. It's a shame that the settlement is no longer there, but it was a very pleasant ride indeed. If the weather is this good tomorrow, I shall take advantage and go out again, I think.'

'Well, the fresh air will be good for you but really, Alexander, I cannot imagine why ever your father would permit you to mix with those dreadful people in the first place. I mean ... peasants! And you do realise that, really, they are all ... Papists, at heart.' She virtually had to spit out the word. 'Hardly the sort that you should be associating with, especially considering you are to be a bailiff yourself one day. Your father must have been mad to allow it.' It really was beyond her.

He gritted his teeth. 'Well, I don't think he saw the harm. They were mostly good people – at heart.'

She raised her eyebrows and turned away from him. Nothing else was said for the rest of the evening until after supper, when he retired early, to read in his room, he said.

The following morning, Alexander rode into the town. He slipped from the saddle and, leading Cyflym, walked through the market. There were no customers at the baker's stall so, hoping for an opportunity to speak to her, he stopped and bought a couple of buns and asked if she knew where the settlers had gone. They all knew Fitz and Pat, and Mamgu was well-known for her midwifing and her tales – and for the gelding of horses. Everyone's grandmother.

'I can tell you this, my lovely, but don't you go saying nothing on who told you, mind.' He shook his head. Absolutely, not – he would say nothing.

'Well,' she looked around to check that nobody was earwigging, 'It's said that they was all murdered in the night, they was. It's only a rumour, though, and you can't go saying it's anything more, but most people round here believes they was murdered as they slept.'

'No! Really? But who would have done something so terrible?'

'Well, that's funny, that is, 'cos nobody really knows.'

She gave another furtive glance all around her, craning her neck this way and that, and leaned nearer to him.

''Nobody seems to know who they was. They reckons it could 'ave bin some sort of soldiers. Summat to do with the Army. Nobody do know for sure, though. It was all secret, like.'

'Indeed. But how do you know all this.'

'Well, I thinks it have come from servants up at the Big House over there, up past Cefn-yr-Afon. What used to be Cefn-yr-Afon. You know how these things spread. They hears things up there 'cos no-one takes no notice of 'em, just being servants and that, and they comes in for provisions and goes off to The Bear an' 'aves a bit too much ale, they do, so their tongues do get a bit loose. It's said as they going to be wanting their own people on the land and build proper houses for 'em, 'ventually. Everyone knows it, they do, but don't nobody say nothin', mind. All just rumours, it is. But you lookin' like such a nice young man ...'

'I thank you,' Alexander replied. 'You need not worry. I will say nothing to betray your confidence. I thank you for your time – and the buns, and now I really must bid you farewell.'

He gave the old crone an extra couple of pennies for her trouble, then led Cyflym out of the Market Square and mounted.

He could barely comprehend what he had heard. All those people, Mamgu, Sarah, Herbert, Fitz and Pat! Murdered! He fell forward in the saddle, resting on Cyflym's neck. Cyflym knew the way home. Home it would not be for much longer. Whoever had committed the atrocities, Cefn-yr-Afon's settlers had been murdered on the orders of the people at the Big House, he had no doubt – and, by implication, his father was in on it. His own father, Robert Lawson! He was the bailiff, after all. Probably arranged it. People handsomely paid to keep quiet – and who listens to rumours among the riff-raff? No wonder he could afford to send him to that school, let alone the stabling for Cyflym.

There would be no record. No record that the settlers ever even existed; all records of tithes destroyed. That would have been his father's job, for sure. No proof that the settlement was ever there. Right now, Alexander despised Robert Lawson as much, if not more than Fitz and Pat had despised Herbert. Then there was his mother, with all her sickening airs and graces and ideas way above her station. Robert's aunt had married well; that side of the family were comparatively wealthy and, while never resisting the opportunity to mention the family connection, keeping up the pretence that she and her husband were anywhere near their equals in social standing was a strain. Then, of course, that dreadful horse of Alexander's was a constant reminder of the fact.

Alexander despised them both. No, he could no longer stay at home. He disowned his parents and his entire, hateful Puritan family. He would leave tomorrow and head for Newark to find Miriam and the Summerlees.

Alexander chose his moment, under cover of darkness, as everyone slept. All was quiet and he entered the kitchen, taking a little food that would not be missed. He packed his things, slipped out and hid them in the bushes at the side of the track, out of sight of the Lodge, so not to draw attention when he took Cyflym out for his ride the next day. His precious book containing Mai's flowers was safely in his saddle bag.

Waiting until his bed had been made up, he wrote a note and placed it on his pillow: 'Gone away. Do not seek me out. I shall never return.' Nobody would think to look for him until he failed to appear for dinner that evening, by which time he would be well away. He doubted his father would try and look for him anyway. Robert Lawson knew his son suspected the truth. Alexander considered, correctly, that is father would probably worry more about being found out than keeping his son at home.

The next day, on the pretext of going for a ride, Alexander saddled Cyflym and rode out as usual. When he reached the hiding place, he picked up his things: a few spare clothes, a blanket roll in case he had to sleep out, his razor and his food.

He had grown much taller and muscular in the last twelve months; his voice had properly broken and he could easily be taken for much older than his now sixteen years. He had plenty of money which he had saved up over time – a gifted shilling or two and the odd guinea slipped to him here and there. It had mounted up over the years. Ever since he was a young child, his instincts had always told him to hoard whatever money he had been given.

It was warm, but he put on his feather waistcoat – it still fitted him, just – and made one last trip out to Mai's Oak. As he arrived, he leapt from the saddle, went through his ritual of kissing the M and the heart, and sat down to open the book, going through each flower in turn.

'Pansy,'

'Pansy,' she repeated, head on his shoulder, stroking his beautiful chestnut waves. He thought it was the breeze. He went through all the flowers, and then stroked a dandelion, smiling at the memory.

'Lion's tooth.'

He could almost hear her saying, 'makes you piss!'

She whispered in his ear: 'Fitz and Pat – they did not die.'

Glancing down he noticed a clump of tiny flowers with violet blue petals and yellow centres. He gently picked one and bowed his head.

'Forget-me-not.'

'Never…' she whispered, unheard – but not unfelt.

'Oh, bless your heart, my dear little Mai. I have to go away. Away from all this horror and evil. I am going to Newark. Your sister is there. I promise you that I will find her and tell her what has happened here.'

Alexander turned a few pages in his book and gently added the forget-me-not to the little collection. With reverence, he closed it, tied the twine bow at the front and rose to his feet. Replacing it in the saddle bag, for one last time, he returned to the tree and kissed the heart. He kissed her initial 'M'.

'Good bye, Mai's Oak. Cherish the memory for me.' He mounted up.

'Goodbye, my sweet Mai. I will keep my promise. You will never be forgotten as long as I live.'

Tears flowed again but, deep inside him, there was the vaguest notion that Fitz and Pat, at least, might have escaped the carnage. Perhaps they had stayed out that night. Just a hope.

He would have to live with the knowledge of his father's wickedness and the dreadful question: why? It was a question that would probably remain unanswered. One thing he vowed; whatever he did, never, ever, would he become a bailiff like his father, or his father before him. Never!

As ever, he paused at Peter's Oak and looked around. Not far from the edge of the forest, he could see, through the trees, four great hogs spying him. He recognised two of them immediately. His heart leapt for joy – My Girl and Arabella!

'Oh, you wonderful girls!' he cried, 'You survived. Go! Hide! Hide deep in the forest! Farewell, my dears. Stay safe. Stay safe – all of you.'

He flinched. A glowing shape hovered above them, almost human in form. Mai? Probably a trick of the light. With a soulful smile, he took a deep breath. Cyflym reared up and broke into a canter, then a gallop.

'Farewell, dear Alexander. I will always treasure your memory. Forget-me-not.'

'Never.'

Ever after, Alexander Lawson chose to believe it was the spirit of Mai MacIntyre he saw that day. He never took so much as a mouthful of pork meat again.

Part Two: The Beacon and the Bonfire

Change

Mai hardly noticed time's passing, now. Eventually, two of the spirit guides returned. The not-quite-a-person who had spoken previously repeated her plea: 'Child, come with us. We can give you peace.'

Mai was unmoved. She kept her back to them.

'I have already given you my answer, have I not? I would have peace if you would leave me be. Now please go away!'

'You have nothing to fear, my child.'

'I fear nothing. I simply wish to wait. And I am not your child – whoever you are. I am Mai MacIntyre, daughter of Sarah MacIntyre.'

There was no point in arguing.

'If you have need of us or wish to change your mind, you will be welcome. We will know and we will come to guide you.'

Mai instantly regretted her hostility. She had not meant to be rude, but she did wish that they would just leave her be.

'I thank you. Truly I do,' she replied, 'and I know your intentions towards me are good. But it is my intention to wait until I find my true home and family. I will not change my mind.'

Defeated again, the spirit guides faded into the light.

Mai was not alone. A few other spirits roamed inside the perimeter of what had been the settlement; spirits who had chosen not to enter the Light for fear of having to face the consequences of their Earthly misdeeds. Sarah and Herbert were not among them. Both had entered the Light, immediately The spirits of John and Alys Jones also entered the Light but, for some reason, Sioned and Ioan remained, but they still avoided Mai. She kept away from the settlement area anyway, for the most part, choosing to be in the forest with My Girl, Arabella, and the other two sows, or in the meadow near to Mai's Oak to gaze at Alexander's carving, but she never strayed too far from her Earthly home. She kept away from the site of the MacIntyre hut.

Apart from the snarling cowardly spirits, the whisperers, there were other horrors to endure. Residual images of settlers lingered; those few who had not been killed instantly, horribly injured and mutilated by sword, pike and dagger, as they took the final staggering steps to their deaths. Over and over again the scenes repeated; sometimes weak, sometimes strong, occasionally disappearing altogether, but the images always returned: the stronger the image, the darker and more sinister the atmosphere of the place. On the day of Alexander's last visit, it was very powerful. He could feel it. Mai knew he could. Cyflym certainly could; the chances were that he could see it, too. It was obvious that he could see her. Despite the horrors that were visual to her, if not to Alexander, she had the courage to stay with him, but was it any wonder that dear, gentle Cyflym could not bring himself to tread onto this blood-soaked land?

Oh, Alexander! She so wished to go with him but she had to remain. He had a life to begin anew; his was the life of a breather. She could not and did not expect him to destroy all hope of a future. Yet he certainly would not accede to his father's wishes: to become a bailiff, to do the bidding of evil. Alexander Lawson was a good person with a heart of pure gold. Mai knew that he would treasure her memory: the pansy, the daisy, the buttercup, the primrose, the bluebell, the cela…, cela… – the other yellow one! Forget-me-not. Never.

Mai also knew that her beloved Alexander would find Fitz, Pat and Miriam and they would live on to do great things during their lifetimes. She knew it as she knew that somehow, one day, she would find the family that would love her; the people who would show Mai Macintyre her reason to be.

Time passed, but it held no real meaning for Mai. There was day, there was night, there were seasons. She did not count them. As a spirit, she did not sleep. She felt neither warmth nor cold. She just watched, trying to avoid the whisperers and the dreadful residual images, though she was never far from them.

Years went by. Mai had no means of tracking them. The time came when My Girl and Arabella both passed away peacefully in the forest. My Girl went first. Mai sensed the end nearing as the old girl slowed down and, as the sweet sow lay down to sleep for the last time, Mai snuggled into her, as she had done so many times in the hut. As My Girl's spirit left her body, the glowing orb paused briefly.

Mai smiled her tender smile: 'Go now. It is your time, my dear friend. Farewell.'

The orb shot away into the Light.

Arabella pined, so very miserable on her own. Mai tried to comfort her but it made no difference.

'Come on, old girl! I'm here for you, my love,' Mai would say to her.

It was no good. Arabella didn't have the insight of My Girl who, Mai knew, could sense her presence. Nevertheless, Mai stayed close to her. The other hogs were still there, but Arabella was miserable and unhappy without her old companion. Within days, she too laid down to sleep on the forest floor. Mai snuggled up to the old girl until her spirit departed. With loving reassurance, she pointed the way to the Light.

'My Girl is waiting for you, sweetheart.'

Arabella's spirit, too, sped into the Light.

The other two hogs remained for a couple of years or so. They were a bit younger than My Girl and Arabella, but not much. Mai stayed around them until their time also came, comforting them during their last days and hours. At least the huntsmen and their dogs had not found them.

Alexander never knew it, but his wish that they stay safe had been granted and, after the passing of all four hogs, Mai remained near to the meadow and Mai's Oak; the memory cherished.

The breathers began to do some very strange things. They made places, other than the fields, for people to work in. Men, boys, even girls, and small horses went into huge holes underground, coming out dirty and black. They made a big building, containing fires that spewed out smoke, flames and horrible ash that seemed to shower the entire valley like black snow. 'Foundry', they called this place. She had heard of places like the mine in other places, but had not seen one until now. Foundry was new, though. As far as Mai could see, the people working in these places were much worse off than the poor people of her settlement who worked out in the fields. These new places looked, to her, like the images of hell conjured up in her mind when Mamgu told her tales. Had the breathers done some terrible things to find themselves there?

Around this time, they also started to dig huge long trenches and took water from the river to fill them. She watched closely. Canal, they called it, and they put what they called barges on them. Mai had never seen a barge, or even a boat before, but that seemed to be the silliest thing ever. Why not just put the barges on the water in the river that was already there? Horses walked along tracks next to the canal, pulling the barges that carried the things from the foundry and the place they called 'mine' but to where, she had no idea. Anyway, it was a silly name; they all called it 'mine', but it didn't actually belong to any of the people who worked in it, as far as she could see. Some of them even got themselves killed in it. Mai didn't understand it at all.

Then they made a track of metal; big long tracks, joined from end to end and next to each other with wooden planks between them to keep them the right distance apart. The breathers who worked the canal boats were always picking fights with the breathers building the metal track. They all drank too much ale anyway. Nothing made sense anymore.

When the metal track was complete, they put huge carts on it. The one at the front seemed to eat fire. It pulled a lot of other carts behind it, and they now carried the things that used to be carried by the canal barges. Horses weren't needed any more. Eventually, the breathers stopped using the canal altogether and their boats and horses disappeared. Mai now understood why the canal men were so angry. What they called the railway was used to take all these things, but where did they take it? What did they use it for? That was a mystery.

They built houses – lots and lots of them, but not on the site of the settlement. That had never happened. People moved in. More and more trees were felled. Horses, carts and carriages were replaced with carriages made of metal that didn't need horses. They were very noisy and strange smoke came out of pipes at the back of them. In each of the carriages was a wheel. They seemed to use the wheel to steer it. They didn't need reins. Things they called roads, much bigger than tracks were built for these carriages to drive along. More and more trees were felled to make way for more and more houses, more cars and more roads.

Then disaster struck. 'No! No! No! They can't! Not Peter's Oak!' Distraught, angry, helpless, she could only watch as the great Peter's Oak, along with all the trees in that part of the forest, was felled to make way for new houses.

It was not long before they reached the meadow. They ploughed it up: all her beautiful flowers and the surrounding hedgerows gone! Mai could only watch, helpless, with heartbreak and anger as her own beloved oak, with Alexander's precious carving, was about to be destroyed. Then, one of the men stopped.

'Hey, Mike! Look at this!' he yelled.

Mike came around from the other side of the tree.

'Bloody 'ell, mate. That's you and your missus, that is! M heart A. What's the chances of that!'

Mike was thrilled.

'Hey, Bert!' he said, 'Can we save that bit for my Angie? She'd be well chuffed with that, she would. Look at the bloody date on it! You can just about make it out – 1655! That's about 300 years ago!'

'Wonder who they were.' Bert answered.

'Never know, will we?'

'Young love, eh? They had it in those days, too!' Mike chuckled. 'Pity it don't last. Well, Angie'll be happy as a butcher's dog when I take this home to her.'

So, the great tree was felled, sawn above and below the carving and a slice sawn out, saving Alexander's precious handiwork. If only they'd known how precious. At the end of the working day, Mike took the carving home to his wife. Mai was heartbroken at the destruction of her beloved oak, and she had mixed emotions about Alexander's carving. It was being taken away by someone who had no idea who had carved it, or who it had been carved for: how precious it was. Mai hoped with all her soul that it would be treasured and preserved. At least it was not going to be destroyed, but she would never see it again.

Time continued to roll on, as time does, but Mai existed in a dimension where it didn't matter as it does for breathers. She just waited. The settlement site had not yet been built on. Cattle and sheep grazed there sometimes, but at other times it was just left to scrub. When the bluebells were in flower, she visited the gravesite frequently. It was sheltered by the canopy of the trees either side, but it was only the bluebells that grew on the river bank above the long-forgotten bodies. The trees had been little more than saplings at the time of the felling, to make way for the lime pit. The larger trees were now mature, mostly birch and oak, but no-one ever wondered why that clearing was there. Mai watched over the bluebells when they were in flower. Very close by, the breathers had built some big market places selling strange things. At first, when she saw the huge square holes being dug out and then filled in again with what looked to be grey mud, she couldn't make sense of it, but then it dawned on her, as this 'mud' set hard, that it was to make the floors to put up buildings. Although she was quite upset about the amount of land being destroyed, she was amazed by the things the breathers had invented to do it.

They put up signs saying 'Car Park'. She'd heard breathers say the words and she could make them out from the letters that Meg taught her. She knew most of the sounds the letters made; she just could never quite remember the order of their appearance in the alphabet. 'Cars' – that was the name of the horseless carriages that came in all shapes and sizes. Then they built a shop that sold cars. Big new shiny cars. 'Car Park' was where people left their cars when they went into the shops. Then they built a 'pet shop' that sold pretty fish in little glass ponds, pretty coloured birds, rabbits and other small animals. No lions, though. The 'pet shop' also sold all sort of things that were needed to keep them, like special food and housing; but the animals were not for eating, so what were they for? One shop sold carpets. Carpets were for covering the floor but the name made no sense. If 'pet' was the name for the animals which weren't for eating, what had the animals to do with cars? And why was it one word and not two, as Meg had shown her? Still, a carpet was a carpet and she shrugged her ethereal shoulders at yet more breather nonsense. The breathers had become very strange indeed.

The day came when the machines (another breather word she'd picked up, along with bulldozers and diggers) arrived at the settlement. She was spending much more time here now as the breathers with their buildings and roads and cars had encroached on her territory, still only venturing to the gravesite when the bluebells were in flower; the sadness was too much. The memory of Alexander and Cyflym, the woodland with it swathes of Spring bluebells and her posies, made the gravesite, the only place where bluebells grew now, too big a draw for her. During the rest of the year, the sadness prevailed and she stayed away.

'Why din't you go with those spirits? Scared, is you?' the whisperers taunted, though the Jones children still kept well away. Unlike the whisperers, Sioned and Ioan Jones did not generally cause trouble in their spirit form, but they were not yet ready to enter the Light.

Mai refused to engage in the whisperers' childish behaviour. Childish? Yet she was the child. They could never harm her, whatever they said. They were cowards. She just kept away, avoiding them as much as she could.

Mai had whispered in the ears of Fitz, Pat and Alexander, but only to try and influence them for their own safety and good. These whisperers only wanted to cause havoc and disharmony amongst the breathers, as they had during their lifetimes.

The biggest mud floor of all soon went down on the settlement site and the biggest of buildings grew up around them all. She found it difficult to comprehend the size. It had huge glass windows and doors. The breathers' cars had glass windows too. Mai only knew it was glass because she'd heard that windows let in the light. They had them at the Big House and they were made of glass, but she had never seen them until the smaller breathers' houses had been built.

This new market was open 24/7 (whatever that meant). Superstore, they called it, packed with shelves selling all kinds of food and clothes (people wore very strange clothes these days) and so many other things that she simply did not understand. Mai understood turnips and other roots but most of the food she had never seen before. The food on the other shelves – well, what she assumed to be food – came in strange metal and glass containers and strange shiny stuff called 'plastic'.

In one section of the superstore, people sat down to eat and drink things that she had never seen before. That part was called 'café'.

Over in the corner, was a section called 'toilets'; people went in there and soon came out again, but she had no idea why. She never ventured too near because that was the area where the dreadful images of the pogrom were most intense. Even on days when the images disappeared, the atmosphere was sinister and oppressive. On bad days, the breathers and images appeared just to walk right through each other.

Mai was fascinated to see how people made their purchases. She followed them around and watched as they put the items that they wanted to buy into carts on little wheels which they pushed around, taking them to the 'tills' which somebody used to add the totals up and they put their purchases into funny looking sacks. At first, people used coins, but not the coins used in Mai's time, and pieces of paper to pay for their purchases, but some used funny little cards – well, that's what the breathers called them, anyway. Some people said 'pay by card' and others said 'pay with plastic' (the funny shiny stuff). It meant the same. Soon, they were using these cards most of the time although a few people still used coins and the pieces of paper.

The way that women seemed to be in charge of the men as they went around the store fascinated her. Most of the time, the men just followed behind them, quite often getting bossed around. That was funny. Perhaps if women were in charge, fighting would stop, although she had not seen any real fighting since the time of the canals – and, even then, people didn't often get killed. In Mai's time, it was always the men who caused the fighting. If women had been in charge in those days, perhaps her father wouldn't have gone off to war and got himself killed. Perhaps she would have known him and Herbert wouldn't have been in charge of the family. Perhaps her life would have been different. Perhaps. But it didn't matter now.

The whisperers were always on the hunt for breathers to tease; anybody easily prone to anger would do. If one person annoyed another for the most minor of reasons, where they would normally exercise some restraint, the whisperers would say something like, 'Go on, then. You tell 'im!' and the breathers would start an argument. Mai occasionally shouted at them to stop it but they always ignored her as she otherwise ignored them.

Then, one day, completely unexpected, Mai heard a familiar voice behind her.

'Hello, Mai. How are you, my dear?'

'Meg! Meg!' Oh, the joy! 'Meg! It's so lovely to see you! Where have you been?'

'Actually, I am – or was – Sister Theresa. I went to Ireland, where your father and Herbert came from, and then to another place abroad, called France, so I could take my vows. I passed as quite a young woman – only 36 years of age; succumbed to a disease known as white plague in my day. They call it tuberculosis now. I prefer Meg though. Anyway, I have heard that you refuse to come into the Light. You will have peace, you know. I can take you if you will come with me. Why do you wish to remain here? It is a terrible place, is it not? And you are so alone!

'Oh Meg! I know those spirits meant well but I just have to find my reason to be! Why I was born. I know it will come one day.

'The reason you were born may never be known – and the life after is not how I, as a breather, would ever have envisaged, but it is nothing to fear, my dear. And even if you find people you think might be the ones you are looking for, how do you expect to communicate with them? I believe that a very few breathers are able to see us but they are very rare.'

'There is one who comes in here sometimes with a woman,' Mai told her. 'I don't see him often – just very, very occasionally. I hide from him, though, because his aura is so bright. Bright as a bonfire. That's what I call him – the Bonfire! I am sure that he could see me but I have seen him get angry and he's very strong. He scares me. But there may be others like him who aren't quite as frightening. Honestly, though, I am far from fearful of going through the Light. I just do not believe it is my time. There is something more to learn here. I just know it.'

Clearly, Meg – Sister Theresa – would get nowhere trying to persuade Mai to go through the Light with her. She had been coping well for a very long time and would continue to do so. Yet how could she be so sure that something awaited her on this side of the Light? From Mai's experience and logic, it is possible. There may well be other breathers like 'the Bonfire' – but not so scary! Possible, but highly unlikely.

'Well, if you ever need me, dear Mai, I will be here for you. I wish you well. May I visit you from time to time?'

'Oh, please do. I would love to see you.'

'In that case, I will see you again with the greatest of pleasure. Strange place, this, isn't it?'

And she was gone.

Soon after Meg's visit, a woman came into the store; she became a frequent visitor. Sometimes she was alone and, at other times, she came in with an older man. Her father, perhaps? He sat in a chair with wheels and she pushed him around. Sometimes, he put a basket on his lap and they collected things as they went around the store. At other times, when they wanted to buy more, she would push him in his chair and he pushed the bigger cart. They did not behave as father and daughter. Their relationship seemed different. There was something special about this woman's aura. It was like a beacon. Mai always looked out for the woman and every time she came into shop, alone or with the man, Mai followed as far as she dared. She didn't like to go further than the ends of the shelves (the breathers called them 'aisles') for the darkness.

There came a time when the woman no longer came with the man. Whenever she did come into the store, she wasn't the same. She had a sadness about her. Her aura still glowed, she was still the Beacon, but there was something not right. Had the man died?

Nor did Mai see the Bonfire again.

Lady in a Mist Meets Relicneedsmate

2012

Lady in a Mist: Widow, 58, non-smoker, graduate; enjoys natural history, conservation, animals, reading, theatre, art, history; seeks male of similar age and interests.

God! This was scary. Online dating. Not something to which Lizzie Phillips ever envisaged herself resorting. She uploaded the best of the selfies she'd taken to her profile and hoped for the best.

Lizzie was not a gregarious person. She liked the quiet life. Pubs and clubs were not just boring, they were tortuous. On the other hand, neither did she cope well with being single. She was desperately lonely. Her three sons all lived hundreds of miles away and had lives of their own. Since Andrew's death, four years ago, she had been in a relationship with a man who had been a good friend to both her and Andrew. Widowed suddenly, just a few months prior to Andrew's passing, mutual support soon evolved into something more. After a couple of years or so, it ended suddenly – and rather acrimoniously.

The income from Andrew's small insurance policy was not enough to keep her going, so she had to keep her administrative job in a social care company. Boring as hell, barely enough to keep the roof over her head with the outstanding mortgage, let alone maintain it, but she had to keep going. They'd needed the money when he was alive and she needed it even more now. She hated it. She needed something to get her teeth into; to command some interest. This wasn't it.

Lizzie trawled the internet and the newspapers for other jobs but there was rarely anything either suitable or interesting. When she did find something that looked marginally better than her current employment, she was unsuccessful. Whatever they said about age discrimination, it was rubbish. She always lost out to people better qualified, or she was too qualified. What they meant was 'You're too old.' Where did she want to be in five years' time? Good question. Good answer? Retired. Lizzie had had enough.

Fifty-eight was hardly a good age to be wishing one's life away. However, in a couple of years her state retirement pension would kick in and she could just walk away from the bloody job. Keep gritting your teeth, girl!

Then the bombshell hit. The State Pension age was increased. She would have to work until she was sixty-five and a half – over seven years away! Overnight, she became a WASPI woman. Women Against State Pension Inequality! She was devastated.

With the combined income from Andrew's insurance policy and her own full pension, she could have managed. If not, she could have found something part-time that wasn't going to wear her out. Now she had to face another seven years. Seven bloody years! The only thing keeping her remotely sane was her dogs! The prospect soon spiralled her into mental decline.

Lizzie never became suicidal, exactly, but many a night she climbed into bed thinking that maybe it would be better if she didn't wake up in the morning. But for her lovely canine companions, Labradoodles Gemma and Jason, and their chocolate Labrador mum, Sally, who had arrived in her life with the puppies, things might have been different. Sally and the Doodles were an expense scoffed at by most of her work colleagues (why complain of being hard up when you have those dogs to keep?), but being one of those people who understood animals better than people and, truth be told, vice versa, nothing was going to part her from her babies. Yet, despite the warm welcome, every day she would come home from work, shut the front door behind her, and the black veil would descend.

Her work attendance record was poor. Go out for a walk, they say, if you're a bit depressed! Get some exercise! You can't help but get exercise when you have three big dogs. You have to go for a walk. Her friend and neighbour, Fiona, was marvellous, popping in to see them a few times a day while she was out, but Lizzie just wanted to be at home with them. And every day, she still had to come home, shut the door behind her to be enveloped by the ever present past, and the ever-waiting cloud.

She had to try this online dating. Some of the dating sites were hardly appealing: Profile pictures of men wearing only vests and shorts, showing off their muscles (fat). Some, for whatever God-forsaken reason, found it necessary to upload pictures of themselves wet-shaving in front of their mirrors. Really? Mirrors appeared to be particularly beneficial for those who'd been by-passed by the concept of the selfie altogether, despite having smart-phones in their hands. And oh, the range of interests: football, rugby, snooker, zzzzz ... Well, ya gets what ya pays for, but there was nothing in the coffers to spare. Lizzie, ever a peculiar mix of optimist and depressive, kept trying.

To her surprise, she got quite a few likes on her profile and even plucked up the courage to chat online to a few. Sadly, these men were not quite what she was looking for – whatever that was. She would know it when she saw it. They all lacked any real character. She wasn't hopeful but there was at least some contact with the outside world beyond her miserable job.

One day, a day no different to any other, she came home, fed and walked the dogs, put something quick in the microwave, ate another lonely meal, washed up her dishes, made a cup of tea and sat down to her laptop to find that her profile had been 'liked' by 'Relicneedsmate'. That day was to change her life forever, in ways she could never have imagined.

Matthew Prosser was the same age as Lizzie – just a few months older. She liked the look of him from his profile picture, even if he did appear to be smoking – ruggedly attractive, intelligent-looking. Best of all, he only lived four miles away. No travelling involved. He didn't mention specific interests but, intriguingly, his profile said 'works with Spirit'. Hopefully, that didn't mean that he was some kind of religious nutcase but, after all, her darling Andrew had been very devout. She clicked 'like' on his profile and soon they started an online chat and exchanged numbers. She phoned him.

'Hi, Matt. It's Lizzie. Difficult to know what to say, isn't it?'

'Tell me about it! Sorry to hear that you lost your husband, by the way. That must have been so hard.'

'Yes, it was, to be honest. But Andrew was a much older than me – and I don't want to sound miserable. How are you? Your profile says that you have a few health problems.'

'Well, yes. Hope it doesn't put you off. I'm being treated for a brain tumour and I have a mental health condition. I'm bipolar.'

'I'm sorry to hear that, Matt. Yes, it did say about the bipolar on your profile. So how are you coping?'

'Oh, you know, not too bad. Up and down. No pun intended!'

She got the joke. Making a joke at his own expense in these circumstances was pretty special.

'What about the tumour?'

111

'Well, actually, it's inoperable, but this new treatment I'm on – it's experimental, but I'm hopeful.'

Her heart went out to him. Already, it felt as though she'd known him for years, he was that easy to talk to. Among other things, he had been a social worker many years ago, but something had happened which was so awful that he preferred not to talk about it. All he would say was that people had not listened to him, something terrible had happened with one of his clients and he walked. They should have listened. Since then, until the tumour struck, he had been in and out of manual work but had found it difficult to hold down a job with the bipolar.

On paper, it seemed he wasn't her sort at all, but they were on the phone for a couple of hours and arranged to speak the next evening – and the evening after that – and the evening after that.

If any other woman had said to Lizzie Phillips that they were going to meet somebody they had just met online, alone in his flat, she would have said they were stupid, crazy or both, and tried to talk them out of it. Lizzie Phillips was now that other woman but Lizzie Phillips was a woman who trusted her intuition. Her intuition told her that she could trust Matthew Prosser.

A Bicycle, TD Bear and a Shelf that's not a Shelf!

Lizzie's intuition had been right. Matt Prosser was the perfect gentleman. His flat was on the other side of town, at the rear of the upper floor of a two-storey block, converted from a former working men's club. She rang the intercom buzzer and he told her where to find him. He was waiting at the top of the stairs and greeted her with a cordial hug and polite kiss on the cheek.

The flats were not situated in the most salubrious area of town but, inside, it was spacious, pleasant and he kept it clean and tidy.

'Coffee?'

'Yes, please. Black, no sugar.'

'Ha! Same as me!'

He gestured to the sofa and she sat down. The room was L-shaped, open-plan so she could see him as he made the coffee. She opened the conversation:

'It's a very nice flat. How are you doing?'

'Thanks, struggling to keep it at the moment, though.'

He brought the coffees to the sofa and placed them on the coffee table. Being black, it was far too hot to drink yet.

'Yes,' he continued, 'I'm afraid I can't work and have no income at the moment. The housing people have been great but the housing benefit doesn't quite cover the rent. My mum gives me the rest, but there's leccy and gas to pay for. You know. Sounds awful, doesn't it? 58-year-old man having his mum sub him. Do you mind if I smoke?'

She hated smoking with a passion, and it seemed a silly thing to do for someone with a brain tumour. Still, it was his place, after all, so she just shrugged and he rolled a cigarette.

'All I can afford.'

'Well, to be honest', she told him, 'they don't smell as horrible as packet cigarettes and I don't think they're quite as bad for you. Anyway, do you not get any other benefits? Employment and Support Allowance. And then there's Disability.'

'Ah. Story there. I did apply. I got a bit of money while I was waiting for my assessment but I had a brain scan appointment come through for the same day as the assessment. I didn't have enough credit on my phone so I wrote to them to explain and sent them the appointment card with the letter. Then my money just stopped. I went to the Job Centre and they said the letter hadn't been received. So I threw a bit of a wobbler and they threw me out. Never bothered since. Been living on fresh air. Despite having been a Social Worker, I'm not very good at dealing with the authorities. With the bipolar, I lose my rag quite easily. Can't cope with nonsensical bureaucracy.'

'You're not on your own there! But what about food?'

'Well, Mum gives me a bit extra when she can, but I don't like taking it really. Not much fun having to cadge from your mum at my age, as I say. People are kind, though. I often find carrier bags of food sitting at the front door. Never know who they're from. Still owe the landlord a bit – the rent is a bit more than housing people can give me, as I say, but he's been pretty good about it, to be honest.'

'Wow. That's incredible.' She looked up at huge family photograph on the wall. Matt with his ex and two boys.

'Those your sons?'

'No, they're my ex-partner's boys. Brought them up like they were my own. We were together ten years but she found someone else and threw me out. Funny thing, though. I'm always handy if she wants a baby sitter or anything doing.'

'You never married, then?'

'Not her. I was married for seventeen years and she found someone else too. Wanted to be out and about. I was working all the hours God sent – two jobs – to pay the mortgage and keep her in whatever style she wanted, but she must have been bored when I was working so she found someone else. Got divorced. Long time ago but then the same thing happened with this one.' He nodded up to the photograph. 'Ten years we were together. One of the boys told me she'd been seeing this bloke for years.'

'You didn't marry her?

'Nah. Once bitten twice shy. Never again. Just as well as it turned out. Anyway, that's me in a nutshell, what about you?'

She gave him the nitty gritty about her life. She almost felt guilty for having been so happily married to Andrew, although she'd had a couple of fairly disastrous marriages before – but she did have three lovely sons to show for it. She told him about the dogs.

'Oh, I love dogs. All animals, to be honest.'

Wonderful! At last, somebody like her.

Then, out of the blue, he said, 'I'm a psychic medium – seen dead people all my life.'

Lizzie didn't turn a hair. She was quite open-minded about it. He didn't look like one of those overly-dramatic sorts you see on the telly. He told her some funny stories, like the one when, as a teenager, he was so full of himself that, for a dare, he went one night to a derelict house that was reputedly 'haunted'. He sat on an old chair when white figures suddenly descended from the ceiling. He ran from the house, screaming in terror! It turned out to be damp ceiling paper coming away and falling to the floor!

Three hours and a couple more mugs of coffee later, it was time to go. She had to be up for work in the morning. He had been such a gentleman and he even escorted her around the corner to where she had parked her car. He was lovely. She liked him a lot, even if there may not be much future in it. She wanted to be there for him – even if it was just as a friend. He was such lovely company.

She returned a few nights later and as they sat drinking coffee, chatting away about this and that, he suddenly came out with:

'What's all this about a bike, then?'

'Bike? What bike?'

'When you were a kid. You had a bike.'

'Well, yes. But most kids have bikes.'

'I know. Well, I didn't, and I still can't ride a push-bike. I never got anything. Yours wasn't the one you wanted, though. You saw the one you wanted in a shop but you never got it.'

Lizzie had never given that bike a thought since she had left home at the age of seventeen, but he went on to describe it: two-tone blue – a Triumph Palm Beach.

'One of my friends had been given one for her birthday,' she told him. 'Another girl around the corner had the same model in pink but I wanted the blue one. I wasn't a pink kind of girl then! I was nine years old and I was the only kid in the neighbourhood not to have a bike. I'm sure I was. I remember going with my dad to the bank, which was on the end of the local parade of shops. Half-way along, there was a bike shop – and there it was! 'My' bike in the window: the blue one! I was saying, 'Dad! Dad! There it is! That's the one I want!' He just seemed to ignore me.

Matt never took his eyes off her as she related the story.

116

'On my tenth birthday, Dad took me out in the car. I was sure I was going to get 'my' bike, but we didn't go to the shop on the parade. He took me to a place somewhere on the other side of town. He said I could choose a bike from the second-hand ones standing outside. I was so disappointed, but at least I was getting a bike. I chose one that had been given a paint job – more or less the same blues as the Palm Beach. Four pounds, it cost. Can't remember how Dad got it into the car, now. It was only a Morris Minor 1000 but, when we got the bike home, I learned how to pump up the tyres, and change or repair the inner tube if I got a puncture. Yeah. I went miles on it.'

Matt smiled at her. 'Tell you what, it was four quid more than my father ever spent on a present for me!'

'Mmm. That's so sad. You know what? I really loved that bike – probably better than if I'd had the Palm Beach, in the end. Looking back, I think it must have been all they could afford. I'm sure they tried to give the impression that they had more than they actually did.'

'You never really felt a part of your family, did you?' he said. 'Always treated differently. Always on the outside. Like you were looking in through a window.'

'Too true. I was always in trouble for not doing this right, or not doing that right. Even after I left home. In the 1960s and 70s, they were like relics from the 40s and 50s. They refused to accept 'modern' life. Whenever I went back home, one of Dad's favourite sayings was 'when in Rome, do as the Romans do'.

She was impressed with Matt's insight – particularly the bit about the bike. These things just 'popped' into his head, he said.

'I was much the same as you', he said. 'My bloody father starved us all. Gave my mother next to nothing to feed the family and pay the bills. She grew up on a farm, so at least she could grow some veg. We were always

117

hungry though. As long as he had enough for his drink. He used to beat seven shades out of me and my mother – until I got too big for him. I thumped him when he hit her once too often and he never did it again. We were all relieved when he died, really.'

'That's awful. You had it a lot worse than me. At least my parents weren't violent.'

He changed the subject and talked more about his mediumship. People often asked him to visit dying relatives to comfort their loved ones as they passed away. He would always oblige if he was well enough. He never charged anything for his services. He didn't believe in that. Sometimes, he would take some expenses, if it was offered but, to his mind, if he charged, he would feel under pressure to 'perform'. It was a gift and it was against his principles to charge for a gift. But then, a gift was something you could give back. He was stuck with this.

Lizzie thought about this philosophy and said: 'Well, not always. What if you were a musician and made your living from playing in concerts? That's a gift too.'

A very different kind of gift, according to Matt. She could see his point of view.

'I used to do a lot of psychometry, but not so much now.'

'I know the word, but I've never really understood what it meant.'

'Well, a medium holds an object belonging to a person and, just by handling it, can sometimes pick up on memories associated with it.'

All new territory for Lizzie; it fascinated her.

They continued to see each other two or three times a week. They got on really well and the relationship seemed to be developing.

One day, in late September, having given the matter a great deal of thought, she said, 'My son is getting married in November. David, the oldest. You wouldn't like to come to the wedding with me, would you? I have nobody to go with.

'I'd be delighted!'

She was at work when the text arrived: 'Don't come round tonight. Not feeling well.'

That was understandable, but such messages became more frequent. She couldn't quite make out how he was feeling about her, or their relationship, but she knew his heart wasn't in it. It was fair enough, given all that he had to contend with. She didn't want to end it because, with his health problems, he might just need her, but she wasn't optimistic about the long-term course of their relationship.

One Saturday evening in late October, an occasion when she hadn't been rebuffed, Lizzie had arranged to visit Matt. Lizzie decided to take the original teddy bear of her collection with her. TD Bear had a story and Lizzie was very attached to him. She wanted to see what Matt would make of him, so she took the bear to the flat, plonking him on the computer chair in the corner as Matt made the coffee.

They chatted during the evening, but no more than that. Lizzie couldn't make out if Matt was warming or cooling. It seemed like both at the same time. Quite strange. TD sat in the corner. With Matt's odd behaviour, he'd slipped her mind altogether and, when she left, she forgot to take him with her.

She didn't see Matt for another week. More texts putting her off, then one saying she could come around on Saturday evening. Things were going downhill. It wasn't really his fault, so she didn't hold anything against him.

She turned up at the flat and, unusually, it stank of stale smoke.

He made coffee. They chatted. During the time she was there, he smoked a lot more than usual – not like him in her company; it was normally just one or two during the evening. He knew that she didn't like it, but he didn't care. Things were definitely much cooler. There was a strange distance between them. She got up to leave after only one mug; this was definitely goodbye. He stood back. Clearly, he wasn't going to see her to the car as he normally did. A polite peck on the cheek to say goodbye was all she got. Was it her or him? He was obviously not in the mood to discuss their relationship, if relationship was what it was. She turned to the door.

'Hang on! Your teddy bear!'

'Oh, heck! TD! Nearly forgot him again.'

'You have to take him. He needs to go back with the others. His energy is seeping away from him here.'

He went to hand TD to her but suddenly pulled him back.

'Just a minute!' he said. 'This bear. There's something about him. I just can't work it out.'

'What's that?'

'Well, it's where you keep him. He's surrounded by other bears ...'

Well, yeah. He knows she has a collection so that's hardly a revelation.

'... and they're not on a windowsill. They sit on a shelf ... but it's not a shelf. I can't make it out.' He was completely flummoxed.

'Wow!' she was amazed. 'TD and the other teddies all sit together on a sort of bench swing that I made from a couple of pieces of wood I had lying around. I used a couple of curtain tie-backs to hang it from a clothes rail in the alcove in my bedroom.'

A shelf that's not a shelf! How could he possibly have known that? Nothing was said about any further meeting. She gave him another quick peck on the cheek and left.

Lizzie never expected to see Matt again. Determined not to be upset, she took a deep breath, held her head up and strode around the corner to the car, cuddling TD close to her. It wasn't just the ashtray that stank of stale smoke.

Glancing down at him she said, 'Bath for you as soon as we get in, my boy!'

She could have sworn that he was smiling up at her with relief!

Later that night she received a text: 'Sorry. Can't make the wedding.'

And that, she knew for sure, was that.

Mr Right was Mr Wrong and Mr Wrong was Mr Right

Lizzie spent that Christmas alone, crying into her beans on toast Christmas dinner. She just couldn't let the boys know that she was alone or how she was feeling. They had their own lives and she didn't want to inflict her misery on them. In the New Year, she decided to try the dating website again. She was beginning to feel a bit more confident. There was one man she quite liked. She met him once but, following that, he just wanted to meet on video calls. Lizzie liked him, but he was obviously not interested in a real relationship. It went on for about a year before fizzling out. At least it had been some company outside work while she took stock of her life.

At about five o'clock one Saturday afternoon, with nothing worth watching on television, Lizzie picked up her laptop and signed in to the dating website. Her profile had been liked by a man named Simon, from Lampeter in Ceredigion. He was a computer science graduate running his own one man band software company from home. His picture looked nice: not bad looking, wavy dark blond hair and brown eyes. She clicked 'like' on his profile. He was already online and they started chatting straight away. He was desperate to speak to her in person but asked her to phone him. She did.

First warning bell ignored.

He told her that his business was doing really well and he had his own house, bought and paid for.

They seemed to get on really well and he had a great sense of humour, but within the first half-hour he said something she found rather strange.

'You're going to think this is a bit crazy, Lizzie – but I think I'm in love with you.'

Second warning bell ignored.

They arranged to meet up in a tea-shop in Brecon at the weekend. She was surprised to discover that he was somewhat taller than she'd expected, around six feet, and he looked fairly fit, despite a slight paunch. He lived alone; never been married and never intended to get married.

He sat next to her rather than opposite and, for a first date, he was a bit too hands on for her liking, especially in public.

They left the tea shop and strolled along the canal, hand-in-hand. He again professed his love for her although she was not about to reciprocate so soon.

She told him about the dogs. He liked dogs. That was a plus.

After about twenty minutes they retraced their steps and went for a drink in one of the local pubs. Nothing alcoholic as they were both driving. He had Coke; Lizzie, tonic and lime. He asked her to go to his place the following weekend. She could bring the dogs. He had a fairly large, well fenced garden. Mostly lawn.

She agreed.

The next weekend, she piled the dogs into the car and took the couple of hours journey to Lampeter. His house was a modern two-bed semi on the outskirts of the town. Not really her style, as she liked old houses with character, but pleasant enough. The décor throughout was neutral and there was very little on the walls.

He came to her house the following weekend and so it went on; alternate weekends at each other's houses. before long she was plastering their selfies all over Facebook, kidding herself that she was happy.

During the week they talked every night on the phone for a couple of hours.

Sitting at her desk at work, one day during the week, her phone pinged. Text. Matt!

'So glad you've found Mr Right; I was so Mr Wrong.'

She replied: 'Thanks. How are you?'

'Ok. You know.'

She didn't.

The relationship with Simon went on and on, seemingly happily enough, but there was something missing: no quality. He wasn't particularly interested in anything that interested her. No real conversation. Outside of his work, he didn't seem to be interested in anything at all. They didn't do anything or go anywhere when they were together. Quality in a relationship was something she found difficult to define, but she would recognise it when she saw it. She had it with Andrew. She didn't have it here. Simon just didn't want to share his life. It wasn't really Lizzie's idea of a relationship. It was no more than 'friends with benefits' – and even that term was pushing it. Lizzie was beginning to feel used. And she was beginning to resent it. This couldn't go on much longer. There was no future in it. He was never going to live with her. He certainly wasn't going to marry her. Besides, he would never give up his cosy routine in Lampeter, and she could never live his suburban lifestyle. Still, it looked as though it was the best she was going to get.

Why, why, why had she not listened to those warning bells in the beginning? Desperation. Fear of being alone. That's why!

The relationship went on for three years, but then Simon stopped communicating during the week. He wouldn't answer her texts or pick up her phone calls. She sent him text after text asking him if he was alright. He ignored them all.

He was due to come to her place on Saturday. He didn't turn up but she received a text: 'Sorry, it's over. Don't text or call again.'

Just like that. No indication. No warning. No reason.

She responded to the text: 'What? After three years? Just like that? Why? Can't we discuss it?'

He: 'I can't do this anymore. Didn't know how to tell you. Sorry.'

Then he blocked her. Lizzie just sat there for God knows how long, in some state of shock.

She cried and cried and cried. The dogs didn't get their evening walk. She did everything else on autopilot, went up to bed and cried herself to sleep.

When she woke up the next morning, she went downstairs, fed the dogs and made herself a cup of tea. Thinking about it, it would be true to say that she and Simon could not have gone on much longer. Nevertheless, it would have been preferable to have ended it amicably or, at least, on her own terms.

Now she was alone again and, in truth, it was just being alone again that terrified her.

Still, the dogs got an extra walk on Sunday.

On Sunday evening, she thought about Mr Wrong's last text to her. She had seen very occasional posts from him on Facebook, just the occasional share of posts by other people but, other than that, there had been no communication with him for four years.

'Thought I'd let you know, Mr Right just dumped me by text, out of the blue, after three years.'

She wasn't really expecting a reply but, to her amazement, her phone pinged almost immediately.

Matt!

'Sorry to hear that. Don't be a stranger. Give me a call.'

She picked up the phone straight away. They were on the phone for a couple of hours. She asked him how he was feeling. Fine. He didn't want to go into details on the phone, though. He invited her around the next evening.

Lizzie made the fifteen-minute drive to the flat. He was there, as ever, waiting for her at the top of the stairs. He gave her a hug and kiss on the cheek, just as he had the very first time they had met, and they entered the flat. No expectations from either of them; just a resumption of friendship. Nothing had changed, except the huge picture, the shrine, had gone. She said nothing but he noticed her glance at the wall.

'I did try to get over it ... you know, before,' he said, 'but I think I just couldn't cope with the thought of losing another family. I felt such a failure.'

'Now?'

'Oh, I'm well and truly over it.'

'Well, never mind that for now, then. How about you? What about the tumour?'

'Would you believe it? Gone! Shrivelled to the size of a pea! The medication killed it stone dead.'

'Oh, that's wonderful!' she beamed, throwing her arms around him to give him a huge hug. 'Yeah. The hospital appointment before I last saw you ... you know ...'

Her eyes softened and she nodded. It was all in the past, but he wanted to explain, so she let him carry on.

'Well, five months at most, I had. There was nothing they could do anyway. That medication was experimental. Radioactive and all that. They just wanted to see if it affected the tumour at all. Maybe what they learned could help someone else. I was just kidding myself. Then, at the appointment I had before the last time I saw you ... five months, they said.'

'But then it actually worked?' she was asking the blindingly obvious.

He smiled at her, raising his eyebrows. She was overjoyed for him.

'They weren't expecting it to,' he continued, 'but against all the odds, it did! Thing is, Liz, at the time, knowing you'd already lost a husband, I didn't know how to tell you. I mean ... I was going to die. Then there was, you know ... her. Well, like I say, not so much her but that sense of failure, losing another family. I was so conflicted. God! You do all you can to provide for them but it's never enough.'

'So? Where d'you stand now?'

'You wouldn't believe it! I rang her to tell her I'd beaten the cancer and d'you know what she said?'

Lizzie shook her head.

'She said, "Oh, that's good. Can you look after the kids tomorrow night?" I told her where to get off. I'd always known, I suppose. I was hanging on to fresh air by my fingertips. I had to break it off completely. It was toxic. Only came near me when she wanted something, anyway.'

Such callousness was beyond Lizzie's comprehension. He was well rid of her. 'Well, it's done. How are you feeling now, then?'

'Ah, well.'

Uh oh!

'The day before my birthday, in February ...'

'What? This February just gone?'

'Yes. I was rushed into hospital. Only just made it, too. Heart failure. I'm OK now. If I don't overdo it.'

'Bloody hell, Matt. Don't do things by half, do you?'

'You know me! That's not the best of it. I tried to kill myself. I'd survived a brain tumour that was supposed to kill me but there was just nothing left to live for. That's what it felt like, anyway.'

'You did what? And?'

'Pills. Went round to loads of pharmacies and supermarkets collecting paracetamol until I had about a couple of hundred. Bottle of vodka. Coke. And half a dozen sausage rolls. Don't ask. Went out to Worms Head, over on the Gower. Thought it would be a lovely place to end it all. Too many people. So I found somewhere in the countryside with a car park. Nobody there when I got there. Downed the lot. Made myself sick – spewed up outside the car, and went to sleep expecting not to wake up. Next thing I know, there's a copper banging on the window. Did I know this was a gay dogging site?'

'What?' She didn't know whether to laugh or cry. Only Matt! She just sat there and listened as he got it off his chest.

'Yeah. I remembered throwing up and looked down. There he was blissfully unaware that he was standing in my pink vomit! He told me to go home. I pointed to the empty bottle of vodka. He told me he'd be back in an hour and if I was still there, he'd do me for whatever it is they do you with for gay dogging. So I came home and crashed out for a couple of days. Don't even remember driving home. I'm still here. I must have got rid of the worst of the pills and vodka when I was sick. Still, I was well over the limit, in the middle of nowhere, late at night and I'd drunk that much vodka and coke! Actually, I think it was the sausage rolls that made me sick in the end.'

'And saved your life, by the sound of it! Thank God. Why the hell didn't you call me?'

'You were happy enough with Mr Right so there didn't seem much point. We weren't going anywhere, were we?'

That upset her. She could have at least been a friend. She could understand it, though. Somehow. A man like Matt, had just fought the biggest battle of his life and, suddenly, there was nothing left to fight, nowhere to go. There was probably nothing left to live for, from his point of view, at the time.

After that episode, he hadn't been looking after himself. Still smoking his roll-ups and eating the cheapest fattiest food.

'What about your money situation. Any better off?'

'Just the same. Five years now I've been on nil income.'

No wonder he was eating crap!

'Think you should try applying for benefits.'

In the years they had been apart, Lizzie had done a few courses to do with benefits and now her role at work had developed to a point where she could help people in Matt's situation. She still hated work though. New responsibilities but no increase in pay. Her bills went up more than her mediocre annual pay increases every year. All the other stressful issues remained.

'I tried filling in the forms, but I can't see how I'm entitled.'

'Well, I think we should look at it together, again.'

With Lizzie's help, Matt claimed various benefits and was owed a lot of backpay. His financial situation changed almost overnight. At least he didn't have to cadge from his mum any more. The relationship resumed where it had left off. He was more confident of leaving the flat now, so she began to take him to her house, which was a bit of a mess – but he didn't judge. He proved a huge hit with the dogs. Jason's hero, Sally had the biggest crush ever, all doe-eyed and sighs, and Gemma was, well, Gemma!

'Told you I was good with dogs, didn't I? All dogs love me, for some reason.'

He had, too, but this was ridiculous. And funny. And very, very sweet. If your dog doesn't like someone, then you probably shouldn't either. On the other hand, when they do …. And Lizzie had the paws up for Matt in triplicate!

Spectral Spouse

The closer Lizzie and Matt became, the more time they spent together, the more she learned about the spirit world. He told her about how the spirits, those who have passed through the Light, walk among us, next to us, but in another dimension; they call it 'the multiverse'. They are individuals, but they work together as a kind of cabal, co-operating with each other. They visit us occasionally: sometimes seen by the sensitive; sometimes not. They may choose to come back to this dimension if they wish to experience a new life in order to gain empathy in a sphere with which they were unfamiliar; but they are not obliged to do so.

'It's like an education, if you like. You start at primary school and the more knowledge you gain the higher up you go, until you've got a PhD or Professorship or something.'

It was all very fascinating. There had to be something in it. The bike. The shelf that's not a shelf. And Matt was so rational – nothing airy-fairy about him whatsoever.

Lizzie spent her first night with him at the flat. A warm Friday night in August. She had settled the dogs for the night and went around to his place quite late. On Saturday morning, as he got out of bed, he seemed fine but, without warning, he yelled and slammed his hand against the wall. The dark spectre of his psychosis was always there: a demon, perpetually lurking, waiting to pounce.

'What's up?'

'Nothing. Leave me be. I'll be fine. Just give me a few minutes.'

He left the bedroom and a couple of minutes later an enormous bump, followed by a crash from the living room – then silence.

'Matt? Are you ok?' she shouted. Not a sound.

Lizzie hesitated, unsure of what to do. Should she leave him? Should she go and check? She didn't want to panic but what if he'd hurt himself? He could have fallen and knocked himself out. She had to check. She got out of bed, left the bedroom, tiptoed down the hall and, very tentatively, pushed the door of the living room ajar and peeped around.

Matt was sitting cross-legged on the floor, stark naked, with his back to her. His big armchair was tipped over on the other side of the room in front of the sofa. His small glass occasional table, on which had sat his laptop and an empty coffee mug the night before, was on its side with the mug broken on the carpet and his laptop on the floor next to it.

'Matt? Matt? Are you ok?' she repeated. Still nothing.

She placed her hands on his shoulders. He was rigid as a statue. She massaged his shoulders, whispering in his ear, 'You're ok, everything's ok, you'll be fine', and, gradually, oh so gradually, he began to relax.

It took about ten minutes of gentle massage and encouragement, before he started to come to.

'Bloody hell,' he said as he looked around, absorbing the state of his living room, 'what happened?'

'Think it was one of your psychotic episodes.'

'I don't remember a thing. Oh God. That's my laptop gone for a burton, by the look of it.'

'Never mind your laptop!' she scolded as she started to clear up the mess. 'We need to get you to a GP and get you a referral to a psychiatrist.'

She went over to the huge overturned armchair and bent down to lift it up.

'Don't do that!' he yelled. 'I'll do it. You'll do yourself a mischief.'

He got up, righted the chair and moved it back to its proper position with such ease, heart condition or not, that it could have been made from balsa wood.

'Go and get some clothes on,' she told him, 'while I boil the kettle.'

After that, things were back to normal.

On Sunday afternoon, they snuggled up together on the sofa in his living room. She was curious to ask him something.

'I don't suppose you've seen anything of Andrew.'

'No – actually, I have tried, but nothing.'

At this stage, truth be told, Lizzie remained open-minded, but not necessarily one hundred per cent convinced of 'the other side'. Still, whenever she had any doubts, she thought back to her old bicycle and that shelf that's not a shelf. She was sure he was psychic, but there had been no real evidence of mediumship to date, other than what he had told her.

They sat there, quietly enjoying each other's company. Matt suddenly sat bolt upright.

'Bloody hell! He's here!'

'What? Who's here?'

'Your Andrew. Definitely, I just felt him. I know he was here! He just sort of came and went.'

Lizzie didn't know how she should react and all she managed to say was, 'Oh.'

They snuggled down to their cuddle again, his arm around her, as though a visit from one's dearly departed husband was the most normal thing in the world to have happened.

A deep vocal noise came from her right-hand side. Even after eight years, she recognised that voice, albeit just a slow, deep-throated groan. No doubt about it. It was Andrew – but it seemed to be coming from Matt!

She sat up and looked at him. She was not imagining it. She was most definitely not imagining it!

Projecting about eighteen inches from Matt's face was a white, striated, translucent strip. At its end was the shape of a human head, with an utterly distinctive profile: Andrew Phillips – her late husband! Her eyes wide and mouth open, she gasped and the vision disappeared.

Matt shook his head.

'What the hell happened then?'

'What d'you mean, "What happened?" Don't you know?'

'No. What was it?'

She described what she saw but he had no recollection whatsoever.

'Naughty, they're not supposed to do that.'

'Do what?'

'Channel without asking the medium's permission.'

Again, 'Oh.' She didn't know what he was talking about and her blank expression said so.

'Spirits can enter a medium like that, like you just saw, and show their faces, but they are supposed to ask permission from the medium first. Normally, the image of the spirit's face is just superimposed on the medium's. The trouble is, when it does happen, the medium is taken over and doesn't really know what's happening. I didn't have a clue! It takes a lot out them … me! I haven't had a spirit channel through me for about fifteen years!'

'Wow! Are you ok though?'

'Yes – I'm fine. Tell you what, though. Your Andrew is one hell of a powerful spirit!'

That was no surprise to Lizzie. He had a very powerful personality when he was alive.

It all seemed so surreal, but she accepted it. She found it a comforting thought: her Andrew was around. She'd seen him with her own eyes.

They settled down to their cuddle again. A couple of minutes later, Lizzie had the strangest sensation that went from the top of her head, inside her skull, down through her spine and seemed to dissipate from her sternum. Warm and kind of 'twiddly' was the only way she could think to describe it. Matt sat up and turned to her.

'He's just tried to contact you!'

'Oh! That's what it was.' She wasn't fazed at all. She felt utterly safe and secure. It was like the most normal thing in the world and they carried on as usual.

She was now utterly convinced – and she adored Matt.

Matt spent Friday night at Lizzie's house. In the morning, she said, 'I need some stuff from GreenFare. Fancy coming?'

'GreenFare? I try not to go there. I used to go shopping there sometimes – you know, with her – but not anymore. Not if I don't have to. Only ever went in there if I couldn't get out of it.'

She raised her eyebrows.

'Why? Bad memories?'

'Oh, no. Nothing like that. I don't give a monkey's about her. It's something else. Bad vibes and such. Something must have happened on that ground a long time ago. Spirits, whisperers, visions – people horribly mutilated. Some dreadful atrocity occurred there. Must have been hundreds of years ago. But the bloody atmosphere. Horrendous. I'll come along, though. But if the atmosphere's too bad, I'll stay in the car, if that's OK.'

'Yeah, that's fine. The shop down the road's cheap enough but it's crap for vegetarians.'

'Never really thought about it.'

When they were together, he ate what she ate, but he had never given vegetarianism any real thought. They put on their shoes and got in the car. On their way, he said:

'The whisperers don't bother me. They used to try but I think I'm too powerful and I scare them. It's just the atmosphere of the place – it's so dark. Really oppressive. I know something terrible happened on that site. It must have been hundreds of years ago but I see awful things there. Visitors – spirits, like your Andrew, who come from the other side of the Light – well they're fine, but it's mostly residual images.'

She didn't completely understand what he was talking about.

'What do you mean? What are whisperers?'

He explained as they drove along. 'They are mischief makers who stayed this side of the Light because they enjoyed causing trouble; too frightened of having to face up to their misdeeds on this side to go through the Light.

'Actually, it doesn't feel too bad today', he said as they drove into the car park. She parked the car and got out. Linking her arm in his, they ambled across the car park to the store, where they picked up a trolley and entered the shop.

Mai couldn't believe what she was seeing. The Beacon! For once, since the old man had disappeared, she wasn't alone. She was with the Bonfire! She followed them around the store. Why was she with the Bonfire, of all people? The Beacon's aura was almost eclipsed by his, but it was still visible to her. Although his aura was still very bright and strong, it didn't seem quite as fiery as usual. He seemed calmer than he used to be. Mai was still too frightened to reveal herself to him, so she remained hidden. This could have been her chance but even with his slightly gentler aura, she was still too wary of him. She followed them around at a safe distance.

Lizzie and Matt did their bit of shopping and left.

'No, it wasn't too bad at all in there today. A bit of activity, but nothing I couldn't cope with. As long as I keep away from the toilets. That's where the worst of it is. Horrible.'

After that, they did their shopping in GreenFare on a regular basis. Occasionally, if the atmosphere was too dark and oppressive, he waited in the car but, generally, he found that he could go in with her. Mai was always watching, but too nervous of him to approach.

Liver

It was Thursday. Always Thursday. She would get the text: 'Don't come round – not well'. He would disappear for a day or two, or sometimes three. This time, he disappeared for ten days. No communication. He wouldn't take her calls or answer her texts. She was desperately worried and eventually dialled 101.

The police managed to gain entry by yelling through the door, 'Mr Prosser? If you don't open this door, we'll have to force entry. We just need to make sure that you're ok.'

Matt, wearing nothing but his dressing gown, opened the door to two big, burly men, a sergeant and a constable. He was furious. Absolutely, bloody furious. He was a mess. God only knows when he'd last had a shower – or even a wash. Ten days growth of beard.

'Are you ok, Mr Prosser?'

They walked straight past him into the hall and turned into the living room.

'I'm fine. I don't need this. Who called you? Lizzie, I suppose.'

'If you're sure you're ok. Looks fairly tidy in here. You could do with letting in a bit of fresh air though, mate. She was worried about you. You should be glad that somebody does care enough about you to call us.'

That was when something clicked. He was emerging from the psychosis anyway, but the sergeant's words resonated: *somebody cares; somebody cares about me.*

Her phone pinged. She picked up the text.

'Sorry. I'm ok. Really bad one this time. Give me a day or two to pull myself together and I'll call you. And thanks.'

She went to see him a couple of days later and they talked seriously about his bipolar and the psychosis. She didn't like to intrude, so she had never pushed him about it before. It was the first time he'd described the real hell he suffered: the mouths in the walls laughing at him, mocking him; the ethereal demons flying at him, in front of his face; bats flying around him. He'd been to a psychiatrist years before, but the medication just turned him into a zombie. He preferred to lose a day or two every week or so than live like that. This had been a biggie though. Ten days! And she'd missed him.

'I love you.' He was starting to take this relationship seriously.

'I love you, too.' Lizzie was sure, this time.

'Matt, you know, I really think you should try a doctor again. Medication has probably come on in leaps and bounds since you last tried. That was years ago. It must be worth a go.'

They did some research between them, sometimes together, sometimes when they were apart. Then he phoned her at work.

'Hi!' she said. 'You ok?'

'Liver!'

'Eh?'

'It's the bloody liver!' he said.

'What's wrong with your liver?'

'Not mine. It's my Mam, isn't it?'

'What? Her liver? Is she ill or something?'

'No! No! Listen, will you? Whenever I see her, on a Tuesday usually, isn't it? She gives me liver. I cook it on a Wednesday and I'm always ill the day after. It always starts on a Thursday!'

Lizzie had been vegetarian for thirty years but, even as a child, just the thought of any kind of offal made her nauseous.

'I've just been doing a bit of research on a bipolar info website.' He was seriously excited, mania notwithstanding. 'It says that liver's one of the things that can trigger psychosis. It's the bloody liver, isn't it!'

'Hell fire, Matt! In that case, if we can go to the doctor and you get some tidy meds, we might be able to control it better.'

So, they did. And it worked. Not perfectly, admittedly. She went with him to see a new GP and then to a new psychiatrist. There was a bit of experimentation with the level of drugs – and they had to expect a certain number of psychotic episodes but, more often than not, he could feel it coming on and take extra medication. That helped him sleep it off before the hallucinations took hold. He'd wake up feeling a bit foggy, but he was no longer losing multiple days out of his life every week. The only problem was that when a psychotic episode occurred, it could still strike without any warning. It was an unpredictability they had to live with. He still wouldn't be able to work. The combined effects of bipolar disorder, psychosis and his heart condition put paid to that.

He gave up the liver straight away, although it was a bit difficult explaining it to his mother, who was convinced he needed it for his anaemia, even though he was no longer anaemic.

He became interested in Lizzie's vegetarianism and asked her about it. The way she explained about the industrial nature of farming animals, the sheer number slaughtered every single day, animal sentience, everything made perfect sense and this tough hulk of testosterone gave up meat altogether. He'd always been an animal lover but never given a thought to what was on his plate. They even went on to cut out eggs and dairy. Matt Prosser was now vegan. Whoever would have thought? But the next time he went to his GP for a check-up, his cholesterol level was down from 37.5 to 4.35 so he was sticking with it.

Two days before Christmas, they went into town. He wanted to buy her something for Christmas. For some reason, it had to be jewellery. In every shop they went in, she insisted that it was all too expensive. Just because he now had a bit of money, he couldn't go spending it on her like that!

Lizzie Phillips was like no other woman he'd ever known. Refusing to take no for an answer, in terms of the expense, they went into the umpteenth jewellery shop and he convinced her to try on some rings. He hadn't actually asked her to marry him but, when they came out of that shop, she was wearing an engagement ring. They had a lovely quiet Christmas, just enjoying each other's company.

In the New Year, Lizzie returned to work sporting her new engagement ring.

'It was always Matt, wasn't it?' noted Deborah, one of her more erudite colleagues. Lizzie just smiled. Of course it was.

Matt and Lizzie busied themselves organising their wedding for the following October. Lizzie handed in her notice at work. She had just over two weeks' leave remaining and, to her huge relief, she was able to finish work at the end of September. All she wanted was to be with Matt – and her beloved dogs.

It was a lovely, classy affair. The best they could afford, with about forty family and guests.

'Finally, we did it! And I was never going to get married again!' he said.

Superstore Spirit

February 2018

Mai followed from a discreet distance, as ever, whenever they came into the store for their groceries. She was so wary of him, yet she couldn't help but notice that his aura, although still very bright – he was still the Bonfire, almost eclipsing the Beacon – was becoming ever calmer. He just didn't seem quite as scary. Perhaps she could, after all, reveal herself.

Should she? Dare she?

Lizzie was so preoccupied and annoyed with the shopping that she wasn't really taking any notice of what Matt was saying to her.

'Really, Liz, you have… you've acquired a friend.'

'I wish they wouldn't do this! They're always moving things around. Can't find the Frank Cooper's!'

'Lizzie! Sod the bloody marmalade!'

She pulled a jar from one of the lower shelves, straightened up, scowled at him and rubbed her back.

'Found it! Sorry, it's just so annoying, though. They keep bloody shifting things! What d'you say?' as she put the jar of marmalade into the trolley.

'You have a little girl holding on to the bottom of your jacket.'

'What? I do?' She looked around at the apparently empty space behind her.

He nodded. He was absolutely serious. She was happy to take him at his word.

Looking in what she hoped was the right direction, she whispered, 'Hello?' and smiled. It was a bit like playing "spot the ball". Fortunately, there was nobody else in the aisle. Then she had no idea what to do. She looked at Matt, raising her 'what now?' eyebrows. No help there, then!

'She's really shy, but she's been following you for a while.'

They wandered around to the booze section to pick up a bottle of wine. Vegan wines were in the minority, but they found an affordable red and added it to the trolley.

'Think that's it, love,' she said, 'we're done.' On their way to the checkout, Lizzie looked behind her again and smiled at her new companion. A bored-looking operator sat at an empty till waiting for a customer to turn up so she started to unload the trolley. He nipped to the end of the till and began loading the bags.

'Ok? Not a bad day for February, is it?' asked the operator.

'Yes. Lovely, isn't it?' Lizzie answered.

How difficult it must be making small talk with stranger after stranger, like the hairdresser compelled to ask, 'are you going on holiday this year?'

They were a bit too near the toilets end of the store for Matt's comfort and Lizzie could see that he was rather desperate to get away. The check-out operator was utterly oblivious. To be fair, Lizzie would have been too, if she hadn't met Matt. She couldn't see anything anyway. It was just that now, there was, quite literally, a new dimension in her life.

She paid for the shopping, he loaded the bags back into the trolley and they made their way to the exit.

'Is she still with us?' Lizzie was immensely curious and looked behind her again.

'No. She stayed at the end of the aisle. She seemed not to want to go any further. Can't blame her. Too near the nasty end! She's still watching us, though.'

Just before they went through the door, Lizzie turned back, smiled, and attempted an inconspicuous wave at her new friend. Who was to know it wasn't just an ordinary, everyday human she was waving at, anyway?

'I wonder what that was about?' she asked him.

'No idea. But she was following you for a while. It's weird. It's you she's interested in.'

'Wonder why?'

'No idea. Defo you, though.'

Lizzie's new friend remained the topic of conversation on the way home and for the rest of the day. Lizzie wanted to know all about her.

'Well, she could be anywhere between six and twelve. It's difficult to say. She has mousy hair – looks like it's been chopped in a sort of lop-sided pudding basin cut, but a bit's been missed and it's hanging down over her left eye. Tell you what, though. She's skinny. Looks as though she could do with a good meal. She's dirty too, poor little kid. Nothing on her feet. Really sweet little face on her, mind.'

'She must have died so young', Lizzie said, feeling a rush of empathy. Her heart poured out to the little girl. 'How was she dressed?'

'Oh, scruffy. She was wearing a kind of pinafore dress – looked like the stuff sacks are made from. Came down to just below her knees. Think it was blue or grey – can't really tell.' Matt being colour-blind on the blue spectrum, every such shade looked like some kind of grey to him. 'She had a whitish sort of, I dunno ... like a kind of tee-shirt underneath it, I think'

That was all he could tell her.

The next time they went shopping, the same thing happened. The child spirit was following Lizzie.

'She's taking the piss now, Liz. Copying you. She's walking on her tip-toes, like high heels.'

Lizzie laughed, remembering trying on her mum's shoes when she was that age. That was so cute. Again, though, the little girl remained at the end of the aisle when they got to the till.

'Next time, what about going to the café – see if she'll come and sit with us?' It was a thought Lizzie had pondered for a while. 'We'd have to have a coffee first, though. The frozen stuff will start to defrost, otherwise – then we've got to get it home.'

'I think that's a really good idea', he said, 'Hopefully, build up her confidence and we can get to know her.'

So, next time, they bought a couple of coffees and sat where she could see them.

'She's there, watching us.'

He was peering at the fruit and veg shelves.

'You're kidding me! Where?'

'Between the salad stuff and the potatoes.'

Lizzie looked in the direction of the fruit and veg and smiled at the invisible child. They both tried to persuade her to come over with inconspicuous gestures.

'No. She's too shy.' Matt said. They finished up their coffees. The little spirit girl followed them around as they did their shopping.

'I'd love to know more about her.' Lizzie looked around her to make sure that nobody was looking. 'Where is she now?'

'On your left.' Lizzie peered around – all clear of other customers within earshot. She looked down at the child and whispered to her, 'Won't you come over and sit with us when we next come in? In the café, while we're having a cup of coffee?'

'I think she's understanding you. She's smiling.'

Matt seemed quite relieved.

They sat in the café a week later.

'She's there – same place.'

146

'Will she come over, d'you think?' They tried to persuade her from a distance.

'Dunno. She's still very sh …. She's here. Next to you.'

'Oh hi. My name's Lizzie and this is Matt. Can you tell us your name?'

Lizzie was finding it difficult, as there were only the two of them, to make it look as if she was speaking to Matt.

Matt perked up, hard concentration on his face.

'Her name is… Mary, is it? Hang on a minute. No. I think she's saying May.'

He was still 'tuning in' to her. A few moments later, he began to translate.

'She's saying, "I am May, daughter of Sarah MacIntyre."' Pause, '"I was named for the month of my birth,"' Pause, '"I was born in the Year of our Lord 1648."' Pause, '"I never knew my father. I only know that he was Eric MacIntyre,"' Pause, '"and he died in a big battle fighting for the King – I think it was before I was born."'

Lizzie was never any good at doing joined-up sums in her head, so it took a bit of working out, but she got there.

'Wow. You were born nearly 370 years ago! Do you know what day?'

'She's shaking her head. I don't think they did birthdays', Matt said.

'I'm sorry I can't see you or hear you, May. Matt can. He can tell me what you're saying. Where were you born, sweetheart?'

'Here.' Matt said. 'She was born here. She's showing me thatched huts. She lived in a round one. Most of the others, bar one, are square. She's showing me pigs in the hut.'

'Goodness. They had farm animals in the long houses. We've seen them at St. Fagans, haven't we? I didn't know they had them in ordinary homes!'

'She's saying that most houses – well, huts – were square, but the couple where hogs – she's calling them hogs – were round so that the dung didn't collect in the corners. Easier to clean.'

'Well, I guess it would be. How old were you when you passed away, May? Do you know?'

Matt concentrated hard. 'She's saying that, when they put her body in the ground with the others, the man from the church said she had only seen seven summers.'

'Oh my God! With the others? A mass grave? You were only seven years old? Do you know why you died so young?'

Lizzie was pretty choked. She just wanted to give the little girl a hug.

Matt said, 'She's saying "blight". Hang on, she's showing me a rash on her tummy – awful pustules. She says she heard that if the spots join up, she would die. And she did.'

Lizzie gasped. It was heart-breaking. Her mind was working overtime.

'She's saying that she has to go, Liz'

'Will you come and talk to us again?'

'She's nodding.'

Then she was gone.

Over the next few weeks, they got to know their new little friend better. They learned about her family: her mother, Sarah, brothers Fitzgerald and Fitzpatrick, her sister, Miriam, and baby Seamus; they learned about how Mamgu tried to protect her; about the kindness of Sister Theresa, whom May had known as her friend and teacher, Meg. They were horrified to hear about her Uncle Herbert's behaviour; about what she had to eat, and sleeping with the hogs (although that was fine, as far as May was concerned). How could anybody be so cruel?

They learned of the pogrom. Lizzie wanted to cry. May could see the whisperers and the visions. She lived with it every day. Even on days when these things weren't visible to Matt, she could see them. It wasn't as though they could harm her. They were just unpleasant. She tried to stay out of their way, remaining hidden as much as possible.

'I told you something really bad had happened here,' Matt said to Lizzie. 'Blight. What do you think it is?'

She concentrated hard. As much as she liked history, it wasn't one of her strongest subjects. We'll have to do some research. Plague? Cholera? Don't think it was Black Death. I don't think it was the right time, but I'm not sure.'

At home, they put away the shopping and each grabbed their laptops. Lizzie had a suspicion of what it could be.

'Matt? Come and look at this? Is this like the rash that she showed you?'

'Yes – exactly that!'

'Smallpox!' she announced. 'Well, that's one mystery solved. Poor little soul.'

Matt had been vindicated in his belief that something in addition to 'the blight' had happened on that site. The atmosphere of the place and the dreadful injuries to the poor souls in the images he had seen had always told him so.

The resident spirits weren't all mischief-making whisperers. Some of them were just frightened to face up to what they had done as breathers, so chose to hang around, but now behaved themselves!

A week later, Lizzie was feeling a bit under the weather. She asked Matt if he would mind doing the shopping alone. No problem.

Cheese. He was standing in the Free From section, reading from the list Lizzie had written out for him. Suddenly, a vision jumped out at him between the vegan Cheddar and yoghurts!

'Where is she then?'

Matt almost jumped out of his skin!

'Jesus! Don't do that! You scared the shit out of me!'

He looked around, sensing that he and May were not alone. A man was staring at him.

'I'm talking to the cheese! Alright?' Matt shouted at him. During his long and varied working life, Matt had once been a Butlins Redcoat, a stand-up comedian – not what one could call shy and retiring – and certainly not averse to making a bit of a fool of himself. The poor man pulled a face, made a swift turn, grabbed his trolley and made a hurried exit from the aisle.

'She's not feeling very well this morning.'

'Oh. Tell her I'll see her next time, then.'

'See? I did tell you that it's you she's interested in.' he said, when he got home as she laughed her socks off at the story of the cheese.

As May became increasingly confident in their company, an idea was brewing in Lizzie's head. One day, as they were driving home, she at the wheel, out it came.

'Matt, promise you won't think this is a silly idea.'

'You never say anything silly. Well, not often, anyway.'

'Really? You haven't heard this one yet. I just feel so awful about that poor little girl having to live among all that horror. You find it difficult enough, but she's a child. You don't think …'

She paused, not daring to actually say it.

'What? I don't think what?'

'Don't laugh, will you? You know so much more about this stuff than I do.'

'Of course I'm not going to laugh at you.'

He really couldn't have guessed what she was about to come out with.

'Well, you don't think … we could ask her to …'

'Ask her to what?'

'Well … to come and live with us, do you?' She kept her eyes straight ahead, fixed on the road. Who the hell invites a ghost to come and live with them?

To her surprise, he took it completely in his stride. He thought about it for a few moments.

'Well, I don't see why not.'

Was he really agreeing to this crazy idea?

'We can ask her next time, if you like. The thing is, as I understand it, spirits are supposed to have a sort of invisible silver thread, which keeps them to a reasonable distance to where they lived, or where they have a special association. Mind you, she hasn't passed through the Light yet. But then again, they turn up everywhere, so maybe it's just Earthbound spirits. Dunno. Never really thought about it. We'll ask her next time we're there.'

May was overjoyed at the suggestion. Could it really be happening? After all this time? Breathers! They wanted her to be a part of their family!

'Could I? Really? That would be lovely. I would like to. Very much. I will have to ask Sister Theresa if it would be alright when she comes.'

'And you can ride in our horseless carriage.' Matt told her.

'It's a car! I do know what a car is!' she protested.

He relayed her response to Lizzie. They both collapsed in fits of laughter over their coffees.

'You can meet our dogs, too. They're really lovely and friendly,' Lizzie said.

They had to explain that Sally, Gemma and Jason lived inside. Mai was both a little bit nervous and excited. The idea of hounds living inside the house was a bit alien. Hogs, yes. But hounds? When she was a breather, only the people in the Big House had hounds in the house. They took them with them when they went hunting. She'd seen them from a distance. They were huge and they were a bit scary.

'Well, our dogs are quite big, but they're very friendly. Honestly.' Lizzie reassured her.

'And they certainly can't hurt you!' Matt interjected.

Lizzie was so excited, even if she couldn't see or hear her herself. Just to get the poor child out of that dreadful atmosphere and into a loving family home would be wonderful.

Sister Theresa said it would be fine. She was delighted for her. May had been right all along; there would be a breather family who would love her.

The next time they went shopping, they would be picking up more than groceries from the store!

Finally, the morning arrived. Inside the store, Matt looked around him.

'Where is she? Is she here?'

'She's sitting on the customer services counter, waiting for us. She's picked up a pair of shoes from somewhere! Oh my God! That was so weird!'

'What was?'

'That woman at the counter just paid for her lottery ticket and she stuck her hand right through her – and the assistant did the same when she gave her the ticket and her change. Ugh!'

This time, Mai waited for them at the customer service counter while they did their shopping, rather than follow them around.

And then she came home – riding in the horseless carriage.

It's a car!

A Spirit Comes Home

Mai had followed them home before now and peered in through the window. A spirit is only supposed to enter a building if invited, apparently – unless they already reside there, or the building, such as the GreenFare Superstore, is built around them.

Lizzie parked the Mini outside the house and turned around to the back seat.

'Come on then!'.

'She's already in there!' said Matt.

She'd already had her invitation.

They unloaded the shopping and as soon as they got in, the dogs were more than usually excited. Sally was an old soul. She knew that something different was happening. She gave a couple of barks, which was highly unusual for her. Gemma and Jason picked up from their mother that there was something going on, and all three dogs were jumping up and down like mad. It took a few treats to calm them down. She knew they couldn't harm her but, at first, Mai was a little perturbed by their size, particularly Jason, who wasn't much smaller than an Irish wolfhound.

'Just nipping up to the toilet.' Lizzie was bursting.

'What is a toilet?'

'What?'

'May – she wants to know what a toilet is.' Matt relayed.

'It's where you go to pee and whatever. Come and see.'

May followed her upstairs. Lizzie showed her how it flushed.

'You just sit on it, do what you have to do, wipe yourself with the toilet paper, press the button and down it goes.'

When Lizzie returned downstairs, Matt said: 'Where does it go?'

'Where does what go?'

'She wants to know where it goes when you flush the loo.'

'Oh, sorry, May. It goes into pipes under the ground that carry it away. Drains.'

'She wants to know why it's called "pee"? They called it "piss"'

'Well, I think piss is a bit of a rude word, so people just say "pee", now', Lizzie explained.

'Apparently, there was nothing rude about it in May's time.'

Lizzie did a bit of research on the internet. May was right. It was only in later times, when people became prudish about bodily functions, that they shortened it to 'pee'.

There were so many things that Mai saw in the shop but didn't understand: kettle, microwave, television. Now she could see them working.

Television! Oh, television! They watched Wonder Woman, Spiderman, Batman. All the things that kids love. And Harry Potter. At least Matt and Lizzie were Harry Potter fans. She liked the Planet of the Apes series, too: Lizzie's favourites. No, they weren't real apes! It was difficult sometimes to explain the difference between fiction and reality. No, people didn't really get hurt. They just made it look that way. There was so much for a Seventeenth Century little girl to learn about.

Carpets still foxed her. Carpets foxed all of them when they thought about it!

Lizzie was watching a programme about psychic detectives. She quite liked these sort of programmes, but as she sat there watching, she felt a strange, intense vibration to her right side. May wasn't happy. Something wasn't right. Matt came downstairs and walked into the living room.

'What's wrong with May? I think she's not very happy. Something's upset her – I can feel it.'

He furrowed his brow, concentrating.

'What are you watching? She doesn't like it. It's annoying her.'

'It's a psychic detective programme.'

He concentrated again.

'Basically, what she's saying is that these people are making money from being psychics and exploiting people's misery.'

'But they help the police to find the bodies of people who have been murdered.' Lizzie protested, half addressing May, half addressing Matt. 'And I think it helps people to think that people like us, people who actually know about spirits, aren't deluded nutcases!'

May was having none of it. She thought it was wrong and that was that. Lizzie never watched such programmes again. She was even almost convinced by May's argument against it. After all, Matt always refused to be paid for his services.

'You're getting more sensitive to spirit, you know, Liz. You felt that – the vibration, and you knew she was hopping mad!'

'Yeah, but I still can't see or hear anything. Not like you.'

'Well, believe me, sometimes, you really wouldn't want to. If you could see what I see – but I could show you how to scry some time, if you'd like.'

'You've mentioned scrying before, I think. I don't really understand it though.'

It's just a means of seeing spirits. You look into a mirror, not concentrating on your face – you have to find a focal point, just behind your face, like your earlobe or something. You need to relax, empty your mind and the images will come. It's best in the dark. You need to put a few candles – tealights are best – in front of the mirror.

She found the prospect a bit daunting – the idea of seeing dead people in a mirror – but she was all for giving it a go. What could be daunting about it? She'd seen Andrew in real life – or real afterlife. Why should a mirror bother her?

May was fast becoming accustomed to Twenty-first Century life. She was having a ball! She grew more confident each day. She was part of a loving family at last. And, for the first time in 363 years, she had constant company.

'Lizzie,' Matt was grinning. 'she wants to know, now she's part of the family, if it would be alright if she called us Ma and Pa. Ma is made up of the first two letters of her name. So would that be ok?'

Silly question! Of course it would! So Lizzie and Matt became Ma and Pa.

Lizzie, a chronic insomniac, took a sleeping pill most nights but they didn't always work. She could be awake all night. It was frustrating and distressing because it left her too exhausted to do anything productive the next day. Twenty-four hours stolen from her life!

Matt said he would do the shopping after one such night. She always worried about him going out in case he had some kind of episode and got into an argument, although he was settling down, but she just wasn't up to it.

'If GreenFare is too bad, I can just go to one of the other supermarkets,' he told her.

May stayed at home with Lizzie.

He was gone an awfully long time. Lizzie was getting a bit worried. When he eventually turned up, she heaved a sigh of relief. He recognised the question on her face before she opened her mouth.

'Sorry I was so long. I bumped into Sister Theresa. I was chatting to her for ages. She's lovely. She was telling me all about life at the Priory and the settlement and May's family. May's father did die at the Battle of St Fagans, like we thought, but he left months earlier. Probably didn't even know that Sarah was expecting. He was very well thought of, by all accounts. Not like his brother. Anyway, she was really hacked off when she found out that the afterlife wasn't what she'd been led to believe. Felt she'd wasted her time and could have had a better life, maybe even got married and had a family herself. She's thrilled about May finding a home. Theresa said that May had been right all along! She would find her family, despite what all the spirits, including Theresa herself, were telling her. But how did she know?'

'Well,' Lizzie finally managed to get a word in! 'she obviously needed to be able to communicate with somebody, and it had to be us together.'

'Yes, but it's you she wanted. Not me. I'm just the vessel, so to speak.'

'Oh, Matt. I think you do yourself an injustice. We're a team. You, I get, because you can communicate with her. But why me?'

Even May didn't have the answer. She always believed that someone would be out there for her. There was just something special about Lizzie that drew her, but what it was, she had absolutely no idea.

'Anyway, there I was, at the end of the dairy aisle and this invisible woman accosts me. We were chatting for ages. People must've thought I was bloody barking, stood there talking to myself.'

'As you do ...' Lizzie was giggling to herself, even though she was becoming quite accustomed to living in this strange new world.

That evening, they sat down to tea on their laps in front of the telly. Jason was lying on his back jerking from side to side, making his friendly yappy growly noise, almost a doggy laugh. Then he sneezed, and started squirming again. Another sneeze. Matt was giggling as he watched them.

'It's her! She's tickling him!'

Jason sneezed again!

'And sticking her fingers up his nose! That's what's making him sneeze.'

Whether or not Sally could actually see her, they weren't sure but she felt something. Gemma, bless her, was oblivious.

Mai stopped and Jason stayed on his back but looked around him for the source of his amusement.

'Do it again!'

'Matt! Don't be so rotten!'

Lizzie was ignored and May did it again. Jason was loving it but he had no idea where the tickling was coming from.

'Stick your fingers up his nose again! Go on!'

Jason sneezed again. They both giggled. It became a frequent occurrence in the Prosser household. May was settling in very well – and Jason loved his new invisible friend! He was having huge fun!

The following Saturday, they all went shopping together. It was the first time that May had been inside GreenFare since Matt and Lizzie had taken her home. Lizzie was blissfully unaware as she strolled towards the café, straight past a nasty little whisperer. Little Mai skipped behind her with Matt following.

'Where've you been, then?' demanded the horrid spectre.

With her nose in the air as she walked past him, May put on her haughtiest voice and replied:

'*I* have been at home. *I* have a home ...', spectral sniff, 'and a family.'

The horrid little spirit pulled a snide face and was about to pass some sarcastic remark when he sensed something. He turned to see the Bonfire glaring down at him. Whoops! He scarpered, dodging around Matt's aura as he fled to the stationery aisle.

They sat down to their coffees.

'*Somebody*, has been at home. *Somebody*, has a home ... and a family.'

'What?'

Matt explained.

Lizzie said, 'Well, so you have, May. So you have. Good for you.'

'By the way, Liz, there's something I need to tell you. You know when I said she was taking the piss out of you, when she was pretending to be on high heels? She wasn't. I was just watching her walking. There's something wrong with her foot. She can't seem to put her left heel on the ground. I hadn't really noticed it before. Sorry, May.'

'Oh crikey! Poor little girl!' Lizzie was quite upset.

'It happened when Herbert threw me across the hut,' she told them, 'and it went underneath me when I hit the floor. It never got better properly.'

That upset Lizzie even more. How could any adult be so cruel to a little child?

Birthday Revelation

Matt and Lizzie enjoyed their newly acquired custom of visiting the café before the chore of shopping. To Lizzie's delight, Andrew had begun to join them. Before long, they were joined by Lizzie's Auntie Margaret, her dad's sister. Lizzie wasn't really surprised. As breathers, Andrew and Margaret had been good friends, and Lizzie was closer to Margaret than ever she'd been to her own mother.

The month of May was fast approaching. They had to celebrate May's birthday, but they had no idea of the actual date. Lizzie came up with a suggestion:

'What about making it May the first? That's May Day. Very appropriate, don't you think?'

Yes, everyone thought that May the first was an excellent suggestion. They went out and bought a card, some flowers, candles, and the makings of a cake. There would be eight candles, as she would have been eight on her next birthday, had she not passed away. This was sheer joy for a little girl from a very poor household where the concept of celebrating birthdays was unknown. As they stood in the checkout queue, Matt suddenly said, 'Hang on!' and disappeared. He returned very shortly with a tray of pansies, from the Spring gardening display, for the borders.

'She wants these for some reason.' The pansies were added to the trolley, paid for and they went home.

Lizzie wrote out the card, and the next day, May's birthday, made the cake. Everything was laid out on the coffee table with a bottle of wine. Lizzie opened the card.

'Oh dear.' Matt said.

'What?'

'We've spelt her name wrong? It's M-A-I, not Y.'

'Of course! It would be! It's the Welsh spelling. Sorry, Mai with an *i*! We've been pronouncing it the English way, too.'

'She's saying that's fine – she likes it!' Matt reassured her.

The spelling error swiftly corrected, Lizzie asked, 'Why the pansies?'

There was a pause and Matt said, 'She's gone all shy and coy. What? What is it?'

Then, 'She's saying "Alexander"'.

'Who's Alexander?'

After a short hesitancy, little by little, the story of her beloved Alexander came flooding out.

'He went to Newark, to find her brothers and sister, apparently. He had a beautiful horse. She's showing me a sturdy looking sandy-coloured horse. He's got a long white mane and tail and white feathery feet. He's absolutely stunning.'

'Palomino?' asked Lizzie.

'Think so.'

'I made Alexander a waistcoat out of ducks' feathers to go back to his school,' Mai told them. 'Mamgu and Meg gave me the things I needed and showed me how to do it. He was so proud of it. He put it on. He was wearing it the last time I saw him at Mai's Oak before he went to find Fitz and Pat and Miriam. I don't think he knew I was there but I think he hoped, because he was talking to me. He was looking at my flowers in his book. Mamgu dried them to save them for me but she gave them to Alexander after I died, so he would have them to remember me by. She put them in his book and that's where he kept them.'

Lizzie and Matt both had enormous lumps in their throats. Lizzie wanted to say it was sweet, but it was so much deeper than that. A young boy wanted to take her away from her misery. Lizzie had never cried so many happy tears in her life!

Matt was on the internet, looking at pictures of horses.

'Like this one, she's saying. But with the feathering on the feet.'

'Yes. Palomino. He sounds gorgeous. I love horses. I used to ride a lot in my younger days. Jane, my sister, lives near Newark. They have a farm and she keeps horses. You'll love it there. We'll have to go and visit sometime. She swears their house is haunted. They've heard children laughing upstairs.'

'Just a minute.' Matt was fiddling at his wrists. 'Cufflinks? I'm sure she's saying "cufflinks" but it doesn't make sense. What have cufflinks to do with horses? Fast? She's saying fast. Fast cufflinks? Sorry, sweetheart – I'm not getting it.'

Lizzie got it. 'Cyflym! Is it Cyflym? The name of Alexander's horse? Cyflym's Welsh for fast!'

'That's it! She's nodding like mad! Cyflym. Sorry, Mai. I couldn't get it. I don't really speak any Welsh. Ma knows a lot more than me.'

Mai's aura was glowing brighter than ever.

Later in the evening, Sally, as she always did at the appearance of 'Uccle' Andrew, as Mai had begun to call him – and who was now a regular visitor – looked up above the back living room window and began to bark, heralding his arrival.

Through almost uncontrollable giggles, Lizzie said, 'I think the oracle's here! Hi, Andrew! Would you please come down and stop the dog barking? We'll have the neighbours complaining!'

'Uccle' Andrew was such a hoot! They could always rely on him to turn up when a drink was in the offing.

'Margaret not coming?' Lizzie asked.

'She sends her apologies, apparently.' Matt replied. 'She has other commitments.'

'Oh, that's a shame. Never mind. I'm sure we'll see her soon.'

They lit the candles on the chocolate cake and sang 'Happy Birthday'.

'See if you can blow them out, Mai. Go on! Have a go!' Matt tried to persuade her.

Lizzie was filming it on her phone. There was a slight flicker of the flames.

'Try again. Perhaps "Uccle" Andrew can help.' Lizzie chipped in.

The candles didn't go out but the flicker was stronger this time. Anyone else would have said it was just a draught, but it's a rare fellow who can summon a draught to order when he's just sitting on a sofa with a plate of cake on his lap and a glass of wine in his hand. The dogs would have been given a piece of cake for a treat but, however much they begged, they wouldn't be having any – chocolate being potentially fatal for dogs. They had extra doggy treats instead. They all sat down to watch Harry Potter! Even 'Uccle' Andrew enjoyed it.

It was a lovely evening. Mai was ecstatic. Her very own birthday party!

On Wednesday, Matt sat in his armchair, scrolling through his e-mails. Mai stayed close to Lizzie on the sofa. The television was on but they weren't really watching it. Lizzie was curious.

'Mai, do you ever think of your Mum and Dad?'

'She's shaking her head,' Matt said, 'She's saying that she never knew her father anyway and her mother didn't care about her so it doesn't matter.'

'You know, Mai,' Lizzie went on, 'I really don't think that's true. I'm sure that Sarah loved you very much. She must have been broken with everything that happened to her. She just couldn't cope. I know I wouldn't have been able to, in her position. If your father had known what Herbert was doing to the family – and what he did to you – I'll bet he'd have wanted to go back and probably kill him. I think they both loved you very much. Or at least your mother did. It sounds very much like your father didn't even know about you. Try not to be too hard on them, sweetheart.'

Mai didn't react, but Lizzie was sure she was right.

A Psychic Artist

'Matt, I wish I could see her. It's frustrating not knowing what she looks like. All I have is your description and it's a bit vague.'

Matt sympathised, then had a thought.

'Well, there are psychic artists. If we could find a good one, we may be able to get a drawing – or even a portrait.'

The idea excited Lizzie. Even Matt liked the prospect. Mai thought it was a brilliant idea. They set about an internet search.

Lizzie stumbled upon a psychic artist who goes on tour and did workshops for people. She was going to be at The Haven, a spiritual centre and retreat, near the Forest of Dean in Gloucestershire in a few weeks. It was a good couple of hours from their home, but quite do-able.

'Her name's Geraldine Chambers. Have a look at her website.'

Matt opened up Google on his laptop.

'What d'you think. Shall I e-mail her? See what she says?' Lizzie asked.

'Yeah. Looks good. Go for it.'

Lizzie e-mailed, explaining basically what they needed. She got a reply within twenty-four hours and made an appointment for 5 o'clock on the Saturday afternoon when Geraldine was at the centre, delivering one of her residential courses. It was only a few weeks away.

On the day, they drove to Gloucestershire and found their way to The Haven. They sat waiting for Geraldine in a lovely lounge, large but warm; homely and cosy at the same time. The place had a beautiful, wholesome atmosphere. The furnishings were vintage, if not antique, and a picture rail extended around almost the whole room. A log fire blazed in the Inglenook fireplace. It was all very much to Lizzie's taste. Lizzie may not have been psychic, but she was becoming quite sensitive to atmosphere. Geraldine's workshop had over-run, and they had been supplied with coffee by two lovely ladies, volunteers, working in the kitchen. They sat chatting to a charming gentleman, sitting in an armchair by the fire: Geraldine's husband. Mai, like a typical little girl, became bored waiting and went out to play in the field behind the building.

When Geraldine turned up, she was most apologetic; her hands were covered in charcoal.

'So sorry you've had to wait. I'm afraid I don't always have control over how long these workshops take. Do bear with me while I go and get cleaned up.'

She disappeared down a corridor off the lounge and Lizzie and Matt carried on chatting to her husband. They didn't mind the wait. It was such a beautiful, peaceful place that they were happy just to sit there and soak up the atmosphere.

'Sorry about that!' Geraldine was back. 'Would you like to come with me?'

Lizzie followed behind her and Matt tried to beckon Mai, but she was enjoying the outside. He didn't think she was coming. They followed Sandy through the double doors, and along the outside of the building. She unlocked and opened the door to a smaller room.

'Please, come in and take a – oh! We have a little girl!' she exclaimed as Mai rushed through the door.

'Yes. This is Mai', they told her.

'Hello, Mai. Would you like me to help you pass through the Light?'

'NO!' They yelled together, almost in panic, fearful that Mai would be frightened.

'Oh no!' Lizzie explained. 'Sorry, Geraldine. She's not lost or stuck or anything. It's her choice to be here. It's just that she wants to stay with us until we pass. Long story. It's just me. I don't know what she looks like. Well, only what Matt's told me. We were just wondering if we could somehow get a portrait of her.'

'I'm a psychic myself,' Matt explained, 'I could help her if she wanted to go, but she wants to stay with us. I just can't do psychic artistry.'

'Yes, I can do that,' Geraldine said. 'I don't actually have any artistic skills myself. I do it through my guide, Louis. One day, I was sitting in the hairdresser's and I started drawing. I had no idea what I was doing and the hairdresser said that it was her grandad. That's how it started. Oh! We have a lady trying to come through. It's M… Mum. She's saying "Mum".'

'Can't be.' Lizzie said. 'Matt's Mum is still alive.'

'No. It's your Mum.'

'Can't be her, either,' said Lizzie, 'she hasn't gone through the Light.'

'Well, she has now. She's definitely saying "It's Mum". Hang on… she's saying J… Jan? Janet? Something like that? Do you have a Jan or Janet in the family?'

'No. Not at all.'

'Oh, I'm sorry, I'm not very good at picking up auditory messages. Wait. She's saying "with Daniel"? Does that make sense?'

'Yes! Daniel's my brother-in-law.'

'Wait a minute. Jane? Could it be Jane?'

'Yes – Jane's my sister!'

'That's it. She's saying "yes". She's very apologetic about the way she behaved to you. She's just saying over and over how sorry she is. Does that make sense?'

'Well, yes, it does. We never had a good relationship. It was partly my fault, though. We were both stubborn as hell. I just couldn't be the person she wanted me to be.'

'Well, she's certainly very apologetic about everything.'

'Nothing to apologise for. We are where we are.'

Lizzie held no grudges. She wondered why her mum had chosen to come through now, here. Why not speak through Matt? Then it occurred to her that Geraldine was independent and they were on neutral territory. Perhaps that was the reason.

Geraldine would do the portrait and they agreed a sum of eighty pounds for an A4 water colour.

'So what do you think about this spirit guide stuff, Matt?' Lizzie asked when they got home. 'I always thought it was a bit of theatrics: melodrama. Is it?'

'Well, sometimes it is, if they get a bit up themselves, but I had one myself for a long time.'

'You never said. You mean you don't have one now?'

'Well, I think my guide gave up on me when I tried to kill myself. I just wasn't listening. The bipolar and psychosis took over, I guess. But your Andrew seems to have taken his place now.'

'Oh, wow. So who was he? Your spirit guide.'

'He was a native American Indian.'

'You're kidding me! Why are so many of them native American Indians?' She thought this was a bit of a cliché; rather old hat. He sensed the incredulity.

'No, really. His name was Eume. He was a Hopi. They were a nomadic tribe. The thing about native Americans is that they were the humans nearest to understanding what the spirit world is all about, and how to live in harmony with the natural world. They only took what they needed and always thanked the animal they killed for their sacrifice. They made sure that nothing was ever wasted. So different to the way we live now.'

It took a few weeks for the portrait to arrive; Geraldine had been very busy. Lizzie was quite surprised when they opened the package and saw it. Matt said it was definitely Mai, but she had long blonde hair, flowing past her shoulders; she was wearing a green top, and the missing tooth had grown back! And she was clean! Not only that, but it came in A3 size.

'I know we said A4,' Sandy told them, 'but this child has such a huge personality that I felt that nothing less than A3 could do her justice.'

'Aw. She said she wanted to be a normal, modern little girl – and be like her Ma' Matt told Lizzie.

Ma's favourite top was green, but she wasn't wearing it when they visited Sandy. When they told Sandy, she said that was how Mai had appeared to Louis.

'Did I do the wrong thing?' Mai asked

'No, sweetheart.' Lizzie was moved almost to tears. 'Not at all. You can't do anything wrong. Don't be so silly. That is who you are. That's fine by us. We know it's you. You look lovely. Anyway, I would rather see you looking clean and beautiful than sad and dirty. That would just remind you of the bad old days.'

'My hair really was long and fair like that, but my mother had to chop it off because it kept getting singed by the flames when I was turning the spit, and the dirt and ash from the fire made it look a lot darker than it was. That's what I should really look like.'

They went out and bought a suitable frame that complimented the colour of her hair, and the portrait was hung on the living room wall. From then on, Mai appeared to Matt as she appeared in the portrait. A modern, 21st Century little girl.

Sarah

'We haven't seen anything of Andrew for a while, have we?' Lizzie asked.

'No. I was just thinking that yesterday. D'you know where he is Mai? No. She's just shaking her head. Wonder what he's up to.'

'I'm sure he'll come in his own good time.'

On Saturday morning, they were, as usual, in GreenFare's café.

'Guess who's turned up!' laughed Matt. 'We've missed you!'

'Hiya! What've you been up to?' Lizzie asked, rhetorically.

'You won't believe this. He's only managed to find Sarah! He's asking Mai if she wants to meet up with her. He's been helping her to recover. After all this time – even in spirit, she was still traumatised with everything that happened. He's saying she may never fully recover. He's been spending a lot of time with her.'

Lizzie could barely believe it. 'Well, what d'you think, Mai?'

'She's not quite sure.' Matt replied. 'Andrew's trying to explain to her that Ma was right. She was very, very ill. She was never right after that bang to her head, poor girl. She was never right after Herbert moved in and took over the family – as if losing Eric wasn't bad enough.'

'It certainly sounds like she had post-natal depression and PTSD all rolled into one. That's what I thought all along,' Lizzie added. 'Mai, you know, she really did love you. I think she was already very ill and then it broke her heart when Seamus went. When she saw that you were dying, she couldn't cope. She just shut down. Perhaps you should give her the chance. When you're ready, that is.'

'Yeah. That's exactly what Andrew's telling her. She's nodding. It looks like she's up for it.'

Lizzie was so pleased – and relieved. Poor, poor Sarah.

'He's going to bring her here next time we're in. Some spirits are so traumatised by their time in this life that they never fully recover. They never want to return here. Andrew's been working really hard with her. She's still a bit fragile but she wants to see Mai and her new life with us.'

Matt was beaming. They were both thrilled at the prospect of reuniting mother and daughter.

Lizzie and Mai were equally nervous. The last time Lizzie had felt like that about meeting somebody – the 'butterflies in the stomach' feeling – was when Matt took her home to meet his mum; she was sixty-two then – and it was the same feeling that she'd had as a teenager when her first boyfriend took her home to meet his family!

They sat in a far corner of the café where it was quiet but with plenty of seats. Even though it was a Saturday morning, it was early, so the café had not yet started to fill up with customers.

'They're here.' Matt said. 'Hello, Sarah, it's lovely to meet you.'

'Yes,' Lizzie chipped in, 'we're so glad Andrew managed to find you.'

Then she noticed that Matt was biting his lip and welling up.

'No, it really is our pleasure,' he said, 'she's a delight.'

'What?' Lizzie asked.

He took a deep breath and said, 'She's just said "thank you for taking care of my daughter."'

'Oh, Sarah. It really is our pleasure. We're pleased to have her in our home. She's coming on in leaps and bounds – and giving us so much in return. I just couldn't bear to think of her constantly alone in the atmosphere of this place. I'm so sorry that I can't see you – or hear you. Matt has to interpret, I'm afraid.'

'It's ok. She understands.' Matt said.

They chatted about this and that and the weather. Lizzie invited Sarah to come home with them, but Sarah declined. Perhaps next time. Matt thought she might be a bit shy and it would probably be all a bit much in one go.

They finished their coffees. Matt went to pick up a trolley and they did the shopping. Andrew stayed with Matt and Lizzie as they wandered around the store and Sarah and Mai walked ahead of them, hand in hand, talking. Catching up?

They got through the checkout and mother and daughter were still in front of them as they crossed the car park. They stopped at the green Mini Countryman. Matt laughed under his breath.

'She's just said "and this is *our* car"!'

'Are you sure you wouldn't like to come home with us, Sarah?' Lizzie asked.

'She can't today. But next time.' Matt said.

'You'll be more than welcome any time, Sarah,' Lizzie told her, 'we will always be delighted to see you.'

They got in the car after saying their goodbyes. Andrew went with Sarah.

Matt thought that Sarah was still a bit 'delicate'. It takes some spirits a very long time to heal from Earthly trauma, even with the help they get on the other side. Poor Sarah had had more than her fair share of that. Sarah had trauma by the bucket-load.

174

When they got home, after unloading the car, and once the dogs had settled, Lizzie asked Mai how she felt. She felt good. She was glad she had met her Mam.

'See, I told you she loved you, didn't I? She still does. That never goes away.'

Mai glowed. She might not be able to see it, but Lizzie certainly felt it. Pure warmth and joy.

A week later, Andrew and Sarah joined them for coffee, then they all wandered around the store. Lizzie found it interesting that, very occasionally, a breather would walk past them and look hard. Some, not just the psychic mediums, see something a bit 'odd'; they just don't know what they're looking at. It had happened a couple of times before, although nobody said anything. It happened on this occasion too. Matt always found it amusing. One or two people stared at them as they walked by, for no apparent reason.

'You still coming back home with us, Sarah?' Lizzie asked.

Yes.

On the way home, there were three spirits on the back seat: 'Uccle' Andrew, Mai in the middle, and Sarah. Lizzie sometimes found it frustrating that she couldn't see them; she kept checking the rear-view mirror just in case.

When they got home, after the usual fuss-pot nonsense with Sally, Gemma and Jason, and Mai introducing the dogs to Sarah, Lizzie made coffee. Sarah was standing, looking up at the portrait of her daughter.

'She's saying "thank you" again.' Matt said.

Lizzie wanted to give her a huge hug.

In the privacy of the house, Sarah found it easier to open up. They talked for a while. She really didn't know what was going on after the day Herbert threw Mai across the hut. She remembered being struck down as she tried to help Mai, but everything was just a vague blur after that. Could Mai forgive her?

No question of that.

'Sarah,' Lizzie said, 'You know that you are very welcome to come here any time. You don't need an invitation. You are part of the family.'

'She says "thank you",' Matt said. 'I think she's still finding it all a lot to take in. She's nodding. She agrees.'

'See?' said Lizzie, after Sarah and Andrew had left. 'What have I been telling you?'

Matt was grinning. 'She's glowing again. Wish you could see it.'

Lizzie might not be able to see it but she could feel the vibrations. Good vibrations.

Happy vibrations from a happy little girl.

The drive home from their weekly visit to Matt's mum, took them on the dual carriageway that ran alongside the river and past the site of the mass grave where the mortal remains of Mai, Sarah, Herbert, Mamgu and the others all lay. Matt was driving. As soon as they pulled up outside the house, he switched off the engine and turned around to Mai on the back seat.

'There's something wrong. What's up Mai?' he asked.

'What is it?' Lizzie was concerned. This had never happened before. She always enjoyed visiting Matt's mum, but Matt said she was really upset.

He started up the car again, made a U-turn and drove off.

'There's something wrong at the gravesite. She's saying the bluebells won't grow there anymore. Bad smells. We've got to go and find out what's happened. I didn't smell anything as we drove past. Did you?'

No, Lizzie hadn't noticed anything, either.

176

Matt parked as close as he could to the gravesite, in the car park of the 'carpet' shop, and they got out of the car. There was a fence between them and the gap in the trees. The gravesite was on their side of the river with the old rail track in between.

'Smell it?' he asked.

'God, yes. It smells like petrol. Really strong.'

'Diesel. Bet you a pound to a penny it's illegal red diesel! Been dumped. Easy enough to get over the fence. Look down there – it's damaged.'

Mai was heartbroken. Her precious bluebells. Would they ever grow back?

'Well, I think they might eventually. I don't really know, Mai. I suppose it depends on how much has been dumped and whether or not it's damaged the bulbs. But I tell you what. We'll plant some bluebell bulbs for next year in the back garden. Mai's special memorial garden. How about that?'

Mai was delighted, although they were all upset about the gravesite bluebells. In the Autumn, as soon as they were available in the garden centres, Ma bought a couple of packs of native bluebell bulbs and planted them in the garden. Mai felt much better. They all did.

Portal

Lizzie eyed Matt as he sat in his armchair beavering away at his computer. She had a touch of nerves but she was going for it.

'Matt?'

'Yes?'

'Do you think I could have a go at scrying? Especially now my mum's on the scene.'

'I don't see why not. We can have a go tonight, if you like.'

'Think I would like to take the plunge. A bit nervy about it though.'

'No need. I'll be here. It's nothing to be worried about.'

'I know. It's just a bit scary, delving into the unknown, I suppose.'

'Lizzie, it's only scary because people make it so. You can do it.'

'Yeah. But you never know what you're going to conjure up, do you?'

'Not if you've been watching too many supernatural horrors on Netflix, you don't!'

She felt a bit daft, told herself not to be so silly and decided she would go ahead and give it a try.

It was about nine o'clock in the evening, curtains drawn, when they set up a mirror with three tealight candles in front of it on the bureau in the dining room. Matt lit the candles and Lizzie sat on a dining chair in front of it. He told her to take a few deep breaths to relax and clear her mind, then look in the mirror, but not at her eyes. She had to find a focal point – just behind her ear might be a good spot.

'Just concentrate on that spot.'

She had no idea what to expect. Mum, perhaps?

'Just relax and wait a while. You should notice a change in your face, but don't look directly at it.'

She didn't know how long it took but, quite soon, in her peripheral vision, she noticed a shimmering over the area of her face. She recognised the form.

'Anything yet?'

Her voice was quiet, not quite a whisper. 'It's Andrew'.

His distinctive features were superimposed over her face. Then:

'Andrew's gone, but that was definitely him. Wait! Dad... his face... above my right shoulder.'

'Ok. He's just showing himself to you. He's here. Just wait. See if anything else happens.'

Matt was sitting quietly on the sofa, trying to keep out of the way in case he influenced her, but close enough if she should need him.

The image remained for quite a while. Now that could have been her imagination. People say you see what you want to see. Heaven knows what the subconscious can bring out. A few moments later, though, over her left shoulder there was movement. Four male heads, moving around like a carousel. That was strange. She didn't recognise any of them. She thought they may have been late Victorian or Edwardian by their dress, collars and such, and a couple of them had moustaches which appeared to be from that era. Then they disappeared and she had no option but to look directly at her face. Staring back at her was a middle-aged lady, again of Edwardian era. She appeared in sepia, like an old photograph. Lizzie thought the image was very similar to Queen Alexandra, the face long and thin, wearing a puffy sleeved blouse with a high-necked collar, rows of pearls, and hair piled high on top. The style was of the same era, but it wasn't Queen Alexandra! The lady raised her eyebrows and adopted an expression somewhere between astonishment and surprise; haughty, as though she was saying, "Oh!"

Who was this lady? Was she real? Or was she a figment of Lizzie's imagination? It could have been from an old photograph that she'd seen, but she certainly didn't recognise the face. It felt all too real to Lizzie – and, though surprising, not scary at all. It was just interesting.

The images all disappeared. She was particularly bemused by the four gentlemen going around on the 'carousel', more so than her dad and the anonymous lady. Lizzie had a photograph of her paternal great-grandfather, Walter Hedgeman senior, with his four brothers. She fished it out of a box file in the bureau cupboard. One or more of them could possibly have been one of her great-great-uncles, but she couldn't be sure. The others didn't really look like anyone in the photograph, although the manner of dress was similar. The photograph she had was dated 1905.

Lizzie was fascinated by her brief foray into scrying and was eager to try again.

'You need to give it a couple of days or so.' Matt told her. 'You need time to recover.'

Lizzie was open to the sceptical notion that what she was seeing was her imagination, but leaning more to the idea that it was real.

Matt's suggestion was sensible, she thought, so they waited. She was eager to have another go, though. Whether or not it was just her imagination, and she was pretty sure it wasn't, she couldn't wait to try again. A few evenings later, they set up the mirror and candles.

Andrew didn't make an appearance, but her dad did. Matt came into the room. She could see orbs in the mirror, white and green translucent balls of light, flying all over the room behind her. There were various spirits in the room with her, but he said:

'Your mum's here. She's standing behind you; hands on your shoulders.'

Lizzie couldn't actually feel anything, but she said, 'Hi Mum. You ok?' Then she felt a bit silly because it seemed a bit of a daft thing to say to a spirit. Or was it?

'Oh, stop it!' Matt said, talking to her mum. 'She's being really apologetic for the way she behaved towards you when she was a breather. She's really upset. It's why she took so long to go into the Light – knew she'd done wrong, trying to mould you into what she wanted you to be. She's saying she should have let you be your own person.'

Lizzie choked with the emotion. Fighting back the tears, she said, 'It's ok. Really it is. We took the roads we did to end up where we are. I'm happy now. If I'd been the person you wanted me to be, I'd have married someone 'professional' and I'd probably never have met this great lummox by here.'

'Oi!'

Giggles.

'It's true, though. We wouldn't have Mai here. She'd still be stuck in GreenFare, surrounded by all those nasty whisperers and horrible visions. The roads we take in life and the lessons we learn along the way are what bring us to where we are today. Let's face it, I was hardly the best daughter in the world, was I? I just didn't know how to be any other way.'

Bloody hell, that was pretty profound – for Lizzie.

'She's saying that she didn't, either. Aw, shucks! She's saying you've done alright for yourself.'

He felt himself blush.

They both laughed.

'Mum, you know you can come here anytime you like. We'll make up for the past.'

'Lizzie, she's saying she's really proud of you.'

'Why – what have I done?'

'You took in Mai. Just a minute… she's saying that she had the opportunity to foster a little girl who lived around the corner when you were a kid. She'd lost her mum and her dad couldn't cope. She couldn't do it because of her obsession with privacy.'

'Wow!' said Lizzie, 'I do remember something about a little girl who lost her mum – it was around the corner – I didn't know them, though. I was never allowed to have friends in the house, even though I could go into their houses. I never really understood it.'

'She's saying that it was all a bit silly of her. She's proud of you, anyway, for taking Mai in.'

'Well, it's a bit different, isn't it? Mai being just a spirit and all …'

Just? What was she talking about?

It was only a fleeting visit. Mum had to go – they all have roles and commitments on the other side. Mum's was looking after newly passed spirits of children and animals. She was loving it. They said their goodbyes and five minutes later, Matt said:

'Hang on! You're dad's here. He's got Uncle Harry with him. Who the hell's Uncle Harry?'

'Really? Wow! Hiya Dad! Hi Harry! How are you doing?'

'He says his back's better. He's not in pain with it anymore.'

'Uncle Harry was Auntie Margaret's husband,' Lizzie explained. 'He died in 2000. Lung cancer. He was in agony with his back as long as I knew him and a lot longer before, by all accounts. They married late, in

1967. Aw! It's lovely to see you, Harry. Well, not that I can actually see you, but you know what I mean.'

'They've got to go. Just popped in to say "hello". Brief visit.'

'Well, that was a bolt from the blue. Sorry for not mentioning Harry before, Matt. I feel a bit rotten about that. It's all been so much about Mai, even with Auntie Margaret here, the subject never seemed to come up. Auntie Margaret adored Harry, too. He was always a bit *persona non grata* with the family for some reason. They thought his back problems were just an excuse not to work, but apparently not. Dad was one of the worst so it's nice to see them being friendly on the other side.'

'Mai's loving all this. She's meeting so many nice spirits! A bit different to GreenFare!'

They went up to bed happy and contented.

On a very warm July day, Matt was sitting in his armchair in the corner of the room on his computer as he so often was. Lizzie was beginning to get a bit irked and frustrated, concerned that they might be getting into a rut. In the flat, they'd always sat together, snuggled up on the sofa, but that rarely happened these days.

'Matt, why don't you come over here with me?'

He closed his computer, got up and did as she suggested.

'We never seem to sit together anymore. You're always over there on your laptop.'

She didn't see it coming. His voice was deep, and when he yelled it could be frightening.

'Is this it? Is this all I have to look forward to? You, telling me what to do all the time!'

He picked up his mobile phone from the coffee table, stood up and, with his free hand, punched the wooden door to the hallway. She hadn't seen anything like it since that morning in the flat. This was much worse. It really shook her up.

'I … I'm sorry … I didn't mean …'

'You didn't mean … bullshit!'

He held his phone in both hands now – and he snapped the hard plastic casing clean in half, leaving the two parts held together only by a few wires attached to either side. He wrenched them apart, stormed out to the kitchen and chucked it straight into the wastebin. She heard the back door open and he went outside.

Lizzie remained on the sofa, still shaking, unsure what to do for the best. He had never spoken to her like that before.

Once she had recovered sufficiently, she got up to look through the back living room window. He was stock still, sitting on one of the patio chairs, elbows on the table, with his head in his hands. She knew that it wasn't him. He didn't mean it. She wanted to go to him; wanted to comfort him. She waited and watched a while, then went outside to join him.

He was silent. She rubbed his shoulders, as she had done that morning at the flat. He was almost as rigid as he had been then. After a few minutes, he started to come to.

'It's ok,' she whispered, 'you're ok.'

He looked up and leant his head against her forearm.

'What happened?' he asked.

'Oh, not much. You just yelled at me, and punched a hole in the door – and snapped your phone in half.'

'What? I did what?'

'Well, you sort of cracked the door. You can see daylight through it, though. But your phone's in two halves.'

'What? I broke it?'

'Just a bit – you chucked it in the bin.'

'I did? Bloody hell! Are you ok? Uh, oh! Andrew's here. Think I'm in trouble.'

Lizzie wished she could hear the conversation but, then again, maybe not. It was private, between them, so she left them to it. Never a good idea to listen to only one side of a conversation, anyway.

As Andrew talked to him, Lizzie made a couple of mugs of coffee.

As soon as Matt looked a bit more relaxed, she took the coffees out, put them on the patio table and sat next to him, putting an arm around his shoulder.

'Ok now?' she asked.

'Yeah. Just a bit woozy, I think. I'm ok, though. Thanks, Andrew. See you soon. Sorry.'

Matt looked at her.

'He's given me a stern telling off! "What's all this about, then," in his proper Army officer voice. You know?'

Yes, indeed she did know. She'd heard it many times. He was rather 'upper crust'.

'He says it's you I should be apologising to. And Mai. I'm sorry – I didn't mean to frighten you."

'Well, I know what I signed up for', Lizzie told him, 'but I don't think Mai has ever seen you like that before.'

'Poor little thing – she didn't know what was happening, or what to do. She just dashed off to fetch her Uccle Andrew. He can always sort things out.'

Matt was smiling now.

'Lizzie, I'm so sorry. I didn't know …'

'Oh, shut up and drink your coffee.'

'Did I really break my phone?'

'Yep. It's well and truly kaput.'

'Oh, hell. What about the door.'

'Think we'll have to get another one.'

He had little recollection of the episode. He just knew that he'd lost his rag, but he was utterly ashamed of himself.

'I'll make an appointment with the doctor a.s.a.p. Don't think the meds are quite right yet. Sorry, Mai. I know I frightened you. And you Lizzie.'

Will you please stop apologising? I wasn't so much frightened, as shocked. It just came from nowhere. I couldn't have been looking out for the warning signs. I should be more aware. It's done now.'

'I'm going to take some Seroquel and sleep it off. You'll probably be on your own this evening, I'm afraid. Sorry.'

'Oh, for Heaven's sake. It's not your fault. You can't help it. It is what it is. I told you. I knew what to expect when we got married. If that's the worst it gets, I'm sure I'll cope. Stop fretting! Anyway, it isn't happening anything like as frequently as I'd been expecting, so that's a plus. D'you want anything to eat before you go up?'

'No thanks. I'll just drink my coffee. Can you get my tablets for me?'

Sitting alone downstairs – well, not quite alone; Mai was with her, although she couldn't see or hear her – Lizzie decided to watch a film as there was nothing on telly, but she couldn't find anything she felt like watching. She thought that perhaps she might try scrying on her own for the first time. She set everything up. Her phone, set to camera was on hand.

Sitting in front of the mirror, with the tea lights lit, she waited. Her dad appeared, followed by umpteen other images. Orbs were flying everywhere in the background – more than the last time. She snapped as many photos as she could. Images weren't clear but she could make them out, not over her face, which was obscured by the flash, but in various other places reflected in the mirror. The energy was electric. She couldn't believe it.

After a good night's sleep, Matt's head was clear and he felt much more positive. Lizzie brought him a mug of coffee in bed, told him all about last night's scrying and showed him the photos.

'Some of these are amazing! It's the energy, Liz – after I get an episode. That's what does it. It's what I used to be like most of the time – why Mai was so frightened of my aura. The Bonfire, I suppose. The spirits tap into it. There's a portal in the front room. Must be.'

'Well, that makes sense. There were orbs flying all over the place again, too. I turned around and actually saw one fly across the room – not just in the mirror, you know?'

They spent the rest of the day quietly. As dusk was about to descend, Matt sat on the sofa watching television. Jason sat on the pouffe, as if he were human, facing Matt, watching him; concern etched over the dog's face.

Lizzie had to take a photo. She got up and picked up her phone, set it to camera and snapped.

Flash!

'What the hell was that?' she yelled.

'What was what?'

'This!'

She sat next to him and showed him the photo.

He could hardly believe what he was seeing either. It had become too dark to take a photograph of Jason, especially with the huge dog being black, but what they did see was astonishing.

'That's exactly what I saw projecting from your face at the flat that day Andrew channelled through you.'

It was the same white, striated, translucent strip – but this time, much longer. It was coiled around Matt in a figure of eight, or infinity shape. There was a human like head at its end, appearing to inspect Matt.

'Good grief! It's Andrew, I'm sure of it. I'm still too groggy to be aware, but this is strong. He's tapped into the residual energy from yesterday. It must have been powerful. There really has to be a portal in this room, you know.'

Andrew, on his next visit, confirmed that it was indeed him.

Just checking that you're ok, old boy.

The Scrying Game

'Can we have a scrying session this evening, Matt?' Lizzie was really fascinated and had developed quite a taste for it.

'Yeah. If you want. No problem.'

'Mai, do you think you could try to come through in the mirror?'

'She'll try, Liz, but it's a bit difficult – it takes a lot of energy from her. She's not as strong as the other spirits. Still, she's up for having a go.'

Later that evening, they set up the mirror and candles and Lizzie installed herself on the dining chair in front of the bureau. Dad appeared as usual.

After a while, she sniffed, and sniffed again. 'I'm sure I can smell pipe tobacco.'

'Can you? There's a very slight little man smoking a pipe behind you.'

'Is it Grampy Hedgeman or Uncle John? They were both little and they both smoked pipes.'

'It's your Grampy.'

'Hello, Gramps! How are you doing?'

'Yeah, he's good. Oh my God. There's shedloads of 'em here. It's full up! They're lining up all trying to get their say! What? You're kidding me! Oh no! No! It's too much! I can't take this! I've got to go out! I'm going out the back for a while.'

Overloaded with so many excited spirits, all trying to convey their messages at once, Matt escaped from the room apace to the kitchen and out of the back door, leaving his poor wife nonplussed! Her grandad was chasing the spirits away, waving his pipe around. The smell of pipe tobacco got stronger; she could even see the cloud enveloping her, never mind smell it. The energy was tangible.

Lizzie sat there not knowing what to do. Was he having another psychotic episode?

He returned after five minutes or so, pale and shaking: a man in shock.

'I need a drink. You're going to need one too – you're not going to believe this …'

'What?'

Matt got a couple of glasses and the decanter of Scotch from the sideboard and did the honours.

'Eric MacIntyre didn't die at St Fagans. He survived. He was too frightened of reprisals against the family to go back, so he stayed away and started a new life. He went on to have another family. He's your direct ancestor. You and Mai are related.'

Lizzie was stunned. Mai was stunned too. She had no idea. An enormous grin spread over Matt's face.

'Whatever, she's thrilled about it. She's glowing.'

Lizzie, Matt and little Mai needed a lot of time that evening to process it all. Lizzie couldn't get her head around it.

'But there are no MacIntyres in our family. And we've never had anything to do with this area. Our family on my dad's side were all in Cardiff, but my mother's mother came from Ebbw Vale, originally.'

'No, it's your father's side. Definitely.'

'How can it be? I know they were from England, originally. My great-grandfather grandfather moved to Cardiff from Dorset. I know that for a fact, didn't they, Gramps? I knew all my great-aunts aunts and uncles. They all stayed in Cardiff.'

'He's nodding, but he doesn't have the answers, Liz.'

'But how can that be right?'

They were all mystified. It certainly explained why Mai was drawn to her, yet it all seemed so unlikely. The events to bring them together were beyond belief: Lizzie and Andrew weren't able to get a mortgage to buy their council bungalow in Oxford because there was something wrong with the structure and, as Cardiff was almost as expensive as Oxford, they'd had to come this far out to buy a property which was as near to her relatives as they could afford; he'd passed away, and she'd met and married, after a false start, a psychic medium. It was too fantastic. How could she be descended from Eric MacIntyre? She had already dabbled with researching her ancestry, but not taken it too seriously. Now there was a new urgency.

'Must be a female daughter of the family who married a Hedgeman, somewhere along the line.'

Lizzie searched and searched her ancestry but there were no MacIntyres to be found.

When Andrew turned up, the next Saturday evening, they grilled him. He was being typically enigmatic about the whole thing. What he did say was:

'Well, of course you're related. Haven't you noticed the family resemblance?'

That was true. There was a bit of a resemblance, but exactly how they could be related was a mystery that Lizzie thought would never be resolved. Deep inside, she was slightly sceptical. Was he right? Or was it in his head? Surely, he couldn't have, albeit unintentionally, made it up? She'd felt Mai; she'd seen Andrew at the flat; Sally always barked to announce Andrew's arrival; she had the photograph of Andrew's spirit wrapped around Matt; she could always smell the aroma of Grampy Hedgeman's pipe tobacco before Matt; how could Matt possibly have known about Harry and his bad back? Surely, she couldn't have invented all that too? Certainly not with that photo.

No. She believed him – but deep in the back of her mind, was the tiniest, niggling seed of doubt.

Lot of the Psychic's Wife

They were unusually alone in GreenFare's café, except for Mai. Matt looked up, jumped from his seat and ran out of the café without a word, leaving Lizzie just sitting there. She turned around, eyes following him. She was almost panic-stricken as he approached a middle-aged woman accompanied by an older lady, presumably her mother, walking towards the toilet area.

Oh no! What's he doing?

'Excuse me! I hope you don't mind but I have a message for you.'

The couple were slightly taken aback, but then he said:

Thomas says not to worry about him. He's fine – and he's singing again.'

The older lady stood there silent, staring, but the younger woman burst into tears.

Oh God, what's he done now?

The woman pulled a tissue from her coat pocket. Lizzie waited, checking the body language. It looked pretty relaxed.

'Thank you so much!' The younger woman was still sobbing, while the other woman managed to look aghast but produce a huge smile at the same time!

'This is my mum. Thomas was my father. He passed away recently. He'd suffered from throat cancer some years ago. He'd been a singer all his life with a male voice choir. Although he recovered, he was so upset afterwards because he couldn't sing anymore. You don't know how happy you've made us. Did the message come through your wife?'

'No, it's me, I'm the medium.'

'Oh, I'm so sorry. You just don't look like what I would have thought a medium to look like!'

'Ah, well. We come in all shapes and sizes!'

They chatted for some time. It all appeared quite cordial. Lizzie's heart returned from her mouth to its rightful place as she told herself there was nothing to worry about and he returned to the café.

Lizzie heaved a huge sigh of relief as he related the story of Thomas. She always worried when this sort of thing happened in case somebody slapped him, or worse!

Of course, Thomas was not singing in the literal sense. It was his spirit's way of communicating to his wife and daughter that he was there – and he was fine.

Matt didn't always get it right. Treating themselves to a pizza in their favourite restaurant, a few weeks later. A woman in her mid-thirties came in with a young girl of about twelve years of age. They sat at the table directly opposite Lizzie and Matt. The girl had Down's Syndrome and, as with so many Down's children, she was a delight. After their meal, Matt could not resist going up to her mum and saying how wonderful she was with the girl. This time, Lizzie was close enough to hear.

'Hello. I'm a psychic medium. Would I be right in thinking you've struggled to bring up this lovely young lady alone?'

The woman was wearing substantial wedding and engagement rings! Besides, she might have been a learning disability support worker, and not her mother at all – a job Lizzie had, in the past, done herself. As it happened, the woman was the girl's mother.

Oh God, no! Earth – please open up and swallow me, now!

To Lizzie's relief, the woman was not offended, on the surface, at least. 'Well, that's very kind of you to say so but, no, I've been very happily married for a long time.'

Lizzie squirmed in her seat.

Matt, please, for God's sake shut up – now!

Fortunately, Matt needed to go to the loo, excused himself and rushed off; the only time she was thankful for the side effects of his diuretics!

Lizzie called over the waitress and paid the bill, picked up her coat and shoulder bag and stepped across the aisle between the tables to the lady and her daughter.

'I'm so sorry about that. He really is a psychic, and usually he's on the ball – but sometimes, he gets things spectacularly wrong. I wish he wouldn't go up to complete strangers like that, but he can't help himself.'

Lizzie knew that, sometimes, he would imagine something himself and his own emotions impinged on his psychic ability, although why he should have made that particular assumption, neither of them knew. Matt Prosser was not infallible. Fortunately, she had seen enough for herself to know that he was genuine. He just got carried away with himself now and then. It had a lot to do with the bipolar disorder. It was when he was in the manic phase that he was most likely to make mistakes like this. He'd not long come out of the depression that had tipped over into that last psychotic episode and now he was on the way (a bit too far) up! The next psychiatrist's appointment should be through soon, surely?

Apart from Matt's need for different, or extra medication, Lizzie did sometimes wonder how much of the psychic was real, and real it was – of that she had no doubt – and how much was hallucination due to psychosis or, perhaps, from his own mind due to the mania. She loved him regardless, and always would, yet that slight seed of doubt still remained, embedded somewhere deep in the back of her mind.

They sat on the sofa watching something and nothing on the television one evening later that week, she didn't want to upset him, but she plucked up the courage:

'Matt, can I ask you something?'

'Of course you can. What is it?'

'Well, don't take this the wrong way but, you know when you see spirits and whatever, and you're communicating with them …'

'Yeah?'

'Well … how do you know it's actually spirits and you aren't hallucinating, like when you have a psychotic episode. I mean, how do you know what's real and what's just in your mind?'

'It's not easy to explain – and I do know that I get it wrong, occasionally. The thing is, when it's in my head I can feel it inside me. When it's a spirit, I just know it's coming from outside of me. I can't really explain it any better than that.'

She knew exactly what he meant. That day when he'd come downstairs and she'd asked him what was wrong with Mai, she knew that she was upset over something. She could feel the intensity of the vibration, but it wasn't inside her; not like when she had butterflies and her tummy did somersaults, when she was nervous or apprehensive about something. No. It definitely originated from outside her. Definitely outside: Mai's emotions. But how could she be sure when he was getting it right? He had made mistakes, after all. It had happened just that week. Then she thought back to the bicycle, TD Bear and the shelf that's not a shelf, Andrew's appearance at the flat – and all the rest of it.

Lizzie Prosser was satisfied – and anyway, she loved her husband with all her heart. He had a few issues, so he was not infallible. But who is? And he was the loveliest man (easily on a par with Andrew!) she'd ever known.

Ghost

It hadn't been the best of nights for Lizzie. She woke late. Rubbing the sleep from her eyes, she willed herself out of bed and into the bathroom to swill her face. Shower later. She put on the jigsaw puzzle that was her dressing gown – the right sleeve was inside out and the belt somehow had wrapped itself inside. Wasn't she sober last night? She trudged her way downstairs, still not fully alert.

What a lovely, warm sunny day! Matt was already out in the back garden. He'd left some coffee in the pot and she poured some into a mug. A few sips perked her up, as she stood in the kitchen watching Matt through the window. She loved days like this, when his heart allowed him to be a bit more physical. It just worried her that there might be no stopping him and he could push himself into mania. She'd seen it all before. He'd feel fine, push himself, overdo it and crash the next day. That kind of behaviour was often the prelude to a psychotic episode, but there was no telling.

She had no idea how long he'd been out there. She needed to ensure he took a rest, so poured some coffee for him and took both mugs outside, placing them down on the patio table.

'Matt! Matt! Coffee!'

He waved, put down the strimmer, and made his way down the garden to her. Just as she was about to sit down, her mobile phone rang from inside the house.

She nipped back through the kitchen into the living room and answered it. Fiona.

'Hi Fiona! How are you two?'

'We're great. What about you and Matt?'

'Good too, thanks. Well, day by day. You know how it is. Matt seems pretty good at the moment though.'

'Of course. Listen, Mum and Dad are staying for a few days. You're still coming to Sammy's birthday party tomorrow, aren't you? I thought you could stop overnight so you can have a drink in the evening? Bring the dogs – Sammy would love to see them. What d'you think?'

'Sure! Be great to see you all. It'll be a bit of a houseful, though.'

'Well, it sometimes feel like we're rattling around in here, just the two of us since he buggered off – but it's great for get-togethers. Cheers me up a bit. I really miss seeing you and the old neighbours every day, though.'

'Swings and roundabouts since you moved, I suppose. You've plenty more space for visitors but missing the neighbours. Well, if you're sure, then. Hang on! I'll just check with Matt. Not that we've got any plans or anything!'

She went back outside and asked him if he wanted to go.

'Looking forward to it!' he shouted, so that Fiona could hear him.

'Fantastic! I've got a card and present for her already. Can't believe she's five already. Hopefully see you all tomorrow. What time should we come over?'

'About four-thirty?'

It was all arranged and Matt was in a really good mood. She pleaded with him not to overdo it. There was a shedload of work to do yet, but it didn't all have to be done at once.

'I'm fine. I'll know when to stop.'

How many times had she heard that one before? On a high, he thought he knew, but he didn't. Still, it came with the territory.

She made him rest every half-hour or so by making him a cup of coffee. She thought he should have decaf. He was delighted with the progress he'd made out there, and was pretty high when he came in, but he didn't seem overly manic.

Lizzie woke early the next morning, after an unusually good night's sleep. Matt's head was completely under the duvet. She pulled it back.

'Matt? Matt?' she shook him. 'You ok? Matt?'

He turned onto his back and his eyelids opened but his eyeballs rolled up so that she could only see the whites of his eyes. He groaned. Then his arms started flailing around in front of him. Damn! He was in psychosis, fending off bats or demons or something.

'Matt! Matt! Sweetheart? Can you wake up for me?'

His eyeballs rolled down to their normal position as he started to come to. He stared at her through narrowed eyes for a moment as if he was trying to work out who, or what she was.

He began to show some semblance of recognition.

'What is it? Bats again?'

He nodded and in a hoarse whisper managed to say:

'Think so. Tablets. Get my meds for me. Need my meds.'

Lizzie tore downstairs, fetched his dosette box and took it up to him. She opened Tuesday morning's pot, gave the tablets to him and poured a glass of water from the jug on the bedside table.

'I need extra Seroquel. I'll just sleep it off.'

She pulled out the pack that he kept to hand in his bedside drawer, not daring to look at how many he popped from the blister pack. Matt had a very high tolerance to them – so high that it scared her. He shoved all his tablets into his mouth at once and downed them in one with just a single sip of water. How did he do that when she had to take a gallon of water for the tiniest single pill? He settled down to go back to sleep.

Lizzie got washed and dressed, tidied her hair, then went downstairs. They wouldn't be going to Fiona's today. Perhaps she could just nip over later and drop off Sammy's card and present. She wrapped the present, two different unicorn motif tee-shirts, a unicorn jigsaw and a box of sweets. Sammy loved unicorns; she couldn't have too many.

At about one o'clock, Matt came downstairs. Lizzie dived into the kitchen and made him some fresh coffee.

'So how are you feeling?'

'I'm ok. A bit groggy. But I'm ok.'

When the coffee was ready, she fetched it from the kitchen. It was no good saying 'I told you so.'

'D'you want something to eat?' she asked. It was a rhetorical question. He never did after an episode, but she had to ask. This one had been surprisingly short-lived but he was not going to be in a fit state to go anywhere for a couple of days.

'I'll just take Sammy's present over, love. I won't be long.'

'What? Oh God! Sammy's birthday! I forgot all about it. Sorry. No. Listen. You can go. I'll be fine anyway in an hour or so.'

'Well, if you're sure. I won't stay too long.'

'No – I'll be fine. It's gone. Honest. I'm just a bit too groggy from the meds to go myself. But you can stop over. Please. Just give my apologies. Take a bottle of wine with you.'

'Ok. But I'll leave the dogs with you so you're not on your own and I'll have my phone on me. Let me know if you need me. Promise?'

'Yes, I promise! Now stop fussing. I told you. I'm fine.'

There were about half a dozen of Sammy's friends from her school reception class at the party, accompanied by their mums. They had a lovely time playing games and dancing. Fiona had arranged for a kiddie's entertainer, a clown who did magic tricks, and all the kids went home with a bag of goodies. They, children and adults – including Lizzie – were all stuffed with sandwiches, party food and drinks. Fiona had done far too much.

Sammy was worn out. Fiona's Dad, Alan, took her up to bed and read her a story. Apparently, she was out for the count before he got to the end. Fiona and her Mum, Elaine, were in the kitchen clearing up while Lizzie rang Matt.

'I'm fine. Really, I am. Stop fussing, woman!'

Lizzie said goodbye to Matt and popped her head around the kitchen door.

'Need any help?'

'Yes – go back in there and pour us all a glass of wine! We'll be through in a minute!'

Fiona took four glasses from a wall cupboard and handed them to Lizzie, who, with great care, placed them on the huge coffee table. Fiona followed through with a bottle of red wine and placed it next to the glasses. She returned to her mother in the kitchen. Lizzie unscrewed the wine and began to pour.

Alan came downstairs and sat next to Lizzie on the couch.

He leaned over to Lizzie and whispered: 'You'll never guess what Sammy just said to me. She said, "Grandad. I can see the ghost behind the door." I nearly crapped myself!' He did look quite perplexed, poor chap.

'Oh' replied Lizzie, "she probably could. It's a little girl. Her names Mai. She lives with us. She came with me. Sorry!'

'You serious?'

'Yeah. She's been with us a while. She goes everywhere with me. Children are often very good at seeing spirits – that's what invisible friends usually are. So Matt tells me, anyway. They grow out of it. Or adults grow them out of it. I don't know which.'

'Where is she now?'

Mai found it all very exciting; her energy vibrated strongly.

'She's sitting here, on my other side. I can't see her but I can feel her'

'Elaine? Fi? There's a ghost sitting on the couch!' he shouted through to the kitchen.

Fiona laughed. She was used to it all and open to Matt's abilities as a psychic medium. Alan and Elaine were vaguely aware but preferred to ignore it.

Elaine yelled, 'I don't want to know!'

Lizzie shrugged it all off and no further mention was made of the subject. Pity really, all they talked about was what a rotten bastard that Simon was for running off with his tart of a PA and leaving Fiona alone with her little daughter. Lizzie's understanding was quite different. As long as he kept up contributing to the mortgage and the bills, Fiona was quite happy, thank you very much!

A few weeks later, Fiona wasn't feeling very well, and Lizzie drove over to give her a hand with Sammy.

'Can Auntie Lizzie put me to bed and read me a story, Mummy, please?'

'Ok. If it's all right with you, Lizzie.'

No problem. Sammy had her bath and spent an hour downstairs with Fiona and Lizzie. Then Lizzie went upstairs with her and settled her into bed.

'Which book to you want, Sammy?'

'My nursery rhymes book, please.'

'Ok!'

Lizzie pulled the book of nursery rhymes from the bookcase and sat on the little chair next to Sammy's bed. She opened the book, but before she had a chance to start reading, Sammy said, in a hushed voice: 'Auntie Lizzie, do ghosts go like this?'

She held her arms out in front of her, swaying them from side to side, wide staring eyes fixed firmly on the space at Lizzie's left side.

'Why? Can you see a ghost?'

Sammy's eyes never moved from the point at Lizzie's side on which they were fixed. She nodded, precisely and deliberately, as she silently mouthed the word 'yes'.

'It's ok, Sammy. She can't hurt you or anything. She's a lovely little girl and she loves children. She looks like she's moving from side to side because ghosts, or spirits, which is what we call them, sort of shimmer, a bit like glitter. Do you mind her being here?'

'No. She's nice. I like her.'

'Ok, so I'll read both of you some nursery rhymes, then.'

Sammy giggled. Lizzie read the story and, when she reached the end, she replaced the book on its shelf and made sure Sammy was tucked in for the night.

'Night, night, Sam' said Lizzie, as she switched off the light.

'She's going with you.' Sammy was smiling, happy that she'd found a new friend.

Lizzie went downstairs and told Fiona all about it.

'Well, I think it's lovely', said Fiona, 'and a shame people like Mum and Dad can't be a bit more open-minded about it.'

'Oh, I think they're lovely people. Just fear of the unknown, isn't it? At least they don't hold it against me. Don't want to burn me as a witch or anything!'

'Mmm. Listen, I'm feeling a lot better now. D'you fancy a glass of wine? You could stop over, if you'd like, so you don't have to drive.'

'Ok. Stick a film on and I'll give Matt a call to let him know. He's probably expecting me to stop over anyway.'

Fiona looked for a DVD while Lizzie phoned Matt.

'He's fine,' she told her, 'quite happy for me to stop over tonight.'

Sally

Sally was slipping downhill. Imperceptibly at first, but old age had crept up on her. Getting up to go outside could be difficult for her and sometimes Matt had to help her. Some days were better than others. They knew she didn't have long, but neither wanted to voice it. They tried not to think the unthinkable; too hard to contemplate. She wasn't showing any signs of pain. Quite the opposite. She lay close to them and the Labrador smile was always there. She was happy just to be with her people. Jason and Gemma appeared to be oblivious.

It was Matt who came out with it: 'Lizzie, I'm going to have to take her to the vet tomorrow.'

Lizzie nodded, but Sally was having none of it. As though she'd understood, they watched as she got to her feet without help and walked with relative ease to the back door. He followed her. She just needed a bit of help to get her back legs over the dog flap. Somehow, she managed to get back in on her own.

At bedtime, Matt insisted that Lizzie went up to bed. She was exhausted, more emotionally than anything. Mai went with her but once Lizzie was asleep, which didn't take long, she went back downstairs to Sally and Matt. Matt had stayed with Sally stroking her, cradling her head, whispering in her ear.

At 4:15 a.m., she raised her head and looked into his eyes. That soulful look was still there. She lifted her front paw. As he took hold of it, she laid her head to the floor and her spirit left her body and flew straight through the back window. There was an orb waiting for her. Matt swore it was Douglas, the cat. At the top of the steps, her spirit stopped and looked back at him – and she was gone.

A flood of tears and then he had to get busy; it was the only way he could cope. Gemma and Jason could see, but whether or not they understood, he didn't know. He washed her body down, placed it in the boot of the car and covered her with her old blanket.

Early in the morning, he took a cup of tea up to Lizzie, his eyes still full of tears.

'She's gone, Liz. I've put her in the car.'

Lizzie welled up, broken-hearted, and let the tears flow as he told her how Sally had passed.

'She just wanted to hold my hand, bless her', he sobbed.

Lizzie was expecting it, but it didn't hurt any less. Matt's tears were intermittent. He was trying to be strong, but it was no easier for him. He loved all the dogs as much as she did.

Her dear friend; her soul mate through all these years. An exceptional dog and exceptional mother. While other bitches were usually happy to be shot of their pups at around eight weeks old, she mourned their loss. Lizzie remembered the joy ten years before, when this beautiful four-year-old chocolate Labrador realised that she was coming with her babies.

As a spirit, Mai understood these things. Nevertheless, being Earthbound, it didn't stop her feeling the anguish of the loss, either. She had that empathy with Jason, who loved playing with her – daft as a brush without a clue who he was actually playing with! Sally was a different character; a calm, loving influence. Mai's aura was subdued.

At nine o'clock, as soon as it opened, Lizzie rang the pet crematorium where she had taken Douglas four years before. They couldn't have been better treated. The owners of the crematorium felt deeply for the bereaved people who brought their departed pets to them.

Matt and Lizzie returned from the pet crematorium and found themselves standing in the living room, looking out of the window to the back garden.

'She just shot up those steps, Lizzie. I'm sure it was Douglas waiting for her. I could swear it was.'

Lizzie was too choked to say anything.

Matt fussed Gemma and Jason for a minute or so but Lizzie was lost.

'I'll put the kettle on,' he said. She just nodded.

A few minutes later he returned with two mugs. Lizzie was still standing there, looking out of the window, to the steps where Sally's spirit had retreated. She was still numb. She took her mug of tea, barely able even to mouth a thank you.

They stood there, holding their mugs, staring out of that window, waiting for the drinks to cool down. Gemma and Jason were beginning to cotton on to the fact that their mother was no longer there. They both laid down on the floor, quietly picking up on the atmosphere.

Very suddenly, Gemma jumped up, pricked her ears, nose pointing towards the garden. She dashed outside and within a few moments returned with something in her mouth.

'What you got there, girl?' Matt asked her.

She looked up at him and allowed him to take an enormous black crow's flight feather from between her teeth. It must have been almost a foot in length.

'Well, bloody hell! I don't believe it. That's amazing! Thank you, Gemma! You know what this is supposed to mean, Liz?'

Lizzie shook her head.

'Well, if a feather drops in front of you – which it kind of did – after somebody has died, it's supposed to signify a spirit passing over. It's Sally telling us she's ok!'

'Gemma's never done anything like that before, Matt. She's never been interested in fetching anything at all! It could have been Andrew or Douglas or somebody, perhaps. You know, if she's gone straight into the Light, letting us know she's alright.'

'Yes, very likely. Anyway, we shouldn't worry. She's an old soul. She's fine. Here.' He handed the feather to her. 'Give her about three months and she'll be back, for sure.'

Lizzie managed a weak smile and took the precious feather.

'I'm going to keep this safe until I can get a frame to mount it.'

She stroked the feather, fetched her book of 'things to keep' and found a safe page for it. She thought of Alexander's old school book and his precious dried flowers.

'Forget-me-not.'

'Never.'

Forgive Me

July 2019

'Where's Mai?' asked Matt.

'How am I supposed to know? You're the psychic!'

Glance to the heavens. She despaired of him sometimes.

'She's disappeared again. I have a feeling she's gone somewhere with Andrew, mind. They've been communicating but I have no idea what they've been talking about. Mai's been a bit contemplative. She could be anywhere – but pound to a penny she's with him. I've just got a feeling.'

Andrew looked older than Mai had ever seen him. He was sitting in his wheelchair with a plaid-patterned blanket over his knees. The wise old sage.

'Mai, what are you going to do when Ma and Pa pass over? Stay here alone, forever? You're going to have to meet Herbert sooner or later. You're such a courageous young lady. Why not do it now? Listen to what he has to say. I'll be there. I'll be with you. He cannot harm you.'

She thought about it. It was true that she would pass through the Light when Ma and Pa go. Then he would be there and, yes, she would have to meet him.

Mai pulsated with anger at the merest thought of meeting Herbert again. She wanted nothing to do with him. Nothing.

'Let's go somewhere else, somewhere nice and peaceful', Andrew suggested.

He took her to a beautiful meadow on a hillside, overlooking a valley: plush greenery, surrounded by hedgerows interspersed with trees and woodland to one side. Sheep grazed. The sound of birdsong surrounded them – just like the meadow where Mai's Oak used to stand.

'This is called a natural burial ground. It's my gravesite, if you like. It's where Ma buried my ashes all those years ago. She put the casket in the ground herself.'

There were no headstones. It was not a sad place, like church graveyards. It was a beautiful, peaceful place, full of life. He was calm and his tranquillity washed through, over and around her.

'All I'm asking, Mai, is that you just listen to what he has to say. He can't do you any harm and I will be there to protect you anyway.'

'Alright. Uccle Andrew. I'll come. I'll listen. But I'm staying as an orb. If I reveal myself as Mai, I would have to face him. As an orb, I'm round, I have no face. I have no eyes. I don't have to see him. I have no mouth, so I can't talk.'

Andrew took her to him. He had come this side of the light to meet her. She couldn't speak to him. She refused to reveal her human-like image to him. As she had vowed, she remained an orb of light.

Andrew created an invisible bubble around them, into which no spirit from outside could enter. They had privacy. Herbert began the conversation.

'Dear, dear Mai. Why will you not speak to me? I am a spirit now. I know how much I wronged you, wronged your mother, wronged your brothers – even baby Seamus. I wronged the memory of my brother. I used a childhood injury to avoid taking the King's shilling and going off to fight. I wasn't brave like Eric. I knew it then and, believe me, I know it now. I have been shown the consequences of my actions. I have no explanation for my behaviour other than, deep down, I knew that I was a coward and I held great jealousy and resentment for your father. I knew I was not fit to tread in his footsteps. He was a great man.

He was everything I wanted to be but was not. I have no right to ask for your forgiveness but – and please believe in my sincerity when I say this – I am truly, truly sorry. I make no excuses. I, and I alone, am responsible for my actions. The only consolation I have is that you found love with Alexander and, by being taken by the blight, you were spared the horrors of the pogrom. Please, Mai, I hope you will find it within your being to grant me forgiveness. If not now, at some future time.'

She still could not find it within herself to speak to him directly. She thought about his words, but remembered his deeds. Perhaps he was sincere, but hers was the mind of a breathing child – not a full spirit. She remained in the form of an orb.

I have no eyes. I cannot see him.

'I believe he is sincere in what he says, Uccle Andrew, but I cannot forget. The memories are still alive within me. I am not yet ready to forgive. I want to forget about it while I am this side of the Light. I may well change my mind when I see things with the understanding of a full spirit but the time is not now. I want my life with my breather family.'

'Uccle' Andrew smiled. Her vocabulary has been developing well with the breathers.

Herbert, nodded.

'Thank you, at least, for agreeing to meet with me, Mai. I understand how difficult it has been for you. I can only offer you my sincerest apologies for the wrongs I did to you and the rest of the family. I could not show you love as a breather, but I give it all to you, and them, now. I have lived with the horror of what I did for a very, very long time.'

For the first time, she made a direct spiritual communication with him: *'Not like I did.'*

Herbert smiled in acknowledgement and nodded again. Andrew erased the invisible bubble around them and the spirit of Herbert Henry MacIntyre dissipated into the ether.

She turned up just before tea-time.

'You ok, sweetheart?' Matt asked her. 'You're very quiet. Where've you been? Something up?'

He concentrated hard on her every word. Lizzie waited, curious.

'She's been with Andrew. Herbert found him. He's seen her new life. He asked to see her. She was a bit frightened but she knew she'd be ok with Andrew. 'The wise old sage', she calls him.'

'Hell fire! Herbert! What did he want?' Lizzie asked.

'Apparently, he wanted to say how sorry he was. He wants her to forgive him. As far as I can tell, he still doesn't really know why he took out all his frustrations on her, poor little thing. He said he was jealous of Eric. But he does want her forgiveness.'

Lizzie looked in what she thought was Mai's direction. This was one time when playing 'spot the ball' wasn't funny.

'Do you think you can, Mai? Forgive him?'

'She's very subdued,' Matt said, 'she's shaking her head.'

Lizzie's heart went out to her.

Matt went on, 'She doesn't feel that she can. Not yet. She wasn't sure how she felt when she went to see him. She thought she might be able to when Andrew told her what Herbert was hoping for, but the mcmories are still too raw for her. She's not ready yet. She still has the emotions of a human child. She told him she will one day, but not yet.'

'What did he say? When she said she couldn't forgive him yet?'

'Apparently, he was ok with it. Understood. He is so full of remorse for everything he did, he said he was prepared to live with it until whenever.'

'I feel sorry for Herbert, in a way, mind,' Lizzie said. 'His life on Earth is over. He really does feel sorry for everything he did. If he'd remained Earthbound, I wouldn't trust him. But he must be genuine. Andrew would never have taken her to see him, otherwise, would he?'

'No, you're right. It's got to be Mai's decision, though, and Herbert understands how she feels. He knows she still has the emotions of a breather child.'

'He must be carrying a shedload of guilt, mind.' Lizzie paused. She looked quizzical. 'That's an odd thing to say, isn't it?' she asked.

'What?'

'He's prepared to live with it. He's been dead over 350 years! But how else to you say it?'

'Yeah. Odd, isn't it? I don't know!'

'Well, life after death, innit?' she chuckled. 'Main thing is, that Mai's ok. You are, aren't you, Mai? I mean, it's ok. Herbert understands. I'm sure that there will come a time when you can forgive him. He knows it as well. And you do too, don't you?'

Matt smiled.

'She's nodding. She's ok. Just not yet. Too much. She's found what she's been waiting for all this time and she wants to leave the matter of Herbert at the moment. Right now, she thinks it would be like muddying the waters. After she's gone through the Light.'

'Well, I guess that's fair enough. It has to be Mai's decision. Still feel a bit sorry for him, though.'

'Don't. He's ok with it. I'm sure they'll make up one day.'

Jason

Matt was right about Sally. In September, she was back. She came with Lizzie's Mum.

'Oh, Patricia! That's wonderful!' Matt was beaming.

'What? What's wonderful?'

'It's Sally! She's been helping your mum with the newly passed spirits. Sally! You're an angel – literally! They say angels have paws, not wings, don't they? Unless they're a bird, I guess!'

'My legs are buzzing,' Lizzie was so excited. 'It's her vibrations. I can feel them – really strong! I've got a happy dog here! It's just the same as when I can feel Mai.'

'She's wrapped around your legs.'

Lizzie placed the palm of her hand down and reached to where Sally was vibrating.

'You've got her!' Matt said.

'I know, I can feel the warmth. It's very distinct.'

Lizzie missed her girl, as did Matt, but she was thrilled to know that Super Sally was a happy spirit.

The weeks went on and Sally usually turned up with Lizzie's mum; most weeks, but not all. She often came on a Wednesday, too. If she didn't turn up, Lizzie always asked her mum how Sally was doing.

'She's fine. A bit busy tonight,' was the usual response.

Even doggie spirits have responsibilities on the other side, it seems.

Christmas came and went but soon after New Year's Day, Jason wasn't his usual self. He wasn't playing with Mai and he was a bit listless. The dogs had their 'off' days occasionally and he didn't look particularly ill.

Matt picked up Jason's lead and the great black dog dutifully went out with him. Two minutes later they were back.

'He got as far as the end of the terrace and stopped in his tracks. Didn't want to go any further.'

'Hell, Matt, that's not like him at all. What's up, boy? Come and have a treat.'

He followed her out to the kitchen. She reached into the 'doggy' cupboard for one of his favourites and offered it to him. He took it but dropped it on the floor, went back to the living room and flopped down onto his side. Matt and Lizzie looked at each other.

'Not well at all, is he? Something he's eaten, d'you think?' Lizzie asked.

Matt just shrugged his shoulders, worry etched all over his face.

'We'll ring the vet in the morning.'

Morning came and Lizzie made an appointment. Matt carried Jason to the boot of the car.

'I'd better stay with Gemma. She's never been on her own before. Is Mai going with you or staying with me?'

'She's coming with me.'

Lizzie had a dreadful premonition. She tried to dismiss it but her stomach was in knots. Feeling quite nauseous, she ran to the car just as Matt was about to close the hatch door.

'Hang on!'

She climbed into the back, put her arms around her beloved Jason, gave him a hug and a kiss and said, 'Mummy loves you very much.'

Once she'd climbed out of the car, Matt closed the door and got in the driver's seat.

'Keep me posted.'

She watched him drive up the road until he was out of sight, then she went into the living room, sat on the sofa and, with an arm around Gemma, stared into space until the phone rang.

'It's not necessarily bad news. The vet can't find anything wrong, but she's called for the radiologist. She'll be here in about twenty minutes. She'd gone home but the vet asked her to come back. I'm in the waiting room. He's just pooped on the floor here. He never does that. Liz – there was blood in it.'

Everyone in the waiting room said what a beautiful dog he was. Matt just cuddled him, choked, while they waited.

Lizzie's phone rang.

'How is he?'

'It's not good news. They've found a massive tumour on his spleen. It just bled out. They've got to put him to sleep.'

His voice was cracking. They couldn't lose two dogs in six months!

'I'll call you when it's done, Liz.'

She could barely breathe. Not her beautiful baby Jason, too?

Lizzie screamed, then balled her eyes out.

The vet and the nurses could not have been kinder. Matt couldn't hold back his tears. The nurse shaved Jason's leg where the needle was to go in. They said he'd probably been ill for a long time, but he was such an exuberant character, he never showed it. Jason looked up at Matt. *Just do it, Dad*, he was saying.

Jason sighed away one last breath and his spirit shot from his body. Mummy Sally was waiting for him.

'Nooooo!' Mai screamed, unheard to all but Matt. Distraught, she shot up to the ceiling. Bang! One of the halogen ceiling lights exploded.

'What the hell was that?' yelled the vet.

'You wouldn't believe me if I told you.'

He just couldn't hold the tears. The vet asked the nurse to bring in the card machine so that Matt could pay without going back through the waiting room. He paid the bill and the vet said they would ring the pet crematorium to arrange for Jason's body to be collected. She let Matt out by the back door, avoiding the sympathetic gaze of all those people.

Walking back to the car, Jason's blue collar and lead in his hand, one of the other dog owners from the waiting room passed him.

'It's rotten when you lose a pet, isn't it, mate?'

'Don't you dare call him a pet. He wasn't a pet. I've just lost my best friend.'

Sitting in the car, he cried his heart out for a while. When he was ready, he took a deep breath and phoned Lizzie.

'It's done. He's gone. We're coming home.'

A week later, they made the trip to collect Jason's ashes. This time, the heart-shaped urn was black with silver paws.

'He'll be back. Give it another three months. He'll be back with his mum.'

He was – but, unlike his mother, Jason was having a bit of trouble getting the hang of becoming a spirit. He was hilarious. Lizzie was a bit cheesed off that she couldn't see him whizzing around like a helicopter! Wow, this was fun! Or not quite understanding that he didn't need to eat any more; Guzzleguts just could not get his spectral head around why he couldn't have any food or treats when Gemma was eating. Such a young, beautiful, daft spirit – just as he had been as a breather!

Mai was the best as Jason realised who had been tickling his nose. *Oh, it was you!* Their spirits melded and

Lizzie picked up on Matt's joy as he watched them. They were always great playmates, but now Jason could see her.

Sally and Jason visited most Saturdays with Lizzie's mum. On the other side, Sally helped Lizzie's mum caring for newly-passed spirits, human and animal, as they recuperated from the shock of passing over. Sally was now training her son to do the same – and his daft antics were a huge hit!

Andrew always turned up on Saturday evenings, as did Lizzie's dad. They got into the habit of watching a film, either on Netflix or from their DVD collection, and having pizza and other vegan junk food nibbles with a bottle of wine on a Saturday evening.

Gemma grieved deeply for Sally and Jason, so Matt, Lizzie and Mai focussed all their love on her, fussing over her as much as they possibly could. Wow! She had all the attention to herself. Poor girl had always been pushed to the background by the enormity of Jason's character. She was at a loss, in one sense, but she now had her Matt and Lizzie all to herself and that compensated.

Still, the physical loss had taken its toll on Lizzie. She just didn't feel the same.

Part Three: Lockdown

Shield

After losing Jason, and within months of Sally, Lizzie needed a pick-me-up. She had the itch to take up music again. Dad had been a pianist. She'd played the violin as a kid but fancied taking up the piano. She'd had weekly piano lessons in addition to the violin for a couple of months but wasn't keen on her teacher, so she had dropped it. She browsed the internet. She found a lovely looking Yamaha Clavinova on eBay, put in a bid and won. She was amazed. Two lovely young men brought it all the way to South Wales from Walsall. It was in mint condition. She found a piano teacher and had a few lessons. She was loving it, but there was a cloud on the horizon.

Matt and Lizzie were hooked to the BBC News, as they had been since the Brexit debacle. By March, all the focus was now on this new virus sweeping the country – and the world: Covid-19. It didn't just look bad; it was terrifying.

There had been much talk of a national lockdown and Matt and Lizzie were of the opinion that the country should be locked down sooner rather than later. The delay worried them both.

Lizzie had an appointment at the hairdresser on March 12th. She sat there, feeling very frightened and uncomfortable. She wasn't frightened for herself, but for Matt. She was terrified of picking up the virus and taking it back to him.

She got home and heaved a sigh of relief.

'Matt, I can't do this anymore. I don't care what the Prime Minister says, we're not waiting. We're locking down – now! It's got to happen before long anyway. I don't know what I'd do if anything happened to you.'

He didn't argue.

'Perhaps we should see if we can arrange for deliveries from GreenFare', she suggested.

Matt went online.

'Ok, hang on, I'm just looking now. There you are, they've got a regular slot, but not for a fortnight.'

'Book it. There's nothing else for it; I'll have to go out this afternoon and do a fortnight's worth of shopping to see us through, but that's it. Neither of us is going out until this is over.'

He booked a regular slot. She went to GreenFare which, to her surprise and relief was pretty empty. She whizzed around the store, doing the quickest two-week shop in history, and got home as fast as she could.

She rang her piano tutor.

'Alistair, I'm really sorry, but I'm afraid I'm going to have to cancel my lessons. I can't risk going out with Matt's health conditions. We're staying in from now on.'

'Oh, that's ok. I think I'm going to have to cancel all my students' lessons in the next week or so anyway. Hope it doesn't last too long and we can start up again soon.'

'Me too. Good luck.'

'You too.'

She was not happy about having to cancel but her background and her few lessons with Alistair at least gave her something of a springboard to carry on trying to progress on her own.

They did everything online. Apart from the weekly grocery delivery, the pet superstore delivered dog food in bulk, the pharmacy in the village delivered their medication, and anything else – stuff for the garden mainly – came from Amazon or eBay. Everyone was very understanding and helpful.

Matt was not on the 'extremely vulnerable' list, so he wasn't required to shield.

'Blow that for a game of marbles!' was Lizzie's response. 'They haven't seen you trying to breathe soup like I have. You're always well enough to go out whenever they see you. That's the trouble with these good days and bad days things. They only see you on a good day. If you're ill I just ring up and postpone your appointments. I don't think they know how bad you really are.'

Lizzie wasn't taking any chances; healthier people than him were dying every day. She had been widowed once and she wasn't about to lose another husband!

Finally, on 23rd March, a national lockdown was announced, by which time cases were rising at a ridiculous rate, with more and more people dying.

Everything they needed was delivered without fail. They didn't really miss going out. Not that they went out much anyway; perhaps once a month for a pizza meal; occasionally a proper restaurant. The only annoying thing was that they couldn't travel to see the family, but there were phone and video calls. Not the same though, was it? They spent a fortune on the garden and it was a lovely Summer. They even managed to put in a wildlife pond and plant it up.

She sat under the arbour, reading a novel, occasionally looking up to glance over to the pond.

'Matt! Matt!'

'What?'

'Quick! Come and see this!'

A beautiful, bright blue Emperor dragonfly hovered right in front of her face. It was huge! It appeared to study her face intently as she watched it: one of those 'what the hell are you?' moments!

'Wow! That's fantastic!' gushed Matt. 'It's called a dragonfly, Mai.'

'Has she seen one before?' Lizzie asked.

'Yeah, she's seen them, around the stream behind the settlement, but she didn't know what they were called.'

'Isn't it lovely?'

'She's glowing.'

'So's this dragonfly!' Lizzie said.

At that moment, Mr Dragonfly must have decided that Lizzie was neither threat nor potential food because he completed his assessment and flew away, directly over the pond. Or could this magnificent creature possibly have been studying Mai?

As a breather, other than her time in the meadow with Alexander, Mai never had any opportunity to appreciate the joys of nature. As a spirit, she had the time to do so, and especially enjoyed it with Lizzie and Matt.

Summer transitioned to Autumn; more days of low atmospheric pressure. Matt's heart always suffered during low pressure, and being physically unable to do as much as he'd got used to doing over the previous few months, he was slipping into a down phase of the bipolar. The two conditions of heart and bipolar fed off each other in a cycle. It was tricky to deal with. There were short-lived highs and lows during both manic and depressive phases, so they never knew what to expect. He was careful to avoid a repetition of the episode when he snapped his phone in half and punched the door. Whenever he felt what he called 'twitchy', Matt took extra medication – enough to knock him out – and went to bed. Sometimes, he was up there for a couple of days.

She brought his food and drink, but he didn't eat very much. He just went to sleep wearing his headphones, listening to some inane Netflix programme on his computer. It shut out the demons to some extent. Of course, even when he was doing well, the dark spectre lurked, and an episode could hit from nowhere. Fortunately, that became a rare event.

It all took a toll on Lizzie. She was down herself at times. That was when those seeds of doubt at the back of her mind would creep in. She dismissed them. The bike, TD Bear and the 'shelf that's not a shelf' – yes, she had seen Andrew for herself, the photos. Then there was Grampy Hedgeman's pipe tobacco; always smelt by her before Matt.

It was not all in his head. Definitely not!

You've Upset the Cat!

One quiet, peaceful Saturday afternoon in late October, when the weather had improved – a good day, health-wise, for Matt – the spirit of Douglas, the cat, was curled up on top of the display cabinet. She had arrived early and dozed, as cats do, waiting for the arrival of the rest of the troops, as Lizzie referred to their spectral visitors. Lizzie was reading her Norah Lofts; Matt, sat in his armchair doing whatever Matt did on the internet. Facebook.

'Aw, there's a post here you shared about Douglas. Big cat, wasn't he?'

'Yes, well…'

'What d'you mean I've upset the c… Jesus! What the fuck?" He sprang to his feet. The laptop crashed to the floor.

'What's the matter? What happened then?'

He reached around to his back, rubbing it.

'Bloody cat just scrammed me!'

'Eh?'

'Look at this! I've been scrammed by a bloody dead cat!'

'What d'you mean, you warned me?'

'What?' Poor Lizzie was utterly confused.

Matt stood in front of her, lifting his tee-shirt.

'Can you see anything. Has he … she, sorry! Has she marked me! Mai said I've upset the cat. How did I upset the cat?'

Lizzie was inspecting his back. Indeed, it did show the mark of a fresh scram, two parallel claw marks, about four inches long.

'You're bloody kidding me!' she said. 'I can't believe that!'

'How d'you think I feel? Why did I upset her?

He listened for Mai's answer.

'Apparently, I called her 'he'. She didn't like it. With you calling her Douglas, I forget she's a girl sometimes.'

'Well, I made a mistake when she was a tiny kitten – but she was very much a lady. There was nothing masculine about her – except her name! By the time I realised the error, she was already answering to Douglas!'

'I don't think there's much ladylike about this!' Matt protested.

'That's true! Better bathe it and put some Germolene on it. Just in case. Do you think there'd be any germs in a scratch from a dead cat? It's been a very long time since she used her litter tray! It is a bit of a sore-looking wound, though.' Lizzie laughed. 'I've got to take a photo of this first, though. It's very red!'

'Oh, great!', he moaned, holding up the back of his shirt as she picked up her phone and took her photo.

They went to the kitchen. Lizzie bathed the scratch and spread some ointment along it.

'I can't believe she did that', said Lizzie, 'Where is she now?'

'Up on the unit again.'

'I did try to warn you.' Mai said, sounding a bit too triumphant for Matt's liking.

'Lesson for today: don't insult the cat!' laughed Lizzie.

'Don't! Just don't!' he said. 'It's not funny!'

Oh yes it was!

Mum was first to arrive in the evening. Sally and Jason were with her, as usual. She normally turned up at about eight o'clock. Dad followed soon after. Andrew usually turned up at about nine.

'You should see what Douglas did to Matt, Mum.' Lizzie was desperately trying to suppress a giggle.

'Don't worry, she's heard all about it. Somebody's blabbed – haven't they, Mai? And you needn't look so smug up there. I can clear spirits, you know!'

'Matt! Don't even think about it!'

He could. But he wouldn't. Lizzie knew it. They all knew it. Above all, Douglas knew it.

'Andrew's late. Oh, hang on. He's here. And Meg's with him!'

'Hi Meg. Lovely to see you. Well, I can't see you, but you know what I mean.'

'She does. She's smiling. She's got something to tell us.'

'What is it?' Lizzie was half asking Meg, half asking Matt.

'Wait a minute... Go on, Meg. What? Never! Really? Wow!'

'Well, that was informative.'

'Mai's absolutely glowing here. Meg's only found Eric. Except his name isn't Eric MacIntyre. He changed it.'

He carried on listening to Meg for a few minutes. Lizzie was desperate to hear what was going on.'

'You're not going to believe this! He didn't die at St. Fagans as everybody believed!'

'Yes,' Lizzie interrupted, 'we've heard that.'

'Well, he was badly injured, but not killed. He escaped. He hid, too terrified for the family's safety to go back … you know … in case of reprisals. Thought they'd all be killed. He was taken in by a local widow. She hid him and they did a flit when he was well enough. You won't believe this.'

'What?'

'Wait for it. He took on this woman's husband's identity. You're really not going to believe this – his name was Richard Hedgeman. So that's where your

Hedgeman comes from! Meg has told him all about us. He wants to meet Mai and you but he's a bit on the shy side. It's going to be a bit strange for him, meeting breathers. He had no idea about Mai until Meg found him. Meg's asking if she can bring him on Tuesday evening?'

Lizzie was ecstatic.

'Oh! Absolutely! Hardly going anywhere, are we? No, we'd love to meet him! Would he mind if we asked him some questions and recorded the answers, Meg?'

'She's saying that he wouldn't mind at all. You can ask him anything you like. He can't wait to meet his daughter – and his however many times great granddaughter! And he's livid about the way Herbert treated Sarah and the children. He's a tough guy, but a loving family man.'

Lizzie was delighted that Eric had now been found – even if he was Richard. And he was a Hedgeman. Kind of.

'See? Told you, didn't I, Mai? Your father would have loved you if he'd known about you.'

After all this time, Mai was going to meet her real daddy. The father she had always believed didn't care about her. The father she now knew loved her, even if he had only just found out about her existence. She couldn't wait!

Matt got the pizza, vegan sausage rolls and the other food from the oven and poured the wine.

'Are you staying, Meg?'

'She'd love to. And you, up there...' he said, looking up at the cat, 'just bloody well behave yourself!'

'Sorry Meg,' Lizzie said, 'but you wouldn't believe what happened earlier.'

'Oh yes, she would. She's heard all about it!'

Mai!

They all enjoyed Saturday night – they always did – but, by Sunday morning, they couldn't wait for Tuesday evening!

Richard's Story

'It wasn't so much conscription as feeling honour bound to take the King's shilling. We were poor as poor could be. They told us that if Cromwell was in charge of the country, there would be misery: no gaiety, no singing and dancing, no Christmas. But how would that affect us, the poor? It didn't matter who was in charge; whether it be King or Cromwell. It would hardly affect our lives of subsistence. Except on the Sabbath. We didn't go to the church. We had nothing to give. Only the wealthy, better offs and their servants went to church. They had gaiety; they had singing and dancing; they had Christmas. We used to do our singing and dancing on the Sabbath and Christmas Day. It was the only bit of relief we had from the drudgery. Everyone worked hard in the fields from dawn to dusk, six days a week. Only on the Sabbath could we relax. Cromwell was not going to take it from us. It was alright for them, living in luxury with all their wealth. So most of Wales, the poor, anyway, was for the King.

We took the shilling and they gave us a chit to put in our pockets which meant that we would be paid handsomely after the War was over – and, if anything happened to us, our wives would get the money. It was a chance to earn a little extra, so off I went with a few of my neighbours. Herbert had injured himself as a child; an arrow to his left shoulder in an accident. It was never as bad as he made out. He just used it as an excuse to get out of working. He had erected a makeshift hovel for himself in a field, but he said he would look after Sarah and the family if anything happened to me. Like a fool, I trusted him.

We found ourselves in Tenby, under Colonel Poyer. We were there defending the garrison for months. We had no real training as soldiers, and no arms to speak of – just what farming implements we could take with us. All I had was a dung hook. Leaving Sarah alone with three children was something I fretted about, but Fitz and Pat were getting to an age where I hoped they could help her out a bit and we lived in a community where most people helped each other anyway. Still, if I had any idea that she was with child again, I would probably not have gone.

From Tenby, we were ordered to march towards Cardiff. There were a few minor skirmishes along the way, but we survived them, mostly due to our numbers. Thousands of us, there were. We were involved in another skirmish on the fourth of May, 1648, with some of Colonel Horton's troops on their way to quash the Royalists. There were only a few of them and we survived that alright - but the big Battle of St Fagans took place a few days later, on the eighth. The Battle started at about seven o'clock in the morning and before ten o'clock it was all over. We outnumbered them by thousands, but they were so well-trained and better armed than we were – more horses too. We stood no chance. We were in hand-to-hand combat, but they had canons as well. When they ran out of canon-balls, they used rocks and stones.

Men lay dead and dying all around me. My leg caught a direct hit from one of the large stones from a canon. It was badly broken below the knee. I could see we had lost the Battle and I thought all survivors would be slaughtered. They say now that they let them go home free men if they promised not to take up arms against Cromwell's forces again. Yet I saw with my own eyes, many of our men slaughtered, hung upside down like butchered animals, insides ripped out, entrails trailing, bleeding out. I did not believe for one moment that they would let us go home free men. It was my belief that, even if they did, they would hunt us down like animals. How could I walk like this, anyway? I would have been killed like those other poor souls.

I truly feared that even if I could ever return to my wife and children, they would come for me and slaughter us all. I had to survive, but all I could think of was the safety of my family.

I lay among many dead men. There was much smoke in the air. The smell of it mingled with the stench of blood, guts and death all around. I took my chit from my pocket and placed it in the pocket of one of my dead comrades in the hope that it would be found and that I would be taken for dead. I recognised the man from one of the other settlements. I knew he was a single man with no family so I swapped his chit for mine. Word of my death might then get back to Sarah and she would receive my pay.

Under cover of noise and smoke, despite the agony of my broken leg, I managed to drag myself to a ditch at the edge of the field. A few of the survivors did. As I rolled into the ditch, a huge thorn from the hawthorn hedge sliced into my face; it made a great gash down my forehead, over my eye and along my cheek. How it failed to take out my eye, I do not know.

I covered myself with branches and grass, staying still by day and inching myself forward by night. They sent flush squads with pike staffs and sticks to poke under the hedges and in the ditches to seek out escapees. Some were caught, but some were missed. In that respect, I was one of the lucky ones, for I saw those who had not willingly surrendered brutally slaughtered. Yes, they said they would let us go if we surrendered and promised not to take up arms again but, after all the brutality I had seen, how could I believe them? How could I possibly trust them?

I hid in that ditch for four days, inching my way along, but being careful to remain hidden. When all was calm, I looked over and saw a settlement. By now I must have been dying of thirst and hunger, let alone the agony of my injured leg and torn face. Perhaps I would receive mercy here, for I would surely die anyway. Under darkness, I heaved my way out of the ditch and managed to inch my way along the field for what seemed like an eternity. I was growing weaker by the minute. I could see a firelight coming from one of the houses on the edge of the settlement and, with all the strength and purpose I could muster, dragged my painful way towards the house. I was almost to the door but there, I fear, I must have collapsed into unconsciousness because the next thing I knew was daylight, my face was being bathed with water and a kindly woman was speaking to me. She had found me when she came out to collect the kindling for her fire.

As I started to regain my wits, she asked if I could get myself inside, before anybody saw me. She knew instantly that I had been injured in the Battle and that I had fought for the Royalist side. Very painfully, I did manage to crawl inside her house and between us, we managed to get me hauled into her cot. She had two young sons of about eight and nine. She told them that I was their father, back at last from the first War. The boys were sworn to secrecy, lest word get out and the bad men came after me. They barely remembered their real father. Those lads were good; they did not wish their father to be lost again. It was my good fortune to have looks, colouring and build, not dissimilar to her husband, she said.

Richard Hedgeman had gone off to the first War in 1642, and never returned. Elizabeth believed him to have been killed. It was not that unusual for men to return from war years later and she would be able to pass me off for him, returned as such, but not while my wounds were so fresh. It would be obvious to everybody that I had just been injured at St Fagans.

So, Elizabeth Hedgeman hid me for ten weeks and the boys, Maurice and Edwin, kept the secret.

She tended my wounds but in no way could I stand with my broken leg so I had to remain abed until it mended itself. I could never have repaid her kindness. Without doubt, she saved my life, at risk to herself and the children, but that was the kind of woman she was and I will be ever grateful. She wasn't Sarah though. I was kept hidden for almost three months. When I could finally walk fairly comfortably, even though with a stick and a hefty limp, we had to make a decision. Hiding me much longer would prove difficult and, while the children were convinced that I was their father, neither Elizabeth nor I felt safe about trying to convince adults who would probably remember the real Richard Hedgeman. I could not go home, for fear of the danger in which I would place my dear Sarah and my own children, but I could not stay here.

Elizabeth had a sister and brother-in-law in whom she felt it was safe to confide. I could not wander as a vagrant, my injured leg the way it was, she said, so there was nothing other to be done than for us all to go. Her brother-in-law, Robin, managed to procure for us a mule and cart which he helped us load with Elizabeth's few possessions: table, stools, cots, crocks, and we put the children on the cart, leaving the village behind us, heading for Newport. Elizabeth had a little money, but it would soon run out.

We were able to rent a small hut and I earned a meagre living by learning to make and mend fishing nets on the docks. It was something I could do sitting down, as I could still only walk with my stick, my leg being crooked where it had broken and not fixed properly.

We were poor, but getting by happily in Newport. We must have been there for eighteen months, when we heard rumour that Cromwell was itchy about dissidents in Wales, which was still primarily for the King, even though he'd had him executed the year before. We heard these rumours that he was sending soldiers and mercenaries to wipe out anyone who had fought on the royalties side. He was terrified of more insurrection. Although we weren't sure if the rumours were true, we thought it would be safer to live in England. We sold half our possessions and bought a rowing boat to take us over the channel to England. We had sold the mule and cart but had sufficient to buy another at the other side of the channel and we made our way to Bristol.

Over the time we were in Newport, my leg had got stronger, although it was still crooked and I walked with a hefty limp but, by now, I had dispensed with my stick. I earned a living laying hedges. Before he went off to fight, Elizabeth's lost husband had been a layer of hedges, as had his father before him. His father had been known as Alan the Hedge, or Alan the Hedgeman – later just Alan Hedgeman. I knew how to lay a hedge alright and, now, I too was Richard Hedgeman. We didn't stay in one place too long, travelling where I could find work, and making camp. Then we found ourselves in Bath. Here, I did quite well for myself, and we managed to rent another small wattle and daub hut. We had to, because Elizabeth was with child. This is where, on September 30th, 1651, my son, William Hedgeman was born. We were not there long. Work was becoming scarce so, in the Spring of 1652, we started travelling again.

We found ourselves in Coker. There was plenty of work here. Although I still had my limp, I was much stronger and able not only to lay hedges, but to do more strenuous agricultural work. I rented another wattle and daub hut and just in time, for in late October, Elizabeth had another son. We called him Gordon. Our sons could not have been more different. William was quiet and thoughtful, while Gordon was the wilder of the two.

We decided that we would stay in Coker, with work round about quite plentiful. The boys grew up. Gordon took up stonemasonry and the other boys thought that they would try it too. William made a great success of it and began his own business. He was much liked and became well respected as an employer. He believed you get nowhere without hard work.

Gordon tried his hand at entrepreneurship and he would make a success of his ventures to begin with but, the moment he had money in his hand, rather than investing, he would spend it on visiting taverns and, shall we say, disreputable ladies. It is said that he fathered a number of children, all bastards. He wandered away and we lost touch.

William was different. He was a shy sensible boy with a great sense of responsibility; not like his brother at all. At the age of sixteen, he married a girl of Spanish immigrant parents. They moved back to Cardiff to start up a new business (The age of the Cromwells, father Oliver and son, Richard) was long past, thankfully, and Charles II was now on the throne), and they had their first child, a daughter called Isabella. She only lived five days. She died of what they called 'the grip'. They went on to have four more children, three sons and a daughter: Simon, Walter and Richard, named for me, and Maria – but she later anglicised her name to Marion. They never forgot little Isabella, though. She was always spoken of.

I tried not to think of what had become of Sarah and the children, but I believed with all my heart that my brother, Herbert, would care for them. I just did the best I could for my new family.'

So there it was. The answer to the mystery of Lizzie's ancestral origin. Strictly speaking, they were not really Hedgemans at all. They should have been MacIntyres!

Missing Links

Lizzie knew a fair bit about her ancestry. She traced it back to her fourth great-grandfather, William George Hedgeman, who was born in 1775 but she got stuck, struggling to go back any further. She had, more or less, given up, but it was always in the back of her mind. Richard's information, discovering her true relationship with Mai, gave her new impetus. Lizzie was born a Hedgeman, so she was concentrating on the male line.

It was always a puzzle to Lizzie how many people knew so little about their ancestry. She'd known all her great-aunts and uncles and had listened to the old family tales as she grew up. Her great-grandfather, Alfred Walter Hedgeman, was a stonemason, and had moved from Sherborne, in Dorset to Cardiff. He was already married to her great-grandmother, Emily, but the children of the marriage were all born in Cardiff. They were anything but wealthy but had managed to bring up all eight of their children, including her Grampy Hedgeman; no mean feat in Victorian times. The children all lived good lives, well into old age. She never knew her great-grandparents, but she was very proud of them for that achievement.

What Lizzie didn't know, was how they ended up in Cardiff from Dorset. A deeper look at the 1881 Census revealed the answer. Walter senior, her great-grandfather, was an apprentice stonemason. Living in the same street was another stonemason and his family. On the 1891 census, by which time she knew that they were in Cardiff, she discovered that Walter and his brother were lodging in Cardiff with this same man. By now, Walter was a qualified stonemason and his brother an apprentice. At that time, Walter and Emily had just two children. The other family had four.

Lizzie's great-aunt and uncle, Annie and Arthur, lived in one of those houses. She often stayed with them when she was a child. In the 1960s, the house was just as it would have been in Victorian times: two up, two down, scullery with a range and a privy at the end of the garden. Being just the two of them, they were quite comfortable. But how could so many people live in such a small place – and not even the same family?

Still, it solved the mystery of how the family ended up in Cardiff, but how was Lizzie going to trace her ancestry all the way back to Richard – and Mai? She estimated that Richard was somewhere in the range of her twelfth to fifteenth great-grandfather, making Mai her thirteenth to sixteenth great-aunt.

By digging a bit deeper, and with a bit of patience, Lizzie managed to get as far back as a William Hedgeman born in East Coker, Somerset, in 1747. Prior to that, she could find no trace. They would have to ask Richard.

Mai was very excited at the prospect of another visit from her father, but was being rather enigmatic as to why. She knew something Lizzie and Matt didn't. They would have to wait until Saturday evening to find out.

On Saturday evening, Meg and Andrew turned up, but they were not alone. Sarah was with Richard. Meg and Andrew had colluded to reintroduce them and they were overjoyed to be back together. Lizzie's heart melted; such an emotional moment. Richard, had his wife back, and the daughter he never knew existed. Even Matt welled up.

Sarah understands why he never returned home and he's saying that if he'd known what Herbert was doing to his wife, sons and daughter he'd have gone back, regardless, and probably have killed him!' Lizzie hoped that was metaphorical. 'He never even knew about the pogrom until now.'

Sarah's spirit was still very fragile. It would always be so. Richard felt huge guilt at the consequences of his leaving the family, even though it was not his fault. He vowed that he would never leave her side again.

Mai glowed, overjoyed to be with both her parents.

'Richard,' Lizzie said, 'I've got back to a William born in East Coker in 1747, but I can't get back any further. Any ideas?'

'I really don't know much more. Think I'll have to ask my son, William. He'd have more idea than I would.'

'That would be great. Ask him to come along with you next time.'

Next time:

'He'd like to come along, but he's a bit nervous about the prospect of meeting breathers. To be honest, I was at first, but he's much more reticent than I was! I'm trying to persuade him that it's alright – with your family and everything. He just can't get to terms with spirits and breathers talking together. Do you know what he said? He said, "What me, conversing with a roomful of breathers? Don't be ridiculous!" I'm sure he'll come around, though. He is curious.'

'Oh, bless! That's so sweet. Isn't it breathers who are supposed to be afraid of ghosts? And anyway, we are your family too!'

'I think we're perceived, on the other side, as being akin to trail-blazers.' Matt said. 'Other than mediums passing on the messages, this kind of relationship has never been known before, apparently.'

And there was Lizzie thinking it was all perfectly normal!

The following Saturday, Richard and Sarah arrived, but Meg was not with them.

'You'll have to excuse the boy,' Richard announced, 'he's a bit on the shy side. He'll definitely be here next time though.'

The boy!

'We're pretty harmless, aren't we?' she asked him.

'He's laughing.' Matt told her.

Lizzie showed Richard the old photographs of her great-grandfather Walter Hedgeman and his family.

'He's saying put twenty pounds on him, and he's the image of my William!' said Matt.

Lizzie was now absolutely confident that she was on the right track.

The following Saturday, they were all there, Lizzie's troops, including William who, initially, was a bit overawed by the whole thing. He had never been inside a breather's home since he passed – well, none of them had – and here he was, talking to them and seeing something of the way they lived in the Twenty-first Century. Television, films, comfortable furniture.

'He's bowled over by it all,' Matt told her.

After a bit of general chit chat, Lizzie brought up the subject of her ancestry again.

'I'm trying to find the links between me and Richard and Mai,' she told William, 'but I'm stuck at the William who was born in East Coker in 1747. Before that, the trail goes cold.'

'Ah, well there's a bit of a problem for you there. There won't be any records, I'm afraid.'

'Why's that?'

'Um … bit of a family scandal. My son, Walter, ran off with a married woman. All a bit embarrassing, really. She left four young daughters to run away with him. Norfolk, I think. It was a terrible shame on the family. They did have a son, Cedric – my grandson. He was a good lad. Did

239

well for himself in business, mind you. He came back to Coker to try and restore the family name, but I think you'd have to speak to him. I'll see if I can find him and bring him with me. It was more after my time, I passed in 1720, before Cedric's children were born. We never heard from Walter again, though. Cedric will definitely be able to tell you all you need to know.'

It was a huge revelation. Richard's great-grandson, Cedric Hedgeman, could surely fill in the blanks. Even if there were no official records, it didn't matter to Lizzie. She knew the truth about the link between her and Mai. She tried searching again. She had found the record of the baptism of William Hedgeman, born in East Coker in 1747, but the information was so scanty, she could not be sure it was her ancestor; just the name of the father, barely legible, George Hedgeman and the mother's name, so faint that it could not be read at all. There were a couple of other William Hedgemans born in the 1740s, not far from Coker. She thought that the one actually born in East Coker in 1747 was the most likely candidate but she couldn't be sure.

Matt dished up the food, Lizzie poured the wine and they settled down to watch 'The Bourne Supremacy'.

Lizzie had a thought; suddenly worried about Richard, as they watched a fight scene.

'Richard, all this fighting and stuff on the television and the films – is it alright with you? I mean, you've seen it all for real, and it's not entertainment, is it?'

'It's not a problem. I think it's terrific. In my day, there was all sorts of wrestling and fighting for entertainment. If we ever had any entertainment, that was all we had! I think it's wonderful!'

'Well, that was a relief! But what about the ladies?

'Meg? Sarah? How about you? Is it too violent for you?'

No,' Matt reassured her, 'They're both really enjoying it!'

Really? Meg? Sister Theresa, the Nun? And Sarah, who had been hacked down by a Parliamentarian mercenary's sword; they both loved it! Mum wasn't so keen, though. She always was more of a woman for romance. She always arrived on a Wednesday evening, sometimes with the dogs, sometimes without; her night for nostalgia with The Repair Shop on BBC1 and Endeavour on ITV3+1.

Between them all, they'd almost cracked it! They've got Lizzie's ancestry going all the way back to Richard and Mai. She counted back.

'Richard, you're my twelfth great-grandfather. Mai, you're my thirteenth great-aunt. All we need now is Cedric to confirm which one of the Williams is the real link.'

'I will try and fetch him with us next time,' William promised.

SAD

There'd been a bit of an Indian summer that year, but as Autumn wore on and daylight hours grew shorter, Matt noticed something about his wife.

'Liz, you're not yourself, love.'

'What d'you mean?'

'You seem a bit down to me. You're fine when you're video calling with the kids, or when the troops are in on a Saturday night, but you do seem quite listless.'

'Do I?'

She thought about it for a while. Matt wouldn't say anything like that if it wasn't true. Now she thought about it, she did feel that energy reserves were lower than usual. She wasn't up to doing much at all. In essence, she was turning into a couch potato. She resolved to shake herself out of it. Matt had enough problems with depression himself at this time of year. That was the thing with bipolar. A manic or depressive phase can last for weeks or months, with shorter-lived bouts of ups and downs during either phase. If she was to care for him when he was in a depressive phase, she could hardly be any help if she was depressed herself.

The last time she'd suffered with a serious depression, after Andrew had passed over, she tried to get out of bed in the morning to go to work and found she could barely stand up, let alone put one foot in front of the other; she actually felt ill. She wasn't functioning very well anywhere. She knew she wasn't right. Six months off work and a course of higher strength Citalopram had seen her right. She was on the medication for a year and was fine once she had come off it, under the supervision of her GP.

'I think you're right, but I don't want to go to the doctor about it – especially with the pandemic at the moment. I don't want to go out at all yet. It's not as if I've got the black dog or anything. And it seems so silly when I'm so happy. I don't want you to think that I'm not. I couldn't be happier. You know I am. I love you so much.'

'I love you too – and I know you aren't unhappy. You know as well as I do that it's nothing to do with whether or not you're happy – unless your pig-sick miserable about something, like you were at work, or when Andrew passed. With you, I think it's SAD.'

'It bloody is sad – you can't be happy about it!'

'Behave! You know exactly what I mean – Seasonal Affective Disorder.'

'Yes', she replied, managing a weak laugh, 'I know exactly what you mean.'

She resolved to keep herself busy, getting out with the dog more, playing the piano, sewing and knitting. Reading was the one thing she really found difficult. When she was like this, she found it hard to concentrate. She'd read a sentence, then read it again, and again. Her mind just wandered off into cloud cuckoo land.

Determined, she kept going. It will all be better in the Spring, and we have Christmas with the troops to look forward to. They would all be there: Andrew, Mum, Dad, Grampy Hedgeman, Richard, Sarah, William, Meg, Sally, Jason and Gemma, of course. And Douglas was also expected to make an appearance. All of them, except Auntie Margaret. Nobody seemed to know where she had gone. She had just disappeared. There was also the guest of honour. Of course, she wasn't really a guest, she lived here – the person who had brought them all together: Mai MacIntyre. Best of all, they wouldn't have to worry about social distancing, or keeping the windows open in the middle of winter! How could she be miserable? She was looking forward to it. She loved having 'the troops' in.

Christmas was a roaring success. They all enjoyed themselves. The spirits loved chilling and putting their 'breather suits' on. They watched 'It's a Wonderful Life', 'The Snowman' and 'Love Actually'. It was all required, feelgood watching, in the Prosser household, particularly 'It's a Wonderful Life'. Somebody knew what they were talking about with that one!

They had a great New Year, too. Matt thought Lizzie was becoming more sensitive to the spirits. She felt her mum arrive and told Matt she was there, sitting next to her. He had to take off his specs. For some reason, the coatings on the lenses blocked his ability to see the spirits and, whenever he was engrossed in whatever he was doing on his laptop (usually some political debate), he sometimes didn't notice their arrival.

'Oh! Sorry Patricia! I didn't see you come in.'

Some of them arrive in funny ways. Grampy Hedgeman was a terror for hiding so that Matt would feel his presence but not know where he was, yet Lizzie could smell his pipe tobacco. Nine times out of ten she would smell it before Matt. Andrew was a real mickey taker, choosing to float above Matt's chair with his arms outstretched in the form of a blessing, as he had always done before Sally passed over.

Even Mum had developed a sense of humour: the first time she visited after Matt had installed the new living room door to the hallway, replacing the one that he punched through, she stood outside in the hall, knocking. Matt heard it; Lizzie didn't. She saw him look up and he said: 'Of course you can come in, you silly woman. Stop acting the fool!'

That was the first time ever, that Lizzie had ever known her mum to act the fool. Mum did find some things funny, but could never have been called the source of mirth – not intentionally, anyway!

So, there they were, happy as could be until a few days after New Year. January the eighth was the first anniversary of Jason's death. Even though he was returning as a spirit, his physical absence had left a huge void in their lives, especially coming so soon and unexpectedly after Sally. Before she realised it, Lizzie was starting to think about Jason's antics and, soon, she was brooding. Then the black veil descended.

What accompanied the black veil was toothache. Really bad toothache.

'I think I've lost a filling – probably got an infection through the hole.'

'Sounds like it, if it is a missing filling. You need to take some pain killers.'

'You know I hate taking pain killers. It's a swallowing thing. I must have one of the worst retch reflexes in the world.'

Other than her daily blood pressure meds, tiny little things, she avoided taking tablets, even Paracetamol, unless she absolutely had to.

Before long, the pain reached the stage where she had to take a couple of Paracetamol; the caplets, which gave her less trouble with swallowing. She was too frightened of Covid to even try to go to the dentist; she wasn't even sure if they were open. She didn't bother to look. What if she picked up the virus and brought it home to Matt?

Lizzie was terrified of anything happening to him. The medics never saw him struggling to breathe when the atmospheric pressure was low. They never saw him with the depression. They never saw the psychosis. These were things that Matt and Lizzie managed themselves. However you try to describe it, let alone any combination of the issues he had and how they interacted with each other, she never thought they understood it. They just didn't get it at all.

Younger, fitter people than Matt were now dying of Covid every day. She doubted he would make it if he caught it. Then, even if he survived, there was a lot of talk of what they were calling long-Covid. As if he didn't have enough to cope with. She certainly couldn't cope with the stress, either.

No. Lizzie would rather have the toothache for the time being. The trouble was, it was adding to the depression. With depression, came silly, negative thoughts that she just tried to brush off. She thought she had.

I'm Here! I'm Real!

'I've got to go up to bed, love. This tooth is killing me.'

'OK, sweetheart. I might stay down here – sleep on the sofa. Give you a chance to rest.'

He knew she probably wasn't going to get any rest and neither was he. It was going to be a bad night. Under normal circumstances, she would have felt really guilty but, at that moment, she just wanted to lie down under the duvet.

'Have you taken some more pain killers?'

'Yes – and I've got a pack in my pocket here.' She tapped the back pocket of her jeans. 'They're not even touching the sides though. Night, love.'

Matt felt utterly helpless.

'Mai's going up with you. The cat's here – she's going up with you, too. Safer with you than me, I think!'

She wanted to smile but she was in too much pain. He just wanted to do something, but there was nothing he could do. He did so much for her already, and she really appreciated everything but right now …

She got herself into bed and tried to get as comfortable as possible. She tossed and turned. And tossed and turned. And then the negative thoughts started whizzing through her brain: what if it's all in his head? What if I'm just seeing what I want to see? What if I'm just feeling what I want to feel? The part of her brain that was trying to show her all the evidence to the contrary was suppressed. She was lashing out at him, because there was nothing else she could do. She'd had three babies, but couldn't remember pain like this. Even when she'd fallen and badly broken her wrist a few years ago, spending the night alone, in dreadful pain, it wasn't as bad as this. Not as she remembered it, anyway.

She started vocalising her thoughts: 'What if it isn't real? Supposing it's all in his head? He's made loads of mistakes!'

He also got most things right but, for now, out of her mind in agony, she didn't care. She had to take it out on somebody.

Mai began to worry. If Ma was saying these things out loud it was getting serious.

Then came the worst thing, or perhaps the best, she could have said: 'What if Mai isn't real? None of it's real! It's all part of his psychiatric condition! It's all a load of bullshit!'

This tirade of doubt was pouring out as she tossed and turned and cried with the pain. The Paracetamol was having no effect whatsoever. Now, Mai began to panic. Lizzie couldn't hear it, but she was screaming at her.

'Ma! No! I'm here! I'm real! I am, Ma! I'm real! You aren't imagining me! We're all real! Please don't say we're not. Please don't say I'm not. If you don't believe in me then what is the point of me? Why am I here? Why was I ever born? Please, Ma! Please!'

For Mai, this was worse than when she first looked down at the women in the wooden hut, washing down her body, and the man from the church who couldn't hear her. Her whole reason to be depended on Ma's belief in her.

Lizzie took the biggest breaths she could manage to try and control the pain, breathing it out. It didn't go away but she began to calm down a bit. She was still tossing and turning, her
    mind in a whirl.

From somewhere, there was a light in the room. She turned over but it went out. Then it came on again. It was the lamp on Matt's bedside table. Then it went out. Then it came on again. Lizzie had a thought.

'Mai? Is that you?' she asked.

The lamp came on for a few seconds and went off again.

'Mai? If that was you, can you do it again?'

The lamp came on. Lizzie groaned in pain. Then she asked her to do it again and the lamp lit up for a few seconds.

'Mai, I'm sorry my lovely. I didn't mean it. Really, I didn't. It's just the pain. I do know that you're there.'

The lamp came on again and she saw a white, glowing orb, about two inches in diameter, roll from the lamp onto the bed. She watched it bounce along Matt's pillow towards her. She fell straight into a deep sleep and did not stir until Matt woke her in the morning with a tray of breakfast.

'How are you feeling, this morning?'

'The pain is completely gone. Not a twinge!'

She told him about the night's events.

'It was Mai. The lamp's not even plugged in. Look!'

He picked up the free plug dangling from the lamp's wire.

'Poor little soul. She's used up so much energy that she's dwindled to almost nothing. That's a hell of a lot for a little spirit to take on. That would take it out of Andrew, so it was amazing for a young little spirit like Mai.'

Lizzie remembered the orb. He smiled.

'The cat. Definitely Douglas. Sending you healing spirit.'

'Oh, bless that dear little cat. I won't have another word said against her in this house! Understand?'

'Yes, dear. Well, between the two of them, they seem to have sorted you out. You know, that little girl loves you so much that she was prepared to almost destroy herself to get you to believe in her. If Douglas hadn't given you that healing energy, Mai would have lost so much of her own that the spirits would have had to come to rescue her and take her through the Light.'

It took Mai a few days to fully recover the energy she had lost. Matt said that she was a bit subdued but was gradually coming back to herself. Ma was on a real guilt trip, feeling bad about it all, but Mai was happy. Ma believed in her again. Ma had never really stopped believing in her.

'She's saying something to you, Liz.'

'What?'

'Ma, please don't ask me to switch the lights on again. It's all I can do to try and blow out my birthday candles. I'm going to be like Pa's phone.'

'What's his phone got to do with it?'

Matt howled with laughter.

'Down to one per cent power!'

By the King's Beard!

The toothache never returned and Matt, Lizzie and Mai got on with their normal lockdown lives.

A couple of weeks later, Cedric arrived with his grandfather, William, and Richard and Sarah. He was a completely different personality to all of them. They were all still quite reserved, although they were beginning to come out of their shells – even the very shy William – as they gradually became accustomed to Twenty-first Century breathers and lifestyle. By contrast, Cedric Hedgeman was full of, well, life! A truly exuberant, happy-go-lucky personality. He was tall, and muscular with shoulder-length, blond wavy hair.

Cedric was not a bit nervous about meeting Lizzie and Matt. He loved the prospect of having so many generations of family all together and getting to know his forebears and descendants. He loved everyone, spirit and breather, human and hound, and everything in the house. He was fascinated by television and couldn't get enough of action movies.

He made a terrific connection with his great-aunt Mai, which they all found amusing: the little girl and the great dashing hulk, as the two of them sat on the floor together playing with the spirit of Jason until the film was put on!

They decided to watch the Bourne franchise on consecutive Saturdays. Sarah and Meg were just as much into it as the men! They were all starting to pick up on modern day life and entertainment. Unlike Richard, Sarah and William, who remained floating near to Lizzie, Cedric plonked himself on the sofa between Lizzie and Patricia. He was completely unselfconscious. Lizzie adored him already.

Lizzie waited for Cedric to settle into things before she broached the subject of his son, her ancestor, with him.

'So, Cedric, can you fill in the ancestral blanks for me. We're as far back as William, born in 1747, if I have the right William. Richard and William think I do but they're not completely sure, either. If he's the right one, his father was George. At least, that's what it looks like on the baptism record but it's so faint it's difficult to make out. That's as much as I know.'

'Yes, that's my grandson, William. I had two sons: George Arthur, born in 1721 and his brother, Henry Richard, was born the previous year. George is William's father.'

They'd done it. Between them all, they had made the link from Lizzie, right back to Richard Hedgeman. Lizzie could have cried with joy.

Lizzie's grandson, Lucas, had not long turned five. He showed her the Power Rangers dressing up costume he had for his birthday. Nana had never seen Power Rangers so, especially for Lucas, she watched a few episodes on Netflix, so she would know what he was talking about. Mai loved it. Anything 'badass'! Our Seventeenth Century spirit was becoming a real Twenty-first Century girl!

'Will you watch it with me, Cedric? You'll love it! You really will.'

Cedric more than loved it!

'By the King's beard!' he yelled, 'What warriors these are!'

Matt keeled over laughing. If only Lizzie could have heard it for herself.

'There's Bumblebee, too! You'll love that as well. And Alita! She's really badass, too – like me!'

Matt groaned. He'd lost count of the times he'd endured them! Anything for their little girl though.

'Well,' Lizzie said to Matt, 'if you've never seen television, let alone CGI or modern martial arts and that kind of stuff before, I don't suppose you could tell the difference between programmes for kids and adults. And what the hell! They enjoy it.'

'Yeah,' he said, 'you're absolutely right.'

Lizzie was so happy. Cedric had shown them the last link in the ancestral chain.

In the morning, over coffee, Lizzie looked at her husband and stifled a giggle.

'By the King's beard, Matt! We've cracked it.'

His eyes rolled to the ceiling: 'Behave yourself!'

She laughed.

'Seriously, though, we've got all the links back to Eric MacIntyre, alias Richard Hedgeman. Is that the reason that Mai knew she couldn't go through the Light? Was it to bring her mother and father together again?'

'These things aren't predestined, Liz. Nothing is. The spirits can only try to influence events – to guide. Trouble is, breathers hardly ever pick up the message. It's so wonderful that Richard and Sarah are together again, though. I think there's been a lot of influencing going on, on the other side, though. Looking at the events that brought you all together.'

'Us', said Lizzie, 'brought us all together.'

He smiled, nodding in agreement.

'Hang on, she's saying something. What is it, love?'

His head was cocked to one side as he listened. He looked very serious.

'Oh, Mai! Of course you can stay! This is your home!'

He looked at Lizzie.

'The poor little girl was worried that she would have to go through the Light now that she's found her real mum and dad. She just wants to stay with us in this world until we go. She wants to enjoy her happy family life here and still be with her real parents whenever they come. She's glowing so bright I'm almost surprised you can't see her.'

Lizzie grabbed a tissue from the box on the coffee table, wiped her eyes and blew her nose. Tears of happiness. She passed a tissue to Matt. He needed one too.

Mai was here to stay.

Family

Every Saturday night they came: Richard, Sarah, William, Cedric, Mum and Dad, the dogs. Meg and Grampy Hedgeman had developed a great friendship, soulmates, and they frequently turned up and left together. They also acquired a new member of the family. Sally had disappeared for a while. Lizzie was a bit concerned.

'Who's Ben?' Matt asked.

Lizzie went over to the bureau and pulled out an old calendar with photographs of the breeder's dogs that she'd been given when she collected them. She turned to a picture of a much younger Sally with a dark grey standard Labradoodle.

'Here you go,' she said, 'the love of her life. He's responsible for Jason! They really loved each other – got up to a bit of the naughty business just before she went to stud, so there were two great black standard doodles included in a litter of what should have been just medium chocs and creams! Anyway, what about Ben?'

'She's gone to keep an eye on him. He's going to pass over soon.'

'Oh no! Not Ben too!'

A couple of weeks later, the breeder, Susan, announced on her Facebook page that their beloved Ben had passed over. Lizzie was quite upset and sent her condolences in a private message.

It wasn't long before Sally brought Ben to the family gatherings. Jason showed no interest in his biological father, but Ben took a real shine to Gemma, even if she couldn't see him or understand what was going on. Whenever he was there, she sat where he sat, snuggling up to his spirit. She just didn't know it. Canine whispering?

Matt and Gemma came in from their evening walk.

'We have company. Dogs.'

'On a Tuesday? Sally and Jason?'

'Nope! Jason and Ben.'

'What? No Sally?'

'No. She's busy. You won't believe this. The farm dogs were out again. They were coming to have another go at us. These two just came out of nowhere! Straight through my legs and went after them. Chased 'em off good and proper, they did. Ben led the charge but Jason was so brave! He's so proud of being his Dad's son, too!'

Lizzie was flabbergasted.

'I thought Jason wasn't bothered about him!'

'Well, they've got to know each other better and formed a really strong bond now. Something's clearly been happening on the other side.'

Wow! Lizzie was proud of the two of them! Those farm dogs were a nuisance, chasing after people, even biting a couple of times.

'They have been reported to the police, I think. There's been a lot about it on the village Facebook page.'

'Yeah. Tell you what though; they won't be coming after us again. Ben's so protective of Gemma. You'd think that she was his own daughter!'

'What a star of a dog!'

'And son of Ben is now his apprentice!' laughed Matt!

Courage in the Raw

5th May 2021: Mai's birthday

Celebrating Mai's birthday was now an annual event. Mai's actual birthday, Sarah had informed them, was the fifth of May. So, from now on, that was the date to be reserved for the celebration of Mai's recurring eighth birthday.

Lizzie made a chocolate sponge cake, as she did the first two birthdays that Mai was with them. Except last year. When the pandemic was really bad, they forgot to order the makings for a cake when they did the online shop, so they just put the candles left from the year before on the party style vegan sausage rolls! This year, they made sure they got it right!

Mum, as usual, was first with all the dogs. Douglas, the cat, was there, still under orders to behave herself! Andrew was unusually early and Dad arrived just before Richard, Sarah, William and Cedric.

'Oh dear', Matt said, 'I feel a bit underdressed! Cedric's very smart in his best leather jerkin, by the look of it.'

'Putting us all to shame!' said Richard.

Cedric thought he might have overdone it.

'No! You look great! Really smart.' Matt assured him; one of those frequent moments when Lizzie really wished she could see them.

Lizzie poured the wine and Matt brought in the cake, with its eight birthday candles around the edge and a figure eight sparkler in the centre.

'Shall I light the candles?'

Lizzie nodded and he pulled out a lighter, putting the flame to the wick of each of the eight candles in turn.

'Aah...'

'What?'

'I should have lit the sparkler first. Think it's too hot. Ouch!'

'Silly bugger!' Lizzie said. 'Don't worry; just light it afterwards.'

Lizzie was ready with her phone to catch it on video as they sang 'Happy Birthday to you'. The room was buzzing with energy.

Matt turned to Mai. 'Come on, then. Try blowing them out, Mai.'

They sat back and watched as the eight little flames flickered sideways.

'Woah! That was strong. Have another go!'.

The flames flickered again but Matt thought he might have contributed to it when he moved his hand.

'Try again, Mai. Matt! Keep your hand still!'

There was a definite flicker, but not as strong as previously. Lizzie called up the troops. Mai was running out of energy.

'Come on folks! Can you help her? Ready? One, two, three, blow!'

The candle flames waved in all directions as all the spirits rallied around the cake. For a moment, Lizzie thought that they would actually blow out – but they didn't.

'That wasn't me! It was definitely them!'

Matt blew out the flames. He cut the cake and they settled down to watch 'Rise of the Planet of the Apes'.

Cedric adored his eight-year-old great-aunt! She adored her big beefy hunk of a great nephew. They sat on the floor; spirits almost melded together as they played with Jason. Cedric was like a big kid.

When the film was finished, Lizzie was starting to fade.

'Sorry, folks', she said, 'I think I'm going to have to love you and leave you. You coming back tomorrow, Mum?'

'You kidding?' Matt relayed, 'She's not missing Endeavour for anything!'

Lizzie grinned.

'Ok, see the rest of you on Saturday, then. Night, night all. Don't forget – you can come any time you like. You don't have to restrict yourselves to Saturday!'

She blew them all a kiss, left them to it and went upstairs to bed. Mai stayed with the troops to enjoy the rest of her birthday.

'Cedric! Cedric! You've got to see Alita. It's brilliant.'

Oh God! Not again! Still, it's her birthday. Matt pulled Alita from the DVD case and switched the discs.

Cedric loved it. He was all for any kind of action movie. This was fantastic!

'I can see why you like it,' he told her, 'Quite the battler yourself, aren't you?'

She laughed. She loved that. She loved him. She loved them all.

Then Cedric got serious:

'You know, Mai, I talk a lot about fighting and swashbuckling and how I would have loved to have taken part in the wars. I always say I missed my time. I love watching those kind of films when I'm here. But the truth is that I didn't have to live through it. I never had to show that kind of bravery and courage – not like your father; not like Richard. He did it for real. He had the courage to stand up for what he believed in. Would I have had that kind of courage, faced with the same circumstances? I don't know. I do wonder, sometimes.

'But you… you have inherited your father's courage. You could have gone through the Light. You were an innocent. It would have been easy for you to go with the

259

guides. Yet you chose to stay among the horror and the misery of that terrible place because you believed there would be something better. That took great bravery. And because of what you did, wonderful things have happened.

'I tell you this: you have taught the spirits something. Even your brother, William, probably the most sceptical spirit of all, has learnt it! Spirits and breathers can be together, spend time together like this. It's something that has never been seen before.'

He looked up to his grandfather. William Hedgeman agreed. He now loved to put on his breather suit!

Mai hung on Cedric's every word. He had not finished:

'Mai, about Herbert. You are not yet ready to forgive him. I understand that. While you are on this side of the Light the memories are too painful and you wish to forget. But when you go through the Light you will see the greater picture.

'So, for now, I want you to promise me something. I want you to promise that you will never be vengeful. Always keep the purity of your soul.'

Yes. She promised. She would never be vengeful. Badass is just for films.

'You have inherited your father's courage – courage in the raw – and look what that courage and your determination has achieved. Your family, breather and spirit, has been brought together, and we all love you.'

That was the best thing of all for the very special spirit of a very special little girl: her whole family, a loving family, all around her.

Mai MacIntyre had discovered her reason to be.

It was supposed to have been a private conversation, but Matt couldn't help relating it to Lizzie, for which he was mildly rebuked by Cedric on Saturday evening when the full contingent of troops arrived

Lizzie soaked up the warmth of the atmosphere.

'Matt, this is so lovely. But I do wish the others could be found – it would be even more wonderful if we could have Miriam, Fitz and Pat – and Alexander, of course – just to complete the family.'

'Well, I know that Meg has been trying to find them on the other side.'

Matt glanced across the room to Meg. Wearing an enigmatic smile, she placed her forefinger to her ethereal lips.

He leaned towards his wife.

'Shush.'

Postscript

The spirit of Herbert Henry MacIntyre is utterly contrite. His remorse is genuine. He bitterly regrets the wrongs he did during his lifetime. He looks on with relief and satisfaction that Mai, Richard and Sarah have found each other, and happiness, at last. He needs Mai's forgiveness but understands why, as yet, she is unable to give it. His soul is incomplete without it, but he is confident that, one day, it will come to him.

Until that time, Herbert Henry MacIntyre contents himself to wait – as long as it takes.

* * *

A Little Note from Mai

I hope you liked reading my story. I had a hard life, but there were some people who loved me and cared for me, so it was not all bad. I have learned a lot since I came to live with Lizzie and Matt. I am very happy now.

Thank you and lots of love from

Mai xxx

Acknowledgements

Many thanks to my husband, for your unwavering support, your advice and for giving me the time to write.

Thanks also to Michael Heppell and my dear friends in the Write That Book Masterclass 2021, for comradeship, advice and support. May we long continue to be friends.

To you, the reader, for purchasing this book and reading Mai's story. It means a great deal.

But, above all, to the amazing spirit that is Mai MacIntyre, a little girl who simply wanted to be loved and have her story to be told.

About the Author

Rachael Trask describes herself as a woman of a certain vintage who's been around the block a few times. Beginning life in Cardiff, she moved to the East Midlands with her family at the age of fourteen. After thirty-five years away, including two spells abroad, she returned to Wales in 2002 and currently lives happily with her husband, a psychic medium, and their dog in the countryside of the South Wales valleys.

Rachael has three grown up sons and three young grandchildren.

Other than writing, she enjoys natural history, dogs, horses, reading, history, and trying to teach herself to play the piano. In 1995, as a mature student, Rachael graduated from Oxford Brookes University with an honours degree in Environmental Biology – her garden is an unintended testament to wildlife conservation!

Printed in Great Britain
by Amazon